The skeleton fe
Dust rose from the

Before the Cimm_____ _____ eyes, leg bones joined above and below knee caps, and legs set themselves into hip sockets while feet settled in at the other end. Ribs, spine, arms, skull—all skittered across the floor or rose into the air, and all somehow found their proper place.

In the time a hungry man takes to gnaw the meat from a chicken leg, a pile of bones was a complete skeleton—but no longer standing stiffly on guard. It moved as freely as any living man of flesh and blood. Conan thought he had seen everything . . . then the skeleton bent, rummaged through the pile at its feet, and came up with a short spear.

The skull face turned toward Conan and the jaws—still furnished with a full set of strong white teeth—clacked twice. Then the bones rattled, and incredibly the skull wore a death's-head grin.

By sheer force of will, Conan cudgeled his wits into order and raised a wild Cimmerian war cry. The skeleton clattered the spear against its ribs, as a living warrior might have struck his spear against his shield.

Then living Cimmerian and skeleton advanced. . . .

Conan Adventures by Tor Books

CONAN

AND THE DEATH LORD
OF THANZA

—— BY ——

Roland J. Green

A TOM DOHERTY ASSOCIATES BOOK
NEW YORK

This is a work of fiction. All the characters and events portrayed in this book are either products of the author's imagination or are used fictitiously.

Conan and The Death Lord of Thanza

Cover art by Keegan

A Tor Book
Published by Tom Doherty Associates, Inc.
175 Fifth Avenue
New York, NY 10010

Tor Books on the World Wide Web:
http://www.tor.com

Tor® is a registered trademark of Tom Doherty Associates, Inc.

ISBN: 0-812-55268-7

First edition: January 1997

Printed in the United States of America

0 9 8 7 6 5 4 3 2 1

Prologue

Some of the wildest country in the Hyborian kingdoms lay between two of its most civilized realms.
Between Aquilonia and Nemedia a long range of
mountains, beginning in the north at the Cimmerian
border, slashed southward to the Tybor River.

Had it not been for these mountains, Nemedia and
Aquilonia might have been a single realm. Had it not
been for these mountains, honest folk in the eastern
provinces of Aquilonia and the western provinces of
Nemedia would also not have had to look to defending
their flocks and fields, homes and families, lives and
honor, as often as they did.

Yet had they lived an easier life, they might also not
have grown hardy, self-reliant, full of good sense, and
without patience for witlings. The hunters and farmers
who grew to manhood within sight of the mountains
made splendid soldiers for the hosts of both realms,
and for other realms as well.

It was not only the mountains themselves that made

the folk who lived in their shadow hardy. It was those who lived in the mountains: outlaws, bandits, common footpads, wild beasts of whom bears and wolves were among the least fearsome, and (or so it was rumored) other creatures who were not of the gods' making.

On maps in cities distant from the rocky or green-clad summits, frowning slate-hued cliffs, and deep forests that could and did swallow armies, these mountains were called the Border Range. But each village in their shadows had its own name for the portion closest to them and for each peak within that portion.

Toward the southern end of the Aquilonian side of the mountains, however, one name came most readily to all tongues. It was "the Mountains of Thanza," and it was not uttered lightly.

No one living in the reign of King Numedides of Aquilonia could say exactly what "Thanza" was or had been. Most agreed it was long departed, but whether for two centuries or two millennia men argued long and loudly. There was even more dispute as to whether it had been a man, a tribe, a realm, or even a god briefly residing in the world of men.

All tales and talespinners agreed on one thing. "Thanza" had been potent in magic, making forests walk and mountains fly. Like Acheron, it had in the end fallen from the very potency of its black sorcerery.

Also like Acheron, some of that sorcery was said to linger in odd places in the mountains—places which no sensible man approached closer than a day's journey.

The men of the caravan descending into Aquilonia from the Pass of Oteron were prudent, or would at least have called themselves so. Furthermore, they had little choice over the way they took from the pass down into the lowlands. Four trails twisted westward from the Pass of Oteron, one of which almost deserved the name of road. At least it was passable to light carts with stout teams in good weather.

So far, the caravan had possessed all of these. They also possessed numbers and weapons, including not a few mercenaries adept with the deadly Bossonian longbow.

Most of the caravan's goods rode loaded on a score of packhorses and mules, but the cart in the middle held a chest too heavy for any beast of burden short of a Vendhyan elephant. The cart also would have been too heavy on this road for its eight-mule team, had it not been cunningly built around the chest.

The axle on which the two iron-shod wheels turned ran through an iron tube riveted to the underside of the chest. The poles to which the mules were hitched were hinged to stout timbers. The chest was bound by iron bands similarly riveted in place. The two teamsters and the pair of guards sat on boards mounted on the iron bands.

In short, there could be no easy stealing of the chest. They who sought the chest needed to think of either dismantling the whole cart in the face of well-aimed arrows and well-wielded steel or dragging the entire apparatus off into a forest where a squirrel barely had room to pass among the trees.

Many eyes turned to the cart when their owners thought the twelve men guarding it were not looking. The twelve were a closemouthed lot who doled out words as if each cost them a Nemedian silver royal. Clearly they were guarding not merely the cart but a secret. As clearly they would have preferred to be on the road by themselves, had traveling these lands in such scant strength not been plain madness.

Now the road wound across nearly level ground, where once, long ago, men had dug proper drainage ditches to either side of the road. The ditches were barely an arm's length deep now and half overgrown with brush. Beyond the brush the trees began, mostly pines thicker than two men and soaring up out of sight into the shadows aloft.

Men looked up into those shadows, then hastily turned their eyes back to the road ahead. They told themselves that the strange scurryings in the brush were squirrels, and that the hootings were owls confused by the gloom under the canopy of trees as to the time of day.

They told themselves these things while they gripped their weapons or the leading reins of their animals so tightly that their knuckles stood out white against tanned and travel-soiled skin.

Among the eyes watching from within the shadowed forest was an intensely blue pair. They were set above a high-arched nose in a tanned, thin face that few ever called beautiful but fewer still readily forgot.

Save perhaps those who had given Lysinka of Mertyos mortal offense, and whose last sight on earth had been her eyes.

There were those who said that Lysinka was not wholly human, although they were careful to hold their tongues where she might hear them. No two agreed on what other blood might flow in her veins, and there were some who said it was ice water and not blood.

Nonetheless, she had in the past ten years won a reputation second to none among the "brothers of the hills," as those who lived beyond the law in the borderlands called themselves. Her forty men and women were not the largest band among the brothers, but much the best disciplined and among the best-armed. Bands twice the strength of hers gave way when they met. As for picking a quarrel with her, one band had slain their chief outright when he talked of such folly in his cups.

Lysinka's face now held an irritation that verged on anger. She had all but stripped her camp to bring thirty of her people to the caravan road. At least there was no loot in the camp now, or none worth the blood-feud that a raid would bring upon the attackers.

With thirty fighters it should have been simple to attack the caravan from both sides and both ends. Neither man nor beast should escape. She had sought complete victory—and then her guide had led the band astray for the best part of an hour before regaining the trail. Now there could be no crossing the road without being seen, thus no attack from both sides.

Lysinka looked at the two fighters, a man and a woman, who were tying the guide to a tree. The man already bore signs of the chieftain's wrath. Then Lysinka whirled about so fiercely that the single waist-length braid of her blue-black hair swung like a whiplash.

"You!" she snapped. "You still say that it was a mistake, your taking us down the wrong trail?"

"I say it, and it is the truth." The man's voice was steady in spite of his wounds, and he met her eyes without flinching.

"Ever heard of trial by battle?" Lysinka said more quietly.

"Against you?" The man laughed. "How could justice come from that? You are my master with every weapon either of us can wield."

"Of course," Lysinka said, with a mirthless smile. "I

was thinking of setting you free, to join the fight. If the gods leave you standing at the end of it, we know their judgment. If you die, likewise.

"But do not even think of fleeing, not where I can hear it! Then your death will be certain but not swift."

"I would have expected no less," the man replied. He seemed readier to laugh than to plead.

"Do I have so few secrets now?" Lysinka said, almost smiling again. She seemed to be asking the trees and the sky rather than men.

"If there was less known about you, Lysinka, " the man said, "fewer would go in fear of you. Men fear the unknown, to be sure. What is known to be deadly, such as the great bear, the asp, or Lysinka of Mertyos, is feared even more."

Lysinka laughed softly. "My friend, you have not earned freedom. But you have earned my oath—your death will be swift and clean, no matter what you do."

The exchange of courtesies came to an abrupt end as a messenger slipped into the clearing. Like all but the rawest of Lysinka's fighters, he had learned to walk so cat-footed that he was among the others before they heard him.

"The caravan is close to our chosen place," the messenger said. He was a youth barely old enough to shave, but he spoke with assurance. It was known among Lysinka's fighters, friends, and foes that she did not care for those who cringed to her.

"Cut him loose," the chieftain said to those binding the guide. "Do not let him out of your sight, or your blood will answer for it."

Without waiting for a reply, Lysinka shifted her quiver to an easier position across her muscular back and followed the messenger.

*   *   *

The caravan's guards numbered some forty, and few of them were witlings or lacking weaponscraft. Such did not live long in the borderlands; or if they lived, no caravan wishing to reach safety would hire them.

However, Lysinka's thirty had the advantage of surprise. It was an ancient Khitan king, known as both sage and warrior, who had first put into words this piece of war-wisdom:

"Surprise halves the strength of the defenders and doubles that of the attacker."

But the king spoke only of battles in which magic played no part. In moments, the battle around the caravan ceased to be such.

Arrows whistled from behind trees, seemingly aimed at the caravan's arches. Dim light and bad shooting sent more than a few arrows astray. Bossonian bows leaped into muscular hands and returned arrow for arrow. The return shafts did even less harm than the attackers', aimed as they were against archers cunningly hidden among trees instead of exposed on the road.

But four of the caravan's dead were from the twelve around the cart. Two others reeled about, past fighting for today.

From the forest, Lysinka saw the cart suddenly exposed. So did those among the caravan guards. Greed and curiosity turned them from guarding their master's goods to seeking the chest. Renegade guards and bandits from the forest collided in a desperate close-quarters fight that boiled up around the cart.

Through the tangle of fighters stalked Lysinka. Long-limbed and swift, she chose to fight with broadsword and dagger rather than weigh herself down with a shield, and she foreswore armor except a helmet and greaves. Her true armor was her sure sight, her swiftness, and the sharpness of her steel, which had kept her alive through more deadly fights than she had years.

She had cleared a path almost to the cart when the magic struck.

It was not magic that announced itself by thunderbolts, blinding light, flames, smoke, or pungent odors. Indeed, it was a moment before Lysinka or anyone else noticed that the iron bands locking the chest into the cart were beginning to glow.

The glow brightened, then wavered and crept down to the sidebeams of the cart. At the same time, the axles on either side of the cart snapped into showers of sawdust, as though instantly turned rotten by woodborers.

The chest thumped to the ground as the iron bands melted through and clattered free. The wheels tottered and fell over. Then the hinges where the trail poles joined the cart frame blazed like miniature stars, so that for a moment men ceased fighting to clap their hands over their eyes.

When they opened their eyes again, they saw the chest soaring toward the treetops. It trailed smoke, and some said afterward they saw pieces falling from it. But it was still something as heavy as a half-grown bull, and it was flying faster than any bird when it vanished beyond the trees.

It was only then that Lysinka and others noticed that the cart's remaining guards were all sprawled on the road. The four pierced by arrows looked dead, but two had not been mortally stricken.

As for their six comrades, none of them bore any wounds or signs of violence, save a trickle of blood from the mouth of one and the nose of another. Their faces turned to the sky they would never see again, they lay as still as the ground itself.

Lysinka's orders and the flats of her blades rallied her men. But in the face of such magic, and with none to rally them, the caravan men fled as if the death-pits of Acheron yawned at their heels. Abandoning honor, arms, and their masters' beasts and goods alike, they fled frantically up or down the road. They would have fled into the forest, had the trees allowed their passage.

When the last terror-stricken shrieks and pounding feet faded and silence returned to the forest, Lysinka stood amidst her ashen-faced men, hands on hips. She softened her glare and her voice as she saw they were still there, and all of them armed.

"For this loyalty, my thanks."

"Oh, it was nothing," came a familiar voice. She turned to see the erring guide. He had a pouch, not his own, tucked into his belt, and was sheathing a short sword with an arm that streamed blood. "A wise man fears you more than any mage ever hatched."

Lysinka laughed. "Have that arm tended to, at once. Now, did anyone see which way that cursed chest flew?"

No one answered, which made her think that perhaps "cursed" was not the best word she could have chosen. Then a woman spoke up.

"It was flying north by northeast, the last time I laid eyes on it. But the gods only know how much it could change course out of our sight."

"Well, if they do, they'll not be helping us unless we do our part," Lysinka said. "We'll gain a bit of silver off the leavings of these wretches. I'll have our spies spread it around among the farms and villages to loosen tongues about strange things flying hither and yon."

"Is it wise, to let so many know that we're on the trail of that chest?" someone said.

Lysinka wanted to snarl but forced her voice to cold politeness. Free speaking was the law of her band, and now would be the worst possible time to break it.

"The tale of that chest will be all through the Thanzas before those wretches stop running," she said. "Do you want some hedge-wizard or mushroom-grubber to find it first? The more who know that Lysinka's fighters seek the chest, the fewer will seek it—or dare to keep it·if they do find it.

"You've a reputation bought fairly, with steel and blood. Who will stand against it? No one I know."

They accepted that pronouncement as from the lips of an oracle, Lysinka observed with pleasure. Within, she was less joyful.

North by northeast led into the wildest parts of the Thanzas. There were rumors of sorcerers lurking there, likewise bandit chiefs with the wits and the strength to match Lysinka.

She knew what she risked by seeking that chest. Soon, her fighters would know. But they could do nothing else. Otherwise they risked that hard-earned reputation. Then they would have neither the prize of the chest nor safety from the vengeance of rival bands.

To be sure, Lysinka knew she might in the end be traveling alone. Even this did not make her pause. She would rather be dead than live to hear it said that Lysinka of Mertyos had turned from danger.

One

The Tybor River rises in the southern end of the Border Range, within the region men call "Thanza." Fed by melting snows from the mountains and by streams from the well-watered plains of three kingdoms, it swells rapidly. At last it merges with the briskly flowing Red River to form the mighty Khoratas, which marches through Argos to find the Western Sea in that land's capital of Messantia.

The Tybor's currents are not the swiftest, nor is it wholly free from shoals and rapids. But it is navigable almost up to the mountains, and for much of its length it forms the natural boundary between Ophir and its mighty neighbor to the north, Aquilonia.

On a night in early summer, a man crouched on the Ophirean bank of the Tybor and studied what lay before him. He studied it with eyes of the same ice-blue tint as Lysinka's.

The eyes stared out of a weather-beaten, harsh-featured face, past first youth and not unscarred but still showing a fierce alertness and a keen intelligence. Blue-black hair streamed down to the man's shoulders. The hand that held a branch aside, to give him a better view of the river, was calloused yet sure in its every movement.

Then silently he returned the branch to its original position, and still silently he rose to his booted feet. He was garbed in heavy woollen breeches somewhat the worse for sweat and brambles, a similarly battered shirt of dark green linen, and a belt that supported broadsword, dagger, pouch, and waterskin.

As he stretched to his full height, one could see that he was all but a giant. Only among the Æsir and Vanir, and some tribes in the Black Kingdoms, did more than a handful of men reach his height. Everywhere else men had to look up, to meet those chill blue eyes—if they wished to do so.

The man's name was Conan, and in the many lands where he had wandered and fought, he was known simply as Conan the Cimmerian.

Conan was on the bank of the Tybor River because of his latest adventure, which concerned a certain potent jewel known as the Star of Khorala. In the end, Queen Marala of Ophir had fled for safety to her Aquilonian kin while King Moranthes struggled to guard life and crown from enemies who sought both.

A land rent by civil strife was commonly a good hunting ground for the Cimmerian. He had few scruples about separating those with overmuch wealth from some of it, or splitting a few skulls in the process.

Also, in such times good mercenaries could command a high price, and Conan was both a doughty fighter and a seasoned leader of men. He had been a fighting man since he was fifteen and a captain before his twentieth year, battling in more lands than he had years.

But for every bulging purse waiting to be lifted or mercenary band seeking a battleworthy captain, there was another Ophirean who would think of the price on the Cimmerian's head. King Moranthes had set it at a thousand gold crowns, enough to make a man wealthy for life.

When a man thus found himself worth more dead than alive in a certain land, it was only common prudence for him to seek the greener pastures of other lands.

The quickest way out of Ophir led to the Tybor and across it to Aquilonia. The mightiest of the Hyborian kingdoms was a well-ordered land, with an army that could swallow all the baronial bands of Ophir with the ease of a frog snatching a dragonfly on the wing. No Ophirean in his right senses would pursue Conan there, and no Ophirean witling would last long against Numedides's men.

Of course, a land with *too* much peace might mean lean pickings for a warrior, but Conan had yet to find any such land. Even among the merchant houses of Argos there had been intrigues aplenty to bring his sword out of its scabbard and gold into his purse. It seemed unlikely that in so wealthy a land as Aquilonia, there would be no opportunity for a keen eye and a swift blade; the more so, in as much as there were tales that Numedides's grip was slacking. The pleasures of ruling had long meant more to him than the responsibilities, and such took its toll. When the royal lion grew weak, the lords and cities often turned into wolves.

Conan had seen this in a dozen lands and profited from it in most. Aquilonia it would be—even if at first

he had to turn an honest coin by taking up his father's
trade of smithing!

First, however, there was the matter of crossing the
Tybor River without anyone on either side seeing him.
This meant the use of a boat. Cimmerian strength and
endurance would let him swim, but rivers rusted the
best weapons, and building or navigating a raft would
take too long.

Boats, however, did not grow on trees along the
Tybor like oranges in a noble's garden in Zamboula.
From where Conan stood, the bank was bare of boats
and nearly bare of signs of human habitation.

Conan slipped from his hiding place and began
casting along the bank, like a lion prowling for a roe-
buck on the plains of Stygia. Only the most alert
observer could have seen or heard him more than five
paces away—and the Cimmerian could close that distance before most men could draw a weapon.

Clouds veiled the stars and dimmed the moon, but
Conan also had the clear night-sight as well as the
stalking skill of a great cat. The few times the moon
silvered a path across the Tybor, he found the nearest
cover and watched for signs of pursuit.

He expected none. A man could empty a jug of
good wine in the time it would take to reach the
nearest village. Its folk would hardly be abroad
tonight. As for those seeking the blood price for
Conan, the last band of those whom he had encountered was feeding the ravens two days' travel to the
south. By the time anyone found them, he would be
safe in Aquilonia.

The third time the moon came out, Conan thought
he saw something black jutting from the bank and not
shaped like a fallen tree. The fourth time he was closer
and recognized a boat. A crude one, hollowed from a

log, but it had paddles and a carved ornamental stern. It also had two guards.

Conan moved within striking distance. He needed no further aid from the moon to see that the men were armed and wore leather cuirasses and rusty Nemedian-style open-faced helmets. Not Ophirean soldiers, or even lords' levies. Likely as not, they were men about some business even less lawful than the Cimmerian's.

As Conan crouched in the shadows, seeking to overhear the men above the chuckle and sigh of the water, a light blinked thrice from the far bank. One of the men raised a dark lantern, aimed the open side toward shore, and manipulated the rattling shutter.

A signal and a reply. Clearly the far bank held the mens' friends. Conan would find no warm welcome from the stolen boat. He moved forward cautiously, in search of a better view.

It was then that he saw the ship.

She was a fair-sized vessel, the Tybor being deep enough for ocean-going ships at least as far as Shamar, two days upstream. With sails spread on both masts, she was barely making steerage way.

River pirates.

Conan would have wagered a sack of silver that these men were nothing else. The oncoming ship was their intended prey. The two men were most likely scouts intended to sight the ship if she took a course close along the Ophirean shore.

The hunters had just become the hunted.

Conan waited until the two men were close together and staring out at the river. No one, it seemed, had ever taught them that even when all seems quiet, sentries should not stand too close together.

The first man heard the Cimmerian just in time to turn halfway around before Conan struck. Conan shifted the aim of his blow from the back to the belly, so the man only doubled up and collapsed, instead of having his spine broken.

The other had time to draw a short sword before Conan's second punch crashed into his jaw. The sword flew from the man's hand and the man himself flew backward off the bank into the river. The current and the weight of his armor dragged him out of sight in a moment.

Conan knelt to search the first man for valuables or weapons. Then the fellow followed his companion into the water. The Cimmerian climbed into the boat.

It had four paddles and no steering oar, but Conan was as at home on or in the water as on land. This had not always been so, Cimmeria being landlocked, but the years of wandering had changed him. Much of his seamanship Conan had learned at the hands of a lady named Bêlit, now only ashes drifting on the currents of the Western Sea but still holding a warm place in the Cimmerian's memory.

Conan thrust the past from his mind, slashed the rope holding the canoe to the bank, and thrust hard with the paddle.

Conan's first thought had been to steer straight for the ship to warn her crew. Then he considered that an armed stranger paddling out of the night might be taken for one of the pirates and so be sprouting arrows before he could prove otherwise.

That was if the ship's crew had much fight in them at all. If they did not, it would be best to give them a wide berth—and meet the pirates straightforwardly.

The paddle blades' angle changed; the canoe swung about and headed for the point on the opposite bank from which Conan had seen the signal light. It was a moderately safe wager that the remaining pirates set out from there.

When Conan finally sighted them, the pirates were within easy bowshot and the moon was veiled once again. Conan counted four or five canoes, with as many men paddling in each one. He crouched low, to give the appearance of one of the men on the bank, both of whom had been a head shorter than the Cimmerian.

But his weapons were ready and every sense at its keenest. Now, if those sons of mangy she-asses could be just a trifle slow with the bows they must have—

Someone raised an arm, signaling from the leading canoe.

Conan raised his own right arm in a brief reply, entirely to buy time.

The pirate started waving his arm frantically. Conan dug his paddle into the water. The pirate chief clearly suspected that something was amiss but did not dare a shout and alert the oncoming ship. This might give Conan just a trifle more time.

Arrows flew before he rammed the chief's canoe amidships, but in the dark, archers shooting in haste hit only the river. A moment later the bow of Conan's canoe drove in among the paddles of the chief's craft. A man cursed as a flying paddle broke his arm—then gasped as one of his own comrades silenced him with an arm around the throat.

This brawl did little to achieve silence. Conan rose to his feet with a thundering Black Coast war cry, then leaped from his canoe with a Cimmerian curse on his lips. His own canoe overturned and his plunging weight drove the pirate canoe down until water slopped over the gunwale.

Then Conan was among the pirates, wielding a dagger and a stout club taken from the pirate on shore.

He would save his broadsword for when he had room enough to use it, hard to come by in a canoe.

Dagger and club were enough to kill two men in the space of three breaths and drive two others overboard. This left Conan facing the pirate chief, and with room to draw his sword—except that another flight of arrows hissed by as the Cimmerian drew.

He needed to be close so that the archers in the other canoes would fear to slaughter their chief along with the enemy sprung out of the night. Conan gripped the gunwale of the canoe and lashed out with both feet. He caught the pirate chief in one knee. The man's scream drowned out the crunch of bone.

The Cimmerian leaped atop the man and grappled him barehanded. The chief had the courage to draw a dagger, but Conan hammered his wrist against a thwart until once again bone shattered. The chief bared his teeth, startlingly white in a hairy, filthy face, and tried to bite the Cimmerian. Conan slammed the man's head hard against the bottom of the canoe once, then a second time for good measure, and the chief went limp.

The next moment, Conan flung himself over the side, a heartbeat ahead of more arrows, most of which plummeted straight into the canoe, except for a few that fell far to the side. A wild gurgling scream accounted for one of the swimming pirates who would swim no more.

Conan thrust club and dagger into his belt and dove deep, under the canoe now crewed only by the dead. When he rose again, the ship loomed higher than before, and lanterns glowed on her deck where darkness had once ruled.

The Cimmerian was within arm's length of another canoeload of pirates who seemed so intent on their archery that they were ignoring both the ship and his presence.

They paid dearly for that error. Conan surged out of the water, gripped the canoe's side with both hands, and flung himself backward. The canoe capsized, bodies splashed into the water to the left and right of the attacker, and another heave brought the canoe back to an even keel.

One pirate had not gone over the side. He crouched, facing Conan with a long dagger in one hand and a quiver slung across his back. Conan snatched up the handiest weapon, the pirate's fallen bow, and parried the first thrust of the dagger with the stout wood. That gave him time to draw his own club, a trifle longer than the dagger.

The man twisted aside from the first blow and thrust at Conan again. The second swing of the club broke the man's right shoulder, but he was stout-hearted enough to shift the dagger to his left hand. Then he screamed, as the Cimmerian lifted him with both hands and hurled him into a third canoe. The pirate crew toppled in every direction, two of them going overboard as their canoe's suddenly wandering course took it within reach of Conan.

This time Conan did not need to leap. His weapons could reach far enough. He flung the club, taking a pirate in the temple. Helmet cracked, skull shattered, and the man toppled limply over the side. The Cimmerian gripped the bow of the other canoe with his free hand and heaved.

Conan's canoe nearly sank as the bow of the other canoe leaped out of the water. The remaining men in it reeled, one unfortunate enough to land within reach of Conan's sword. The Cimmerian dropped the canoe, sending another man overboard, and slashed two-handed at the nearest prey.

The sword was the best Nemedian work, fit to kill at a stroke even one-handed when properly wielded. With both the Cimmerian's stout-thewed arms driving it, the blade sheared through the man's shoulder blade, rib cage, and belly, to jar against his hipbone. He was dead before he struck the river, and the last man in the canoe hurled himself overboard with a howl of stark terror.

Conan was also in the river a moment later. A flight of arrows hissed through the air where he had been, save for one that scored his ribs. He had taken worse hurts from enthusiastic bedmates, and he knew of nothing in the Tybor to be drawn by the scent of blood.

He heard a second flight of arrows hiss into the water as he dove deep. When he broke into the air again, he remained low, his nostrils just above the water. The ship was looming closer still, her decks now blazing with lanterns like a town square at festival time. She was also now under sweeps as well as sail, four on either side.

The men aboard must have thought to outspeed their foes rather than outfight them. Well enough, save that their torch-dazzled eyes had missed something the Cimmerian saw clearly from his vantage on the dark river.

A long, low canoe was creeping in from the port quarter of the ship. Conan judged it to be carrying at least ten men, enough to clear the ship's decks easily if most of her crew was below at the sweeps.

The Cimmerian had done all he could do as a lone wolf in the river. It was time to fight among allies with a deck underfoot. He judged distance carefully, then dove again.

When he rose a second time, one of the sweeps was within arm's reach. He gripped the blade with both hands and hauled himself on to the shaft. Hand over hand he climbed the shaft of the sweep, until he could reach out and find a grip on the ship's side.

The timbers were weed-slimed and splintery, but the Cimmerian's grip was strong. Moreover, finding handholds on a ship's side was child's play to Conan even before he sailed with Bêlit—to Conan or any other man who grew up climbing the cliffs of Cimmeria.

As Conan climbed, archers in the large canoe saw him. Three arrows *thunked* into the wood around him, a fourth grazed his shoulder, a wound even more trivial than the mark on his hip. He gripped the railing, vaulted over it, and crouched on the deck as the next arrows whistled by.

"Ahoy!" came a shout from aft. "Who in the name of Erlik's chamberpot are you?"

Conan remained crouching. "A friend who'd rather fight for you than with you. Or swim alone." He looked about him. "In Mitra's name, get the men up from the sweeps. Your deck's bare as a tavern dancer and the pirates are coming up from astern!"

"Who are you to give me—?"

The man's indignation ended along with his life, as a pirate archer put an arrow into his throat. Conan sprang up, caught the man as he toppled, and lowered him to the deck.

"Ahoy below!" he shouted, loud enough to raise echoes from the nearer shore. "Drop the sweeps and man the decks! The pirates are boarding!"

Before anyone below could reply, a grappling hook hurtled over the railing and caught in the frame around the mainmast. A second caught the railing itself. Conan slashed the rope to the first hook with his sword, then clutched the second hook and heaved.

Two pirates were already climbing the rope. One fell back into the canoe, landing across the gunwale. The crack of his spine snapping reached Conan's ears. The other pirate lunged upward and seemed to fly over the railing. He landed rolling with a cat's agility and came up with dagger in hand.

For a moment, Conan had no weapon in hand— save the grappling hook itself. He parried one dagger thrust with the hook, then closed and ripped upward. The man screamed like a damned spirit and fell, clutching spouting gashes in belly and thigh with desperate, futile hands.

Moments later men began swarming up from below, just as the ship ran in among the surviving canoes of Conan's earlier opponents. Pirates swarmed aboard from both aft and forward, but Conan's warning and stand had bought the crew just enough time to reach the decks.

Even then the pirates had the edge in numbers and in steel. But the sailors were fighting for their lives, marlinspikes and sheath knives have never been despicable weapons, and the crew also had Conan. As men in many lands had learned to their cost, in a fight he was worth five ordinary men.

The Cimmerian buried the grappling hook in the skull of his first opponent. It stuck there, so he kicked the dying man overboard and drew his sword. He had to face a second opponent before he could draw his dagger, but he had the advantage in both reach and speed on the man. The pirate's life ended soon after Conan closed against him with steel in both hands.

Conan turned at a warning shout, to parry a murderous blow at his thigh. His dagger locked the foe's sword, and the Cimmerian brought his own blade around to strike deep into the man's neck. A bearded head lolled on jerkin-clad shoulders, and another pirate sprawled on the deck.

Conan now gave way before three pirates who seemed to have some notion of fighting as a team. But as he did, a sailor heaved up a grating under the feet of the middle pirate. He overbalanced and fell forward. Conan's sword was not meant for thrusting, but he kept the point more than sharp enough to go clean through the falling pirate.

This briefly left Conan with only his dagger against two swordsmen, so he continued his retreat. He retreated as far as the water barrel lashed to the deck by the tiller ropes, then slashed the ropes and turned the barrel on its side. A fierce push sent it rolling at the two men. One of them did not leap clear; as it passed on he lay screaming with a crushed leg, until a sailor crushed his skull to end the screaming.

The last man came at Conan with a berserker's speed and fury—and carelessness. He never noticed that the Cimmerian had picked up the fallen dipper from the water barrel. The man's sword met the dipper's iron shaft, sparks flew, and the man howled as the Cimmerian's dagger sank deep into his belly, through a gap in his aging corselet.

Conan now saw that the deck was all but clear of live, fighting pirates. A few were scrambling over the railing or leaping for their lives. Conan ran to the fallen barrel, heaved it aloft and strode to the railing. The large canoe was directly below.

The barrel was nearly empty, or not even the Cimmerian could have lifted it. It was quite heavy enough to shatter the bottom of the canoe. Nearly riven in two pieces, the pirate craft drifted away, its surviving crew clinging. The canoes forward also withdrew with more haste than dignity, urged along by a sailor who had picked up a fallen pirate bow and was emptying the quiver with great enthusiasm.

A man with a neat gray beard and a searching eye who barely reached the Cimmerian's shoulder came up to Conan.

"Many thanks, friend. You named yourself truly. Have you any other name?"

"Sellus," Conan said briefly. This man did not seem to be one to sell to the Ophireans a man to whom he owed his ship and life. But a thousand gold crowns could do more than ale or wine to addle the wits of the wisest of men.

"A northerner, too, by your looks."

"So I have heard," Conan said. "May I ask if I am addressing the captain?"

"The captain lies dead with an arrow in his throat. I am Levites of Messantia, owner of the *Sirdis*. I can reward you as I please."

"I'll not refuse a free passage to Shamar," Conan said. "As for anything more—scum like those pirates, I fight as the spirit takes me. Judge my worth for yourself, and I'll accept the judgement of an honest man."

The owner's eyes studied Conan. The Cimmerian suspected that the merchant was one who knew how to squeeze any coin until it shrieked and would take him at his word.

A smile twisted his lips as he thought of how the merchant would reply to learning that his savior had begun his life in the Hyborian lands as a thief in Zamora. Not the most successful of thieves, but nonetheless one with more in common with the pirates than it would be prudent to admit here.

"The passage is yours, upon my word, and in the best cabin we have free. Also something for your purse, so it need not be slack-bellied when we reach Shamar."

"I could ask no more."

That was hardly the truth, but Levites also seemed a man with whom there could easily be such a thing as too much honesty.

Two

Conan slept little and lightly during the two days it took *Sirdis* to finish her upriver passage to Shamar. Nor did he take off as much as his boots, let alone his weapons.

It was not Levites's niggardliness that made the Cimmerian wary. It was his being a Messantian, and therefore a subject of the king of Argos. Ophir was not the only land where the Cimmerian had a price on his head.

It was a tedious tale for the most part, his sojourn in Argos, and those parts that were not tedious might injure the reputation of ladies, which was against the Cimmerian's notions of honor. But it had begun with his becoming one of the Guardians, the protectors of the city before it gained itself a king, and had ended with his dashing down the quays and leaping aboard the first outbound ship.

Conan sometimes thought he might have risen high in the service of the new Argossean monarchy, had he been one to keep his mouth shut in the face of injustice to old comrades. But if that was a gift, it was not one the gods had given him. He had spoken, the king's judges had replied, and Conan ended at sea, on his way to his meeting with Bêlit.

Wherefore he did not much regret his departure from Argos. He knew this of kings, that they more often than not preferred lapdogs to warriors, and no man in his right senses could call himself ill-fated who had held Bêlit in his arms.

But aboard an Argossean ship, none of this might matter. If Levites had risen through royal favor, he might be eager to bring the Cimmerian to "justice" out of loyalty to his liege. Were he his own man, he still might think of one reward from Ophir and another from his king, for the head of the same man.

Still, Levites showed no signs of suspicion on the voyage, nor was Conan molested, either waking or sleeping. Perhaps it was the sight of the Cimmerian squatting on deck, cleaning rust and Tybor slime from his sword, that kept the peace. Sitting, he rose shoulder-high to some of the crew, and his scars and scowl were enough to make any man cautious about approaching him.

On the third morning, *Sirdis* warped into the docks of Shamar. Conan stood in the pay line with the crew for his reward, where he received much hearty gratitude and invitations to parties at Shamar's taverns. He refused none of them, although he had no intention of being found anywhere near those taverns. But if Levites or anyone in his pay was looking for him where he would not be, that was more time for his trail to grow cold. . . .

* * *

A village stood on the site of Shamar in the distant days before Atlantis sank and the dark shadow of Acheron's evil magic stretched across the land. Water flowed from abundant springs, fish abounded, and steep-sided hills made for easy defense.

When a city called Shamar came to be in a land not yet called Aquilonia, it needed all the defenses nature and men could contrive. Thrice it was besieged from Ophir, twice from Nemedia, and once by the royal host of Aquilonia when the city rose in rebellion. Half a score of times river pirates snatched ships and men from its very wharves.

Yet the city survived, prospered, and grew, repairing the breaches in its old walls, stretching out new quarters across the hills until they in turn needed walls, and in time becoming one of Aquilonia's great cities. Its governor was always a duke, its garrison numbered in the thousands, with horse, foot, and siege engines ready to hand, and its merchants were among the shrewdest and richest in a realm not lacking such men.

How many people it held, Conan doubted that anyone knew. He knew only that it held enough to make it easy for a man to lose himself among them.

It also held its share of pleasure quarters and thieves' alleys, where few honest men ventured at all. It would take more than a thousand crowns to tempt them there in search of one who would assuredly fight like a lion if they were so unfortunate as to overtake him.

Levites had not been so closefisted as Conan had expected. With his own purse and his reward from the merchant, Conan was well-fitted to hide longer than his enemies could seek.

He might even find a frolicsome wench for a night or two.

* * *

Conan was not the easiest of men to forget, but in the quarters where he found refuge, a man was seldom asked his business and a man like Conan was asked hardly at all. He had a brisk set-to with one panderer and his hired bravos when they thought Conan should pay before the woman came with him, and in the end none of the woman's protectors were in any fit state to receive payment.

With the woman, however, Conan was more than generous. For her own safety, he advised her to leave Shamar. It was to put her aboard a ship downriver that he left the pleasure quarters for the first time, on the morning of his seventh day in Shamar.

On the quay, they embraced—almost chastely, to the casual eye.

"Farewell, Brollya," Conan said.

"The gods be with you, Sellus—if that is your name."

Conan's face might have been a stone mask. The wench had her wits about her—but then, he preferred such women.

"I'm no priest to say where the gods are. But I suppose they can't be too far from me, or I'd been long dead."

"Sad for me, had it been so. I knew that Mikros was growing old and foul-tempered, but not bloodthirsty. I am well out of his reach, and you should think on traveling too. Mikros has friends."

"They've poor taste, if they call that heap of ox turds a friend. A good few men have tried to put their daggers in my back and ended with my dagger in their gizzards. I'll lose no sleep over Mikros's bullies."

"Be ye coming or be ye jabbering till sunset?" a harsh voice inquired from the deck above.

"Farewell, then," Brollya said, and stood on tiptoe to kiss the Cimmerian. He put his arms around her waist and lifted her, while she gripped his shoulders. Then he set her gently back on the quay and urged the porter with her baggage on to the gangplank.

The haze burned off the river as the ship headed downstream. Soon all that Conan could see of Brollya was her red hair, glinting as she stood at the railing amidships. He paid off the porter, generously enough to make the man bow extravagantly, then went in search of something to break his fast.

Since Conan reached Shamar, spring had given way to summer. It was already hot, and the water the apprentices splashed about to clean their masters' doorsteps dried almost before they could wield their brooms. Markets, stalls, shops, and street vendors were all in full cry, and down one street Conan even saw a band of jugglers and pipers beginning their act.

He bought sausages and watered wine from one of the stalls and continued on up Tanners' Hill. From the summit of that hill one could see the whole of Shamar, and Conan never spent much time in a new city without doing his best to know his way around it. A few well-greased palms had bought him much useful knowledge; his own eyes would bring him more.

Halfway up the hill, he came to a large wooden board, fresh-planed pine with the ink of its notice barely dry. It hung on the front wall of an inn called the Golden Lion, whose carved sign told Conan that the woodcarver had never seen either a lion or gold in his life.

The Cimmerian stood and read:

COME, YOUNG HEROES!

ALL WHO WISH TO SERVE THEIR REALM AND RULER ARE CALLED TO ENLIST IN THE THANZA RANGERS.

THIS NEW LEVY SEEKS A THOUSAND STOUT HEARTS AND ARMS, TO MARCH INTO THE STRONGHOLDS OF THE BANDITS OF THE THANZA HILLS. FREE THE LAND OF THEIR SCOURGE AND DIVIDE THEIR ILL-GOTTEN GAINS AMONG YOU!

WHILE YOU SERVE, YOU SHALL LEARN THE CRAFT OF ARMS FROM SEASONED VETERANS OF THE HOSTS OF AQUILONIA. YOU SHALL BE CLOTHED, FED, AND ARMED AT THE EXPENSE OF COUNT RALTHON, CHARGED BY HIS MAJESTY KING NUMEDIDES WITH THE RAISING OF THE THANZA RANGERS.

ALL OFFENSES SHALL BE PARDONED FOR THOSE WHO ENLIST FOR A FULL YEAR, AND LIKEWISE ALL DEBTS FORGIVEN.

WHERESOEVER YOU READ THIS SIGN, THERE SITS A MAN READY TO ENLIST BRAVE SPIRITS FOR THE THANZA RANGERS.

COME FORTH, AND BE NAMED AMONG THOSE WHO DESERVE WELL OF YOUR HOMELAND!

KLARNIDES

CAPTAIN OF FOOT IN THE
HOST OF AQUILONIA

Conan read the sign with a bemused look on his face, and not because he found the reading difficult. No man to sit down with a scroll unless he needed the knowledge it held, the Cimmerian could still make himself understood in half a dozen tongues and understand as many more. Aquilonian he had learned early, as the realm's might made its tongue a language a traveler might encounter on any road from Vendhya to Vanaheim.

Bemusement gave way to a broad grin, then to laughter. Conan had seen such appeals in other lands, and even responded to some. He knew perfectly well what this sign most likely meant.

Some local noble was paying overdue taxes or perhaps a bribe to the court, by raising the so-called Thanza Rangers. The men would be the scourings and sweepings of Shamar and the country about it, debtors, fugitives, and every other sort of man who likely deserved naught but a swift knock on the head

The food and wine would be of the poorest, the clothing rags, the weapons castoffs that no smith would own to having made. The men would have no pay, and nothing to show for their work (if they did any) unless they not only reached the hills but defeated the bandits, reached their strongholds, and received a decent share of loot that was most commonly stolen by their captains.

Conan wondered who Klarnides, Captain of Foot, might be. If he was some relative of the count lending himself to this bad jest for gain, Conan would not even waste time spitting on the man if their paths crossed.

If Klarnides was in truth a captain in the formidable host of Aquilonia, he had Conan's sympathy. That and no more, for the Cimmerian did not intend to be found within a league of the Thanza Rangers if he could avoid it. But certainly no less sympathy, as any man deserved, if he was marching to his death or disgrace in the name of duty.

Briefly, Conan wondered why Klarnides was not marching out with his own company. Was King Numedides's host shorthanded of late? There had been rumors that the king's weakening hand had begun to affect his host. Old veterans were said to be retiring in disgust and new recruits buying themselves free, even if this left them in thrall to the moneylenders.

Not his affair, Conan decided. He would be long gone from Aquilonia before it made any difference to him whether the whole host of the realm dropped dead in the streets. Indeed, such chaos as that would unleash might profit a man with a quick eye and a sure hand—

Conan's instincts hinted of the gathering at the end of the street before his eyes assured him of its certainty. He shifted his gaze, and recognized two of the men in the gathering.

One was Mikros the Shamaran panderer. A second was Levites the Argossean merchant. Conan could not put names to the others, but he knew their look. They were the hardest sort of professional thief-takers, probably former soldiers turned bravo—and he had little doubt as to what thief they had been ordered to take.

Conan had learned more than a few of the hunter's tricks well before he left Cimmeria. One of the foremost

among these was *never* to show you knew that your
prey or your enemy had sighted you. So the gaze of the
ice-blue eyes passed lightly and swiftly over Levites,
Mikros, and their men, as if they were merely a dead
dog or a pile of offal lying in the street.

The simplest solution would be to march into the
Golden Lion and enlist, shielding himself behind the
promised pardon. The most wretched, starveling levies
still offered a seasoned warrior more opportunities
than any prison cell!

What stood between Conan and that solution was
something even simpler: the Golden Lion's doors
were all locked, its windows shuttered. If he broke in,
he might still find no one there to enlist him in the
Thanza Rangers, and he would have committed a
crime for which a man might be hanged, in broad daylight before more witnesses than he could count on his
two hands.

It would therefore be well to find some other way of
staying ahead of the thief-takers.

Behind the men was the cross street that Conan had
used to reach the Golden Lion. It ran uphill and down,
and would let the Cimmerian vanish into any of a half-
dozen quarters of the city where thief-takers went at
their peril.

If he could pass that way safely. The thief-takers
might have only a description of him, and Mikros had
been drunk the night of their quarrel. But Levites
knew Conan's countenance far too well for the wanderer's comfort.

It was a pity that Levites was not the sort of merchant to count his money in safety while others dirtied
their hands in his service.

Going the other way, the street branched swiftly
into a maze of alleys. Conan knew little of what lay

within that maze, but wagered that the thief-takers knew hardly more.

Conan turned, with ease and grace, as if turning his back on a dozen armed enemies was no more serious than sending back a jug of poor wine. Only a keen-eyed observer could have known from the set of the Cimmerian's broad shoulders and the hands only a finger's length from the hilts of sword and dagger that he was as ready to fight as a hungry panther to leap upon prey.

It took more than usual self-command for Conan not to look back. But he had seen no bows among the thief-takers, the street was growing too crowded for archery regardless, and as long as those behind could see only his hair and back—

"Stop him!"

Even now, Conan did not break into a run. His hearing was not as keen in a noisy city street as it was in a forest or mountain fastness. It would still give warning of an enemy before the man could reach striking distance.

So Conan continued to walk with the careless air of a country lad in the great city for the first time, bemused by its sights, until he heard booted feet running behind him, drawing closer. Only then did he whirl, his sword out, striking with the flat of the blade at the nearest thief-taker.

The man had a shield on his back and a short sword in his belt. They might have been grave goods in a Stygian tomb for all the use he had from them. The flat of Conan's blade took the man across the throat, flinging him backward into the path of the bravo closest behind him. The two men tangled, toppled, and crashed on to the cobblestones. The first writhed, trying to claw breath into his throat, while the second lay stunned by the fall.

Others came on, but now Conan was running, beginning with a good lead as well. His long legs increased the lead, until he reached a vendor with a small green-wheeled cart of honey-glazed winter apples.

Conan snatched the cart out of the vendor's hands and pushed fiercely. The cart rattled over the cobblestones and overturned squarely in the path of the remaining thief-takers. One vaulted it at the run but came down on a fallen apple, so that his feet flew out from under him. Others piled up behind the cart or slowed to go around it.

That gave the Cimmerian the time he needed, to vanish into the alleys. Once well-hidden in the shadows of the alleys, Conan faced another choice. Go on, out of Shamar and perhaps on out of Aquilonia? Or double back and leave Shamar as one of the Thanza Rangers?

He had to admit that the notice had piqued his curiousity. He had never explored the Border Range between Aquilonia and Nemedia and seldom turned down an opportunity to see a new land. Also, traveling in company he had a better chance to pocket bandit loot if there was any or slip unpursued out of Aquilonia if there was none.

Conan found a momentarily deserted stretch of alley and began climbing the nearest wall. It had even more handholds than the timbers of *Sirdis's* hull, but was in considerably worse repair. Bricks and tiles lay scattered in the muck of the unpaved alley before Conan pulled himself on to the roof.

All that remained was to cross a few rooftops to

throw off the last hardy pursuers. Then he would find himself a secure refuge until the Golden Lion opened.

Conan looked up at the sun. For all that he and Brollya had been awake before dawn (having, in truth, slept little during the night), it was well into the morning. Unless the Golden Lion's customers were all late sleepers, the inn should be open long before Mikros's thief-takers thought of taking to the rooftops in search of their prey.

The day grew hot, then scorching, until most men would have been driven to shelter. But most men were not the Cimmerian, whose mighty frame had endured the damp heat of Vendhya and the Black Coast, the blazing heat of a dozen deserts, and the cold of Hyperborean lands and seas. Conan sat with his back braced against one chimney and his feet against another, listening to the din of Shamar going about its daily business.

At last he heard the sound that he had been awaiting.

"Come one, come all, good folk. The Golden Lion awaits your thirst with fine wine, your hunger with hot pasties, your weariness with the softest beds in Shamar."

This went on for some while, as Conan scrambled from rooftop to rooftop, leaping across the narrow alleys with a cat's agility. He would wager everything in his purse that the crier's patter bore small resemblance to the truth, but he did not care. His business with the Golden Lion had little to do with the quality of its hospitality.

Conan made a swift passage across the rooftops of the maze, but came to a halt at its edge. The gap between the roof where he crouched now (amid billows of reeking smoke from some shop far below, which smelled worse than a tannery) and the Golden Lion was too wide for even him to leap.

Also, it would be in plain sight of a score of passersby below—and of two of the thief-catchers, who stood sentinel, one to either side of the inn's door. A slight youth wearing a red tunic with the badge of the Thanza Rangers stood a little to one side, casting sour looks when he thought the armed men would not notice.

It seemed that Levites's wits were as active as his body. No slipping down to the ground unseen and sauntering in to the recruiting sergeant for Conan.

But the huddled buildings and narrow alleys of the maze extended well to the north, to the rear of the Golden Lion. Keeping low, Conan made his way across roofs of timber and tiles, of slate and shingle, and even a few crumbling layers of brick that might once have been the floors of rooms in towers on the walls of ancient Shamar.

His weight nearly took him through one of those layers of brick, and he heard cries and curses from below, but no pursuit followed. He was dripping sweat by the time he finished his journey, but before the sun reached its zenith Conan had found a safe leap to the roof of the Golden Lion.

Without hesitating, the Cimmerian flung himself into space. He landed asprawl, fingers and toes scrabbling for purchase on the steeply pitched roof and not without bruises and grazes. But he had a safe perch on the roof of the Golden Lion, and now all that remained was to make his way downstairs and enlist in the Thanza Rangers.

He was prying open a dormer window when it opened from within and a maidservant stared out. She took one look at the apparition facing her, a giant in breeches and vest and wearing enough steel to arm a company, took one deep breath, and let out a scream that sent birds fluttering up for many streets around.

Who else the scream might have alarmed Conan did not wait to learn. He flung himself through the window, his broad shoulders splintering rotten wood from the frame. He landed rolling, sprang to his feet, drew his dagger, and gripped the maid by the shoulder.

"Oh, hush, girl," he said with rough kindness. She could not be more than fifteen. "Be quiet, and say I put you in fear of your life. Then none will harm you."

From the look of the girl's wide eyes and mouth, it would scarcely be a lie. Conan crossed the tiny chamber in three strides, listened for a moment at the door, then flung it open and started down the stairs, taking two steps at a time.

If the maid's scream had not warned the thief-takers, Conan's thundering descent of the stairs certainly did. Doors flew open as he passed, servants scattered like chaff on the wind before him, and he heard voices shouting, "He's in the Golden Lion! Head him off before the taproom!"

It was as well to learn from his enemies where he should go. It was not as pleasant to learn that they seemed to be thinking ahead of him. Conan had no illusions about his chances of enlisting in the Thanza Rangers if he shed Aquilonian blood beforehand.

So he came down the last flight of stairs with all steel sheathed and both hands ready to strike or merely push as necessary. One thief-taker had reached the second step from the bottom, and Conan was on him before he could bring his sword around, almost before he could shout.

One stout Cimmerian fist crashed into the man's

jaw, snatching him off his feet. Conan's other hand caught the man by the collar and lifted him. With the thief-taker tucked under one arm and the other hand balled into a ready fist, Conan stepped lightly down the last of the stairs and out to the inn's front hall.

He might have been skewered on half a dozen swords in the next moment, save that the thief-takers could not so use the Cimmerian without similarly slaughtering their comrade. Steel turned aside as Conan strode into the taproom, the thief-taker still under one arm.

"Sellus the Northerner reporting for duty," Conan said, raising his free hand in the traditional Aquilonian salute.

Two men sat at a table near the far side of the taproom. Conan noticed that they were both armed and had their backs to a solid brick wall. The smaller of the two men was plainly some variety of clerk. The larger was not as easily dismissed.

He was nearly as tall as the Cimmerian, and if anything, broader across the shoulders. He wore a leather corselet with cast bronze fastenings and silvered mail shoulder guards, and his head was shaved to reveal a double handful of scars—nor were those the only marks of battle he showed.

"No duties for you today," the man said. "Nor for your friend here."

The thief-taker tried to bite Conan. Conan held him at a distance, making the gesture futile. He was aware of several pairs of hostile eyes gouging holes in his back, but doubted that they would attack in front of such a formidable witness as the shaven-headed soldier.

"Oh, he's not at all fit for duty," Conan said lightly. "He had a dizzy spell on the stairs and I brought him down to find some place where he can sleep it off. *I'm here to enlist in the Thanza Rangers.*"

"Sellus the Northerner, you call yourself?" the big soldier said. "Well, I'm Tharmis Rog, Master-at-Arms of the Rangers. You ever soldiered before?"

"Here and there," Conan said. "I've been a sell-sword in—"

"He's been a thief in—!" shouted someone from behind, then pandemonium erupted.

"Ho! You can't go in—" began another, in a voice so high-pitched Conan was reminded of a eunuch.

"Take him!" a third voice shouted, and *that* voice the Cimmerian recognized as belonging to Levites. He dropped the thief-taker, snatching the man's knife from his belt as he fell. Then Conan sprang over the table and whirled, his back to the wall and the table and the Ranger recruiting party between him and the thief-takers.

Fear of Levites or greed for Ophirean gold drove the thief-takers beyond the bounds of sense. Two charged forward, snatching short javelins from under their dirt-caked cloaks. Before anyone else could move or speak, they threw.

They underestimated both Conan and Tharmis Rog. The Cimmerian's sword flicked out between the two Aquilonians, with the speed of a striking adder. It caught one javelin in midflight with an echoing clang and sent it flying vertically upward. It sank a hand's breadth into an oak beam and hung there quivering.

The other javelin was a clean miss, harming no more than the soot-blackened paneling of the taproom. But Conan's evasion of it allowed a bravo with a scarred face to get behind him.

The man was in easy reach of Tharmis Rog, but the master-at-arms might have been a granite monument.

He merely grinned as he watched Conan whirl just in time to see the long dagger stabbing toward his back and kick hard.

His boot thudded into the man's belly. All his breath went out of him, as he flew over a table, shattering a dirty wine jug, and crashed to the floor amid a litter of overturned stools and benches.

Now Conan returned Tharmis Rog's grin. His reply held no mirth, merely a promise that the matter would not be forgotten.

Whether it was the grin or perhaps satisfaction that Conan had survived some rite of testing, Tharmis Rog now stepped out from behind the table. He greeted a fresh javelin with a stool held out in front of him. The javelin drove completely through the woven cane of the stool's seat but barely scratched the master-at-arms' corselet. As deferentially as a steward presenting the latest vintage to a royal duke, he held out the newly decorated stool to the thief-taker.

"Pray take your weapon, sir—"

"I won't—"

"Oh, you will, little man." Suddenly the courtesy was gone and Tharmis Rog looked more like a bear about to attack. "Take that sticker back and keep it out of my sight. That, or choose between eating it at one end or wearing it at the other."

The thief-taker turned as pale as his Stygian-dark complexion would allow and hastily obeyed.

"Now," the eunuchlike voice said. "What is all this brawling over one recruit? I think I have the right to an answer."

The speaker was the youth who had stood outside, wearing the red tunic. Conan now noticed that he also wore white kidskin boots, and a sword that must have been worth a year or more of Tharmis Rog's pay.

Levites looked at the youth and began to splutter. Tharmis Rog made a noise like a bear feeding and Levites was silent.

"Either explain or get out while we enlist our friend Sellus here," Rog growled.

The danger of losing those crowns loosened Levites's tongue. It also loosened Mikros's. Both tried to talk at once until Rog drew his sword. It made only a faint rasp as it darted free of its scabbard, but he could not have gained more attention in less time if he'd blown a trumpet.

Tharmis Rog and the youth listened attentively to Levites telling the story of Conan's crimes in Ophir and Aquilonia. Conan listened in silence. If he had not found an ally in Tharmis Rog, there would be time enough to do something about it when Levites ran out of wind.

That took a good while, and Rog was again imitating a bear when the merchant at last fell silent. Then he turned to Conan.

"What have you to say to this?"

"It's the way Levites and Mikros see it, no doubt. But they didn't tell you everything."

Conan added a few details, such as his saving *Sirdis* from the pirates, Mikros's treatment of his women, and other matters. As the Cimmerian spoke, the two Aquilonian soldiers both took on a predatory look.

"Mikros," the youth said at last. "You have no place before the law. Hold your tongue or the watch will learn of this." His voice sounded much less like a eunuch's now.

"Master Levites," he went on. "Aquilonia and Argos have no quarrels, and I would be loathe to make one."

"Then I thank you for your honorably returning Conan to—" Levities blurted.

"I am returning no one to you," the youth said. "He may not even be the man you seek. Also, if he did save your ship, it will be known on the waterfront. Our sailors and dockhands will not be happy to handle your cargoes, if you show such ingratitude. Or do you call him a liar in the matter of the pirates?"

Conan threw Levites a look, which said plainly that if the merchant named the Cimmerian a liar, those would be the last words he ever spoke. Levites swallowed and wiped sweat from his brow, for all that the taproom was cooler than the streets.

"He did fight, much as he says."

"Then go back to Messantia and meditate upon ingratitude," the youth said.

Levites looked ready to argue yet again, but Tharmis Rog growled. "Go back, or what'll happen to you and your ships will cost a deal more than a thousand crowns," he said. "There've even been rumors of Argossean merchants buying the pirates' aid against rivals. Now, would you like *that* noised about among the men who've lost shipmates to the pirates?"

The speed with which Levites withdrew showed what he thought of that.

With the taproom at last empty of thief-takers and other unwanted bystanders, Conan swore his oath of enlistment in the Thanza Rangers. To strengthen it, he repeated the whole oath, instead of merely saying, "I so swear" at the end of each sentence. That would prove him willing to be bound more tightly to the Rangers and also prove that he was no witling.

"Now, you're well enough off for boots and weapons," Rog said. "But you turn over all your money. To me, here, now."

Conan's curses rattled jugs and bottles on the taproom's shelves. Finally Rog held up a hand. "It's a lawful order, which you swore to obey. Hand it over, or I'll strike you off the books and you go take your chances with the thief-takers. We'll need most of it to pay for the damage to the Golden Lion."

Conan undid his purse from his belt and flung it down on the table. His look at Tharmis Rog was that of one wolf to another, when intending to challenge the leadership of the pack. Rog returned the look.

"Captain, will you sign for this?" Rog said, turning to the youth. Conan kept his mouth shut as the youth stepped forward and with a quill signed the name "Klarnides" under Conan's name in the ledger.

A collection of street sweepings under a master-at-arms with an itchy palm, who had the boy-captain in his pocket as well. It was not the way Conan would have chosen to leave Aquilonia. But anything else would put a price on his head in the mightiest of the Hyborian kingdoms.

Also, the Cimmerian knew that he could face anything the Thanza Rangers might fling at him, Tharmis Rog included, in exchange for the few days he would need to find a way of deserting. It might even be worth staying with them all the way to the mountains, where a born hillman could cover his tracks from citybred pursuers as easily as a babe sucked in its mother's milk!

But before he departed, both Captain Klarnides and Master-at-Arms Tharmis Rog would have cause to remember "Sellus the Northerner."

Three

"Here, Countess. Something to warm you."

The speaker not only woke Lysinka; his use of the pet name told her that he was one of the handful of old comrades entitled to use it. No one else had ever died for calling Lysinka the "Countess," but cracked pates and broken arms were not unknown.

She unwrapped herself from the layers of oiled leather cloaks and woolen blankets in which she had slept cocooned from the mountain weather. She wore nothing within her sleep cocoon, but the man holding the bowl of porridge did not look away as she emerged nude into the gray morning.

That was the law among her band—a woman might be bare without being willing. Men—even one woman—had died for breaking the law.

"Hullo, Fergis," she said. "Anything happen during the night?"

"Not a cursed thing. You did well to sleep the night through."

"I slept the night through because several strong-willed folk—a red-bearded Bossonian among them—would give me no peace unless I did." She drew an ivory comb from her sleeping gear with one hand and a tunic and breeches with the other.

Fergis had the grace to flush, as far as she could judge under the dirt that now clung to him as to all of the band. Ten days' march into the Thanzas, with no baths save what they could snatch in icy streams, had made them all as grimy as charcoal-burners or chimney sweeps.

More than one of the men had dared to wonder aloud if this chase after the flying chest would lead anywhere save to blisters and bear-clawings. Lysinka hid her own doubts, but let the men grumble. She knew that she need not worry unless the grumbling stopped and the men marched in sullen silence.

As Lysinka pulled on her clothes, she felt a drop of rain on her shoulder. A moment later she felt another. Hastily she snatched for the porridge, knowing it might be her last chance at hot food this day.

She had just finished scraping the wooden bowl empty when the skies opened and the camp seemed to be plunged under a waterfall. Fergis cursed, and from the trees around them other voices echoed his curses.

"Have our people ready to move out," Lysinka said. Her lilting command cut through the curses and somehow even rose above the rain.

Fergis's bushy eyebrows rose. "In this?" he muttered, reluctant to question any of her orders but concerned as always that she should give none the band would not obey.

"We'll be warmer on the move than sitting and feeling sodden and sorry for ourselves," Lysinka replied. "Also, for once we can move without fear of being heard by men or scented by beasts."

"There is that," Fergis said. He raised both fists, thumbs upward, the band's salute to their chieftain. Then he turned away to begin the work of routing the laggards out of their blankets.

Many days' traveling to the south and west of Lysinka's hill camp, the sun shone on a rocky hillside not far from Shamar. At the foot of the hill lay the camp of the Thanza Rangers, but their work that day lay far above, toward the bare, sun-scorched crest of the hill.

The recruiting notice for the Thanza Rangers had asked for a thousand men. Conan had not as yet concerned himself with counting heads, but he would not have wagered a puddle of spilt beer that the camp held more than two hundred.

At least nine out of ten of these were more or less fit to fight. Or at least they would be, by the time Tharmis Rog was done with them.

"Fighters or corpses, that's what you'll be," the master-at-arms had told the first men into the camp, and each new band as they came. "If you won't shape yourself aright, you'll die in the Thanzas. Die hard, too, and slow.

"If *I* kill you here, though, at least it'll be quick and your bones will lie where the gods can find them. Unless you desert, and if I catch you after that, you'll wish the bandits had flayed you alive or thrown you into a pit of quillpigs.

"Do you understand, you miserable whoresons?"

Conan remembered a muttered chorus of assent. Then Tharmis Rog had bellowed:

"Was that men talking or piglets squealing? When I ask a question, I want to *hear* the answer."

The next time and ever since, the "Yes" and the "Aye" had raised echoes.

Rog himself was raising echoes today, as he taught the Thanza Rangers to climb hills in something that one could almost call a line of battle. Conan did not think much of his teaching, but then Rog was plainly enough no hillman.

From his position well uphill from most of the line, Conan could see the better part of his comrades making heavy weather of the climb. Some had already dropped parts of their loads—and their hides would smoke for that, when Rog saw it. The master-at-arms was old enough to be grandfather to some of the recruits, but could best any two of them without working up a sweat.

The Cimmerian was the one exception to that rule. Thus far, the two big men had carefully avoided facing one another. This could not last forever, but both knew that when the fight did come what little discipline the Thanza Rangers had might be shaken to its shallow roots.

It would have helped had they possessed a more seasoned captain or at least one who remained in the camp. But "recruiting duty" kept Klarnides in Shamar, close to its comforts and far from the camp where people were beginning to remark on his absence. There were also rumors of other captains being appointed to the Rangers, even less war-seasoned than Klarnides.

This was no great matter to Conan. It there were no ways for soldiers to work around fumbling or foolish captains, he would have been dead half a dozen times over. Klarnides was at worst a louse in one's breeches. Tharmis Rog might prove a wild boar.

Certainly he sounded like one now. He was bellowing curses to one slight youth, who looked even less fitted for soldiering than Klarnides.

"By Erlik's brazen tool! Do I have to come up there

and run my sword all the way up to your teeth before you climb?" And much more in like vein.

Conan strode back and forth across the slope with a hillman's confidence, pointing out easy and hard ground whenever he could whisper, sometimes only using a gesture or his sword. His evident experience with soldiering had given him an under-captaincy with command over thirty men, but Rog did not care to see Conan dealing with anyone beyond that thirty.

Today, the Cimmerian would have gladly fed Rog and what he cared for to a Stygian temple serpent. The master-at-arms was using a loud voice in place of teaching a few simple tricks for climbing hills, tricks that Conan had known as soon as he could walk. Much more of this and men were going to be falling, rolling, and reaching the bottom of the hill in such condition that it would need a god, not a master-at-arms, to put them on their feet again.

As that thought passed through Conan's mind, the slight youth finally lost his footing. He reeled backward, one foot waving in the air, hands clawing frantically at emptiness. His waving foot struck a boulder—and the boulder, lightly seated in the hard ground, came loose.

Conan plunged down the slope as if his feet had grown wings. With one hand he clutched the youth's hand, as he slammed the other hard against the boulder. It was too heavy for even the Cimmerian's giant strength to hold single-handed, but he delayed its fall long enough.

Only when the youth was safely out of the boulder's path did Conan let it go. It thundered down the hill, striking sparks from other rocks as it flew, trailing a comet's tail of dust and pebbles, crushing bushes as if they were blades of grass, and finally ending not a spear's length from Tharmis Rog.

Rog's bellow made all that had gone before it seem like a hush.

"Sellus! Bring your arse down here at once, if you know what's good for you!"

Conan looked about him, as if he thought the voice was coming from the ground or the sky. One man within easy hearing range whispered, "Best do it, Northerner. Rog's a bad man to cross."

"And my ears are bad, when people tell me what's good for me," Conan replied. Rog's voice had the note of a man who has made up his mind to settle a matter for once and for all.

Then the Cimmerian began his descent. He started slowly, almost ambling until Rog let out another roar, this time laced with such splendid curses that Conan stopped to listen in admiration. He would have to remember some of those ripe Aquilonian phrases if he ever needed to drill Aquilonian street sweepings into soldiers.

For now, what he needed was to speak to Rog before the man worked himself into such a rage that the fight would come at once, in front of all the men.

Discipline might survive a private battle. It would hardly survive Rog's public humiliation.

Also, while Conan did not doubt for a moment the outcome of the fight, he doubted that he could win without word of it being noised about in Shamar. Then others might come seeking Ophirean gold, before the Thanza Rangers marched out of Shamar to some place where Conan could vanish from their ranks without anyone the wiser.

So Conan did not finish his descent at his earlier amble. He came down the rest of the way at a dead run, slanting back and forth across the slope to avoid building up too much speed, leaping over boulders, and reaching the level at a pace that would have done credit to an antelope.

He dashed up to Rog, threw the man a mocking parody of the Aquilonian salute, and snapped:

"Sellus the Northerner reporting as ordered, Master-at-Arms!"

One of Rog's white-knuckled hands was on the hilt of his sword. The other was balled into a fist. His eyes told of his being ready to wield one weapon or the other against the Cimmerian if the other man so much as blinked.

Instead, he said, in a voice shaking with forced moderation:

"Was that boulder an accident?"

Conan replied, with a wintry smile, "Will anything I say matter to you?"

"Are you saying that I'm ready to start a fight?"

"If you're ready to call me a liar, and in front of the men, are you not?"

The phrase "in front of the men" seemed to reach through Rog's fury to touch his soldierly good sense. "We'd best meet tonight quietly, to see who is lying," he said, in a voice that no longer shook with rage.

"I can meet at your pleasure," Conan said. "That little stretch of meadow north of the oak grove?"

"Fair enough," Rog said, and started to turn away. Then he stopped, and without facing the Cimmerian, said, "Oh, and I hadn't planned on killing you."

"Accidents can happen, but I take your meaning. I thought much the same."

Like two wolves who have given and accepted a challenge, the two big men turned away from each other and walked off to rejoin their soldiers.

*　　*　　*

Lysinka knew when it reached her that the message spoke the truth about human tracks. Scouting for the band were the twins known only as the Village Brothers. They might have many reasons for not wishing their names known in the band, but they had also given Lysinka any number of reasons for being glad to have them.

They hardly ever missed the track of humans or the spoor of any natural beast. When commanded to conceal Lysinka's trail, they used equal skill to remove the slightest trace of the band's passage. If they said humans had passed this way, Lysinka knew her band was no longer alone in the pines at the foot of a crag-studded hill with no name.

Hand signals brought her comrades to alertness, and they needed no further orders to array themselves to meet an attack from any direction. Any *human* attack, at least—Lysinka had thrice rejected the services of those who claimed mastery of magic, for she distrusted all such. Yet for two days this forest had held the smell of a place where there might lurk dangers against which steel would contend in vain.

The rain covered even the slight noise the woodswise bandits made in arraying themselves. When a little while had passed and no one had come against them, Lysinka made another signal. The band was to move on, with more scouts thrown out to the flanks, and all weapons ready.

Lysinka's band stalked forward through the dripping forest with the silent intent of wolves on the hunt. Little rain fell on them through the canopy of interwoven branches. From time to time thunder rolled above the treetops, echoing off the cliffs, which they had only glimpsed briefly through the trees.

After a further while spent in this stalking, muscles

cramped and necks stiffened with the constant struggle to look in all directions at once. Lysinka felt an urge to sneeze, and saw Fergis nearly strangle himself in a desperate effort to silence a cough.

The last thing the chieftain had expected was to find a clearing flanking the trail. In that clearing stood a black-clad man, arms folded across his broad chest.

"Welcome to my lordship of Thanza, Lysinka of Mertyos."

Lysinka was so flustered by the warmth and formality of the greeting that she replied in a much less amiable tone.

"If Thanza was ever a lordship, its lords have been extinct for more centuries than you could count without taking off your boots. Who are you to claim it?"

"One who could claim much more, but is content with Thanza." Then he raised one hand, palm outward.

"The tree to her left. The big knothole."

Wsssshttt. The shaft from a Bossonian longbow quivered in a fir tree an arm's length to Lysinka's left. It had split a reddish-brown knothole at about the height of her breasts.

The message was plain. *My archers hold your life in their hands.*

Lysinka did not know if her own gesture would be her last. She was certain that such a threat could not go unanswered.

She coughed loudly—and an arrow sprouted from the turf just to the right of the man. Instead of a knothole, this shaft split a round, pale-yellow mushroom.

The man's eyebrows rose. They were bushy and more gray than black. Then he smiled. Lysinka had once seen an otter baring its teeth just so, before it bit a crayfish in half.

"Well spoken," he said. Then he threw the hood

back from his head and shook out his beard. His beard was thick and more black than gray, while his hair was so scant that it was hard to judge its color. He spoke and stood, however, like a man still in full vigor.

All this told Lysinka nothing whatever about what business he might have with her, and whether she would live to see another sunrise. She forced down her anger. She felt as though she were being dangled over an abyss like a doll in the hand of a petulant child.

The man now thrust his hand into the pouch at his belt. Lysinka forced her own hand away from the hilt of her throwing knife. It would be in the man's throat before he could complete any treachery, even if she died in the next moment.

Instead, the man drew out a piece of iron. Lysinka looked, then stared. It was unmistakably a piece of iron strapping from the flying chest. She recognized some of the runes, even though the iron now seemed gray and brittle, as if it had been fiercely heated, then swiftly and rudely quenched.

"Ah, I see you recognize this," the man said.

Lysinka chided herself for being so transparent. She thought she had retained more of the self-command of her younger days, when she had been adept in the intrigues among the concubines.

"Perhaps I do," she said, inclining her head gracefully. "But I am as a guest to your host. I would not insult you by asking more about it than you are willing to tell, nor accuse you of dark plots merely because you possess something tainted with magic."

"It has been said that you have the manners of a great lady—when you choose," the man said with a grin. "Now hear me, Lysinka of Mertyos. I am willing to tell you a great deal about this chest. We both seek it, and neither of us has much hope of finding it without the other's aid.

"However, I do not propose to tell you here in the presence of your men, in the wild and wet forest. Come with me to my seat"—he jerked a thumb toward the cliff, invisible behind the trees—"and hear of a rare quest."

"I will come well-guarded," Lysinka said, testing the man.

"Come with all your band," was the reply. "I do not fear treachery."

"Nor do I, but I would be a poor guest if I brought that many. Have you a palace atop the cliff?"

"Perhaps it once deserved the name. Certainly it keeps me and mine warm and dry. If you do not wish to bring all your folk, may I at least send down guest gifts to them?"

Lysinka saw that Fergis was now in sight, but standing so that she could converse with him without the blackclad man seeing her face. The "conversation" was swift, a matter of raising eyebrows, touching fingers to mouth and nose, pulling at cheeks, hair, or beards, and so on.

"Very well," Lysinka said. "I will come with ten of my men. You will send down ten of yours with the guest gifts."

"You ask hostages?" the man said, unable to hide surprise and even indignation.

Her self-command had returned. She said, with a bland smile, "It is only just that I offer hospitality in return for hospitality. My men are as honorable as yours."

This left much unsaid, but the man seemed prepared to accept it. Lysinka made one final gesture to Fergis—and smiled as his face fell.

He would not be among those going up the cliff. The band would give less offense to the hostages if he commanded below—and more surely avenge their chieftain, if it came to that.

Four

Conan left camp as soon as he had seen to food, wine, salves, and bandages for his men. All needed the first two, which rather to the Cimmerian's surprise were both abundant and good. The Rangers' noble patron had to be dipping generously into his coffers, if only out of fear of his soldiers turning bandit.

Many needed the salves and bandages. Blisters from climbing in poorly fitting boots or gripping sun-heated rocks, thorn punctures, cuts, bruises, too much sun and too little water—a day's training like this was likely to lay men out with everything save perhaps snakebite and broken bones.

It was two-legged serpents who were in the Cimmerian's thoughts as he left the camp well before he needed to merely to reach the meeting with Rog on time. Indeed, they weighed heavily.

He did not fear treachery from Tharmis Rog, who would have small need to risk dishonor against the Cimmerian. Rog was older than Conan and perhaps a trifle slower, but as large, as strong, and doubtless as cunning a fighter. It would be as well to end the fight before both men had hammered each other past the fitness needed for campaigning.

Nor did Conan fear Rog sending men to do what he would not stoop to do himself. A wolf did not send jackals to pull down a rival.

But there were men in the camp who hated Tharmis Rog or regretted the oath they had taken. Some had been so foolish as to speak openly in Conan's hearing, seemingly taking him for a bluff, blunt-witted northerner with few loyalties and less of the Aquilonian tongue.

Conan remembered those men. He intended to make them remember him, if he could find a time and place where it would not weaken the Thanza Rangers. Meanwhile, such men might well be laying plots to bring Tharmis Rog down, then make it seem that Conan had slain the master-at-arms.

Such men might also have taken the course of telling Mikros where one Sellus the Northerner was to be found. Conan did not imagine for a moment that he had crippled or frightened enough of Mikros's bullies to leave the panderer impotent. He would likely enough meet the man's hirelings again before he left Aquilonia.

And if he met none of these, there could still be bounty hunters from Ophir, Argos, or in time even distant Turan. King Yezdigerd ruled a realm that had no fear of the wrath of Aquilonia, and it was yet another realm where a certain wandering Cimmerian warrior had a price on his head.

Altogether, there were more than enough chances for uninvited guests at this private feast, to make it prudent to approach the feasting hall by a long and winding route.

From many years' traveling and fighting, Conan

had gained the art of learning his way around a stretch of countryside or a quarter of a city within days of his arrival. Already there were parts of the land around the camp he could have crossed unerringly in the depths of night, and this evening the light was slow to fade.

Conan traveled even faster than he had expected, and could have searched all around the meadow had he not feared being seen. So instead he hid himself within the oak grove, under a cluster of bushes that offered further concealment. Perfectly hidden, he even felt it safe to lie down and sleep, for all that he removed neither clothing nor weapons.

After all, if he did not wake in time, Tharmis Rog would surely make enough noise over not finding his opponent ready, to wake not merely the sleeping but the dead.

The ruined castle high on the crags had at last begun to grow closer. For some while, Lysinka had begun to think that she and her chosen ten comrades were doomed to spend the rest of eternity on this stony, winding path up the cliffs.

It helped that the rain had stopped, a rising wind had hurled the clouds away to eastward, and an angry yellow moon shed a trifle of light below. It did not help enough, when the wind moaned and whined around the rocks like the distant murmuring of lost souls, and the cries of nightbirds and bats had no natural ring to them.

Lysinka told herself to rein in her fancies and trust he who called himself the lord of Thanza until he betrayed that trust. No wise chief would willingly sacrifice ten of his men for a merely equal number of foes. His own men would fling him from the cliffs if he did.

Except that Lysinka would be one of the dead. She

was not one to swell with vainglory, but she knew that her band would be maimed past repairing by her death.

Well, if it came to that, she would do her best to take his lordship with her. Then two headless bands might draw off, the one from the other, and her comrades live to mourn her. They would never find her body, not in this wilderness of stone that had driven the trees to retreat like a pack of mangy dogs.

A new note in the wind struck shrill and harsh. It rose until Lysinka wanted to plug her ears with her hood, until the lost souls seemed to be shrieking in rage rather than whispering in loneliness.

She stiffened as invisible fingers seemed to touch her. They plucked and caressed her brow, her ears, her throat, and more intimate places. She found herself breathless yet wanting to scream in rage and terror.

She barely heard a shout from up ahead. To save her own soul she could not have said who shouted. She needed no hearing to see the fate of the man just ahead of her.

In one moment he was bracing himself, one hand on a heavy staff with its butt jammed into a crevice, the other groping for a handhold. In the next moment the staff snapped like a twig. The man reeled, overbalanced, clawed his other hand bloody trying to keep his handhold, then lurched over the edge of the path.

Lysinka tried to shut out the fading sound of his scream and the sight of his blood on the rock. She drew a shuddering breath and found that she was gripping her staff with both hands, as if ready to wield it against an opponent. If anything, visible or invisible, touched her again . . .

The Thanzans ahead of her were making every rite of aversion she had seen in the borderland and a few

she did not recognize. She licked her lips several times
and at last found her voice.

"What—was that the wind?"

"Aye, lady," one man said. He kept his face averted
from her, and the wind piped about them so that most of
his words were lost. But she heard enough to learn of
something called the Spider Wind, which plucked men
from where it would, when it would, as if it were a
living thing with an appetite sated only by human flesh.

Lysinka thought she knew most of the true dangers
and many of the legendary ones of the Thanzas. But
she had never heard of the Spider Wind.

How did one sell one's life dearly against such?

She had not found even the vaguest of answers,
before they reached the end of the climb, and torch-
light and the smell of roasting meat made the terrors of
the climb seem a child's nightmare.

At least for a while.

When Conan awoke, the last light had long since
departed from the sky. Within the oak grove, it was as
dark as the tunnels beneath a temple of Set. Save that
the Cimmerian smelled rich forest soil instead of
ancient dust, heard night birds calling instead of water
dripping, and saw fresh human footprints, rather than
the marks of the sacred serpents.

For the same reason that he had taken the long way
to the scene of combat, Conan had brought sword,
dagger, and various lesser knives. He and Tharmis
Rog would fight barehanded; those they might meet on
the way could well be less honorable.

His sheathed dagger dangling about his neck, Conan
crawled swiftly on the trail of the men. He soon
thought he could have marched along with a drummer
and a trumpeter. The newcomers had so little march

discipline or knowledge of the forest that cracking twigs and rustling leaves made a trail as plain to Conan's senses as that left by their boots.

If matters went on as they had begun there would be no need to warn Tharmis Rog.

For a while, it seemed that matters would go just that way. The men and their pursuer had to be halfway through the grove now. From the occasional word they let drop, Conan knew they were Aquilonian, some perhaps not native speakers. He recognized no voices.

Time for a prisoner to answer a few pointed questions—or the dagger's point, if all else failed.

Deed followed thought as quickly as the Cimmerian could find a man a little apart from his comrades. That did not take long—these men were city folk, to whom a forest was as alien as a city would have been to the boy Conan.

The Cimmerian's chosen prey braced himself against a gnarled, arching oak root, scratched himself and bent over to tie the laces of his boots. He was thus engaged when the Cimmerian snaked under the arch in the root and snatched the man off his feet.

The man went down face-first. As he struggled to rise and shout at the same time, a massive hand pressed his face into the leaf mold and rotten fungus.

"You can speak quickly or die slowly. Chose."

Conan decided that the man's gasps and grunts promised cooperation and rolled him over, while drawing his own dagger. When the man breathed freely again, the steel was at his throat.

No night-sight much less keen than Conan's could have made out the man's features, but the scar from the right ear across the cheek to the corner of the mouth was unmistakable. Conan had last seen this man writhing on the floor of the Golden Lion after the Cimmerian's boot took him in the stomach.

"Mikros does not give up easily, does he?" Conan said, in an almost conversational tone.

"Ahhh—" the man gasped.

"The worse for your friends," Conan said. "How many are there?"

The man shook his head. The dagger's point pricked harder.

"Ten—a dozen—no more," the man said, eyes huge and showing mostly whites.

"My thanks," Conan said. He cracked the man's head smartly against the root and the bully went limp. He still breathed, but it would be dawn before he regained his senses and days before his head stopped aching.

Conan resumed his pursuit, more swiftly now that he knew whom he sought. He was still well behind the panderer's men when he found a gap in the trees that showed him the meadow. The moon silvered the grass, the fallen trees, and the boulder against which Tharmis Rog sat, his broad back protected by the stone and his sword across his knees.

His head was bowed on his chest, and Conan thought briefly that it would hardly be a fair fight if the man were half-asleep or fuddled with wine. Of more immediate importance, Mikros's men were preparing to attack.

A dark silhouette rose to Conan's left, another to his right. The leftward man was nocking an arrow to a bow, the other lifting a short spear.

Conan cupped his hands, took a deep breath, and bellowed:

" 'Ware, Tharmis Rog! We've another fight before ours!"

* * *

The fare in the lord of Thanza's camp was frugal but well-prepared. After ten days of marching through the forest, Lysinka was ready to praise the cook out of more than mere politeness.

"I thank you on his behalf," her host replied. "But then, he was a good cook when he served me at the manor on the Rhyl. He has not lost his skill by moving to the Thanzas."

Lysinka did her best not to look confused. The Rhyl was a river in Nemedia, several days' ride from the Border Range and well to the north of the Thanzas.

The man laughed. It was a robust laugh and under other circumstances might have warmed Lysinka's spirit. Here on this dark windy crag, she felt more as she had when the Spider Wind fumbled at her.

"I hold the rank of baron in both Nemedia and Aquilonia."

"Then why do you choose to live here, which is really neither, nor indeed any place fit for civilized folk?"

"Perhaps I am not civilized enough. Or at least so my enemies in both lands have said. My life would be forfeit within the reach of either realm's justice. So I live here, with my followers."

"And conjure your food and weapons from the air and the rocks?" Lysinka said.

"Such curiousity can be dangerous, Countess."

"You have not earned the right to use that name, my friend. Indeed, you have not even told me if you have one, other than 'lord of Thanza.' "

"You may call me Grolin," the baron said. "May I ask that you walk apart with me for a short while? I mean no harm and indeed hope that it will be for our mutual good."

Lysinka decided that if the walk led to a certain kind

of wrestling bout, Grolin might well find himself fit for work as a eunuch in Vendhya. But time enough for that if it proved necessary.

Grolin led the bandit chieftain away from the firelight, up a crumbling flight of stairs that he allowed her to mount unassisted, and across a floor that showed gaps large enough to swallow an ox. Safely on what was left of a curtain wall, they had a splendid view out over the nighted forest, tinted unnatural shades of silver, gray, and blue by the moon.

"The chest is what you seek, is it not?" Grolin asked.

"I can hardly pretend otherwise, can I now?" Lysinka replied. Her voice held a bitter edge.

"You did yourself no harm by revealing your desire," Grolin said. "It is one I share. Together, we may attain it."

"And fighting some mad wizard for its possession?"

"You were ready to do that with your unaided steel, Lysinka. Together, we can do better. You have thirty stout fighters. I have a sorcerer. Or at least one who finds this quest worthy."

Lysinka frowned. Grolin was flinging open a door to a whole new world, much too large for her to grasp readily. She said the first thing that came to her mind, to avoid seeming a witling.

"As long as he is master over whoever magiced the chest—"

Grolin stopped her with a hand to her lips. It seemed to Lysinka that he and his men must learn the rules of her band, about touching women, if there was to be peace tonight, let alone during a quest of days or weeks.

After a moment, Grolin let his hand fall. "Your pardon," he said.

"Granted. But is this hedge-wizard likely to be strong enough?"

"I do not know. No sorcerer called the chest. It flew of its own will, called by the Mountain of the Skulls. That is the original resting place of what lies within the chest."

"A treasure?" Lysinka frowned. Within, she was torn between eagerness to make her comrades rich and suspicion that Grolin would be deft in treachery to avoid sharing any gains.

"Some have called it so," Grolin replied, so softly that Lysinka could barely hear him over the moan of the wind. "It is called the Soul of Thanza."

In spite of herself, Lysinka felt the night wind as chill against her as if she had been unclothed. She shivered, but stepped aside as Grolin moved to embrace her.

"What does this Soul do?"

Grolin did not look at her as he replied. "It gives its possessor lordship over death."

Conan expected his shout to bring Tharmis Rog to his feet and the big man's sword out of its scabbard. Instead the master-at-arms only grunted like the sleepiest of boars and shifted his position slightly.

The Cimmerian had no time to marvel at this or ponder the reason for it. He snatched up a rock and flung it with all the strength of his arm at the archer. The rock took the man in the shoulder as he loosed his arrow. He roared with surprise more than pain, but his arrow flew wide.

In the next moment Conan leaped on the spearman just as his weapon flew. Its course was truer, but the archer's cry had roused Rog more than the Cimmerian's warning shout. He moved, just in time to take the spear across the mail shoulder pieces of his corselet. Sparks flew but no blood.

Meanwhile, Conan was trying to end the spearman's fighting, keep the archer from shooting again, and fight the other men who were swarming out of the trees toward Tharmis Rog like dogs at a bear-baiting. Not for the first time, Conan would have given some years of his life for the power to be in two places at once.

His own strength and sheer good luck divided the work between him and Rog. The spearman had no more chance against Conan than a goat against a tiger. In moments he was limp.

Meanwhile, one of the running men darted squarely into the path of the archer's second shaft. He reeled, clutching his throat, which had suddenly sprouted the arrow. Then he fell as the archer let out something between a wail and a curse. That was the last sound the archer made, as the Cimmerian closed with him and split his skull with the broadsword.

Meanwhile, the death of friend at the hand of friend had slowed the onrush of Mikros's other hirelings. So had Tharmis Rog's lurching to his feet and drawing his sword. He held it uncertainly, and Conan saw him rub his eyes with the back of his free hand. He might for now be no more use in a fight than an unschooled boy, but he was still a head taller than any of the men around him.

While some of those men were merely standing and gaping and others trying to form a circle around Rog, Conan struck them from behind. He had both sword and dagger in hand, and also used fists and feet, all with dreadful effectiveness.

He snapped one man's spine with a kick, clove another's arm from its shoulder with the sword, hamstrung a third with a low slash from the dagger, then found himself surrounded. He tried to find an opening that would leave him with no one at his back, but his surviving enemies now seemed to use speed of foot against strength of arm and steel.

Conan kept whirling and striking, but half a dozen of his minor cuts oozed blood and he knew a serious wound was only moments away. At least Mikros would hardly have enough men left alive and hale to track down Brollya, after Conan fell—

A roar like storm-flung surf on rocks half-deafened the Cimmerian. Suddenly two men facing him were jerked aloft, as if by a hangman's noose. Where they had been, stood Tharmis Rog, with one massive hand clamped around either neck.

This time, the master-at-arms had not allowed the Cimmerian to remain in danger longer than necessary.

Conan saw a man to Rog's right raising a knife, leaped to meet the skulker, and knocked down another bravo in so doing. The uplifted dagger met Conan's downslicing sword and flew from the man's hand as the hand also flew from the wrist. The man howled and ran; Conan idly wondered if he would reach a hiding place before loss of blood brought him down.

Now the two big men stood side by side, facing no more than four opponents; Conan no longer counted the two men Rog was holding. The master-at-arms lifted these, briskly cracked their heads together, then flung them away as if they had been offal that soiled his hands and offended his nostrils. Flying through the air, they brought down two of their comrades.

The two bravos left on their feet did not stand their ground. They fled into the trees, screaming as if being burned alive. One of the men thrown down by Rog regained his senses and lurched off after them.

Rog looked down at the other. "I suppose we'd best

wake up this fellow and ask him who sent him out to spoil an honest fight."

"Never mind that," Conan said. "Pardon, I did not mean to give you an order. But I know who sent them." He described the scarred man.

"Ha!" Rog said. "I had begun to suspect the same. As well to be certain." He looked Conan up and down. "Do you still want to fight?"

The Cimmerian replied with a level gaze and voice. "Do you still think that boulder was aimed at you?"

The night birds had begun to sound again after the fight. Rog's bellow of laughter silenced them once more. "After you risked your life to save me, I should go on believing you seek my blood? If I do that, call me a witling and give me to my daughter's care, for I'm past soldiering!"

"Well, then," Conan said, "it seems we have no more quarrel."

"Rightly enough," Rog said, shaking his head. "But we've some talking to do. Shall we do it over some better wine than the camp holds?"

"If I refuse that offer, you may call *me* a witling," Conan replied, with a grin that bared the white teeth in his blood-spattered face. "I don't know where you'd send me, though, for I've no daughters or sons either—that I know of."

If the mountain wind had seemed cold before, Lysinka now felt rather as if she were embedded naked in a block of ice. She swayed and would have fallen if Grolin had not held her upright. She did not notice whether his hands strayed and for some moments hardly cared.

Once again, the need to prove she was no witling drove her tongue into movement.

"Does this mean the possesser of the Soul is immortal, free from death? Or does it mean that he can command death for others, at will?"

"Yes, I think," Grolin said.

"Both? Or do you not know?"

"The legend says both, and legend is all there is about the power of the Soul, when it is in the Mountain of the Skulls. One should not be surprised, when the legends also say that the Soul comes from the time of Acheron."

Lysinka jerked herself out of Grolin's arms. "That musty tale to frighten children! Every time someone meets magic they do not understand, they blame it on Acheron." She knew she said this to lessen her own doubts.

"Sometimes, they do so justly," Grolin said, once again speaking as if he were afraid the wind or the rocks might overhear him. "Acheron rose, wrought mighty magic, and fell. Though it disappeared, all its evil did not. That lingers yet in odd corners of the world."

"Mitra knows this is odd enough," Lysinka said, with forced heartiness. "So are its people. So, even, are the bargains they offer."

"Is it too odd for you to accept?" Grolin asked. She heard greed in his voice but no treachery and, indeed, some gentleness, as though he understood how much he was asking.

"Not that I can say, tonight," Lysinka said. "But the decision is not mine alone. I must put it before my people." She hesitated, then added, "Have you friends in either realm who send you aid?"

"I see your shrewdness was no rumor," Grolin said, a trifle sourly. "Call them enemies of my enemies and you will be right. But they would ask the swine's share of anything we won through the Soul. Nor are they as fair as you."

The flattery was open, but the desire in Grolin's voice likewise sincere. Plainly he expected that the bargain be sealed in the oldest way between a man and a woman.

Just as plainly, she had to come to her decision tonight.

"Grolin, I must go below and my ten with me. In such a matter, my band must meet and speak together."

He looked as if he wished to kiss her or at least pat her shoulder, but he withheld his hand. "Then go, and speak so that they will do the wise thing and join the quest for the Soul of Thanza."

"It was something in my food that had me sleeping there like a drunkard," Rog said. He was hardly sober now, but he and Conan were at a snug country inn, the White Raven, not facing armed bravos.

"Any notion who might have put it there?" Conan said. He had drunk less than Rog because he feared the master-at-arms might need further protection. He hoped this would not extend to putting the man to bed. The Cimmerian had expected to win the fight, but he had less hope of moving the man's dead weight if he drank himself senseless.

"Notions only, but enough to let me know where to start asking questions."

"Best not punish anyone without Klarnides's approval," Conan said. "If he does have the ear of the count—"

Rog spat into the bark chips that covered the floor. The tavernkeeper looked daggers at the two big men but prudently refrained from more.

"That for Klarnides and the other lapdogs coming to join him."

Conan's look framed a question.

"You haven't heard?" Rog explained. He went on to describe two new captains said to be on their way to the Thanza Rangers. If half what he said was the truth, the two newcomers made Klarnides seem a more seasoned warrior than Conan.

"Well, we've settled our quarrel," Conan said. "So come good captains or bad, we can stand together against them and for our men."

Rog's reply to that was to lay his head on his arms and begin to snore. Conan laid out enough brass coins to pay for the last jug of wine and wrapped himself in his cloak.

"Huh," the tavernkeeper said. "Either pay for a room or take yourself and your friend—"

An empty wine cup neatly parted the man's hair— or would have, if he had not been entirely bald. It smashed to powder against the wall behind him.

"We're staying here," Conan said. "We've drunk our fill and paid for it."

The innkeeper wrung his hands. "But those who come in the morning—"

"—will have the place to themselves, *if* you give us something to break our fast when you want us to leave. A few loaves of bread, a plate or two of sausages, any odd fowl you may have ready roasted—"

The innkeeper promised a bountiful breakfast so quickly that his tongue kept tripping over itself, and Conan hardly understood what he and Rog had been promised. Nor, for the moment, did he particularly care.

Tomorrow they could return to the camp and begin working together to make the Thanza Rangers worthy of the name of soldier.

* * *

"Countess?"

The voice was Fergis's. Lysinka rolled over and sat up to contemplate her comrade, who was squatting beside her sleeping coccoon. It was close enough to dawn that she could recognize his face as well as his voice.

"Have our folk voted?"

"Aye."

"How did they vote?"

"We will follow you to join with Grolin."

"That is as well. He will go questing for it, whether we join or not. Together, we will be more than twice as strong as either band. We may win further allies too."

"Aye, and if those levies they are supposed to be raising in Shamar come calling, we'll be better prepared to meet them."

Fergis looked at his chieftain, and for the first time in years she was conscious that she was naked before him. She would not make matters worse by covering herself, however.

"Eh, Countess. Does he want to bed you?"

"You think it proves him a man of poor judgement if he does?"

"Proves him—?" Fergis began indignantly, then gave a short bark of laughter. "Countess, it is between him and you. I have not lost my senses."

Nor, Lysinka suspected, the desire for her that glowed gently within him. This made his loyalty all the more perfect, so that she felt ashamed of baiting him.

"I have not lost mine either," she said. "The Soul of Thanza is said to fight against death. It does not fight against common sense."

Five

Conan awoke in the blackness of the nighted forest with a toe prodding him in the ribs. He had reached for his sword when he saw that the toe belonged to Tharmis Rog.

"Is it time for me to relieve you?" he asked the master-at-arms.

"Not yet, but I hear movement in the mule lines."

"Not our people?"

"Too quiet to be any of our drunkards."

"A deserter?"

"I think all such fools have already left. My wager is on bandits."

"Then why haven't you gone down to the lines to deal with them?" The Cimmerian had been sleeping in his clothes. To join Rog, all he had to do was grip his sword and stand up.

Rog chuckled. "Because I want to see if the lads on sentry duty remember aught of what we told them, back in Shamar. *Then* I'll help them."

"We'll be in sorry shape if bandits take the mules."

"Sellus—if that's your name—they may not have mules in those benighted northern lands you hail from. Around here, a farm boy grows up ignorant of mules only if he's a halfwit. I was a farm lad, and I joined the army as a mule driver.

"Between bandits and those pack mules, my money would be on the mules—"

Before Rog could finish or Conan reply, one of the sentries proved that he remembered at least part of his training.

"Help! Help! Somebody's trying to steal the mules! Help!"

The sentry's panicky squall was no proper alarm, but it did its work just as well. The camp of the Thanza Rangers came alive and awake around Conan and Tharmis Rog.

The two big men listened to the cries, the stumblings and fallings, the clatter and scrape of desperately snatched weapons, and the disordered footsteps of men hurrying toward the mules. When the two thought that enough men were awake and armed, they ran toward the now-braying mules, ready to guide the men of the Thanza Rangers into their first combat.

The Thanza Rangers had taken their time on the road from the camp outside Shamar to this dark camp in the forests near their namesake hills. Conan and Rog working together had wrought prodigies in barely ten days, but Klarnides was not yet much help and the new captains were an outright burden.

For some of them, it had been too long a journey. There were those who were eager for bandit loot, hoped to show off their new-found skills and their loudly proclaimed courage, or merely expected to find desertion easier in the borderland.

There were others who would gladly have been in the Shamar camp or even back in the city. A good half of the two hundred men the Rangers had raised were still there—the half whom Rog and Conan pronounced in need of further training, if they were not to be more dangerous to their comrades or themselves than to any enemy.

Even with a fraction of their intended strength, and that halved, the Rangers could not have delayed taking the field any longer. The word from their patron, Count Ralthon, as that they had to make a campaign this year, even if they numbered only ten.

So Klarnides took a hundred men and one Nestorinus, the least skilled of the new captains, down to the wharves. There Rog and Conan loaded them aboard an Aquilonian river galley. Supplies, mules, packsaddles, and other gear went aboard a hired merchant vessel.

Somehow everything arrived more or less safely and in order two days later, at a small town whose name Conan could never afterward recall. Its only virtue was that it lay almost at the southern tip of the Border Range, with the summits of the Thanzas in plain sight at dawn once the mist burned off.

Klarnides, showing more judgement than Conan had expected, divided the Rangers into two bands of forty, one under Conan and the other under Tharmis Rog. The remaining twenty he gave to Nestorinus, although both men and captain usually marched directly under Klarnides's eye. It was understood that their main task was to handle the pack train and the spare weapons— which, like the rations, were better and more abundant than Conan would have dared expect.

"Somewhere between us and Numedides is a man

with both gold and sense," Conan said. "Any notion who, friend Rog?"

"Notions aplenty, but no more," the master-at-arms said. "Not to be talked about either, until we've done some serious work."

By the time the Thanza Rangers had done serious work, Conan feared that few of them would still be alive to talk about anything. Had he been his own master in this campaign, he would have taken another month training the men. Some showed promise; none yet seemed truly battleworthy.

But Conan was not his own master, and the only way he could become so was to desert the Rangers the moment they reached country rough enough to hide his trail, which would, of course, be the very moment that seasoned war leaders became even more necessary than before.

As he would not slay men in cold blood, so did Conan refuse to abandon these Aquilonian innocents to the tender mercies of the bandits. So he was at the head of the column when it marched north from the river town. He also both ate and slept lightly during the seven days of the ensuing march.

The mules were making such a din that Conan could not have heard heavy cavalry over the shrill braying. With all his battle-honed senses alert, he still could not tell whether the intruders were one, few, or many.

They might even have been a night-spawned phantom of a nervous sentry's untrained imagination—save that Tharmis Rog thought otherwise, and Conan trusted the Aquilonian's ears and experience.

"Hold!" Rog bellowed from behind the Cimmerian. "Bear right and left, you dung-weaned calves! Don't go charging straight into the lines, or the mules'll have you if the bandits don't!"

That shouting must have warned everyone within half a day's journey of Rog's tactics. But it was needed, for the men behind the two leaders were rushing forward like a mob.

Conan looked briefly behind him to see Nestorinus and Klarnides running with the others. Nestorinus looked as helpless as a chip of wood in a millrace. Klarnides at least seemed alert and had his sword drawn, as he raised the standard of the Rangers in his other hand.

He might even have achieved dignity, if he had taken the time to don more than a loinguard and a helmet before rushing out to lead his men into their first battle.

Looking behind him proved as unwise as all Conan's teachers of warfare had ever told him. The ground suddenly dropped out from under him, and he toppled forward. He turned the topple into a somersault and came up on his feet. At once he collided with something hairy enough to be an ape and foul enough to be a midden pit, save that it howled and cursed in a human tongue.

Conan stopped the howling and cursing with a buffet to the bandit's chest that caved in ribs, and finished the work with his dagger. This gave Nestorinus, Tharmis Rog, and several Rangers enough time to scramble down the slope behind Conan. Indeed, they nearly rushed Conan off his feet again and went on to trample the next bandit, so quickly did they enter the fight.

Conan felt more relief at this than over his own survival. If the Rangers had even a handful of men who would rush into the fray, they would likely enough

draw most of their comrades after them. The Rangers
might not clear the Thanzas of bandits, but they could
at least leave the forest on their feet at the end of
summer, instead of greeting the winter from shallow
graves amid the trees.

Another bandit went down, then two more leaped
on mules they had cut loose. The mules neither threw
them off at once nor carried them to safety. Instead
they trotted around in circles, braying even louder than
before.

The Thanza Rangers had few archers—or rather,
few men whom even a green captain like Klarnides
would trust with a bow (at least with Conan and
Tharmis Rog to advise him). One of these archers
must have nocked and shot, because an arrow whistled
so close over Conan's head that had he been a hand's
breadth taller it would have pierced his skull.

Instead it flew on, to skewer one of the stolen mules.
Now the mule did rear, flinging its rider to the ground.
The second mule broke into a gallop, but by this time a
useful number of Rangers stood across its path. A man
thrust with a spear at the rider as he leaned aside, a
club cracked him across the head, and he toppled to
the ground. A single scream marked his passing, aided
by spears, knives, clubs, and boots.

The rider who had been thrown was now back on
his feet. Nestorinus dashed to meet him, then halted
abruptly as the man drew a sword. Conan had his own
weapon drawn, and the captain backed up so abruptly
that he nearly impaled himself on the Cimmerian's
point.

"Watch that, you fool!" Nestorinus snarled.

It was on the tip of Conan's tongue to say that a
coward should take care whom he called a fool. But

Klarnides brushed past both men and stepped up to the bandit.

"Do you—?" Klarnides began, his voice hitting a high pitch.

The word "yield" never reached his lips. The bandit screamed a singularly vile obscenity and moved straight into a thrust.

Klarnides had been raising his sword in the manner prescribed by formal dueling customs and had to jump aside. He nearly went down, and Conan swore that at the youth's next blunder he was going to take matters into his own hands.

Klarnides had only modest gifts for war. But he doubtless had powerful friends, who would not be grateful to those who allowed him to die on a bandit's rusty sword. Conan did not much worry about his future in Aquilonia, but it was home to Tharmis Rog and his daughter, who should not have reason to flee.

Before Conan could take a step, Klarnides's sword swept down into fighting position. The clanging of steel on steel was worthy of a blacksmith's forge. Sparks flew as the bandit fell back, at once on the defense and hard-pressed at that.

Then the bandit's arm lay open and bloody, as did his shoulder a moment later.

"First blood!" Klarnides shouted. "You can still yield."

The bandit's second reply was even coarser than the first. Then he hurled himself forward. If he reached close quarters—

Again, Klarnides needed no help. He sidestepped and thrust in a single controlled movement, and his sword sank deep between the bandit's ribs. The dead man stood for a moment, then collapsed as Klarnides jerked his sword free.

"My thanks for your thoughts as if they were deeds," Klarnides said, bowing as if he and Conan had been meeting in a palace garden. He nearly fell forward, and Conan saw that the captain's face was pale and his hands, covered with the bandit's blood, were shaking.

Klarnides took a deep breath and straightened. "Rally the men and kill any wounded the bandits left behind."

Nestorinus looked so willing to play butcher that Conan nearly ran him through on the spot. Tharmis Rog coughed.

"Er, Captain?"

"What?"

"We need a prisoner. Dead men can't tell us about this band."

"Oh, of course."

Behind Klarnides's back, Conan and Tharmis Rog exchanged brief smiles. It needed more than swordsmanship to make a captain, but perhaps there was hope for Klarnides after all.

Lysinka awoke to see Fergis crouched between her and the fire. That also kept him between her and Lord Grolin. The outlaw baron had invited her three times to sleep on the same side of the fire with him. He had also accepted her three polite refusals with good grace. So far he had not invited her to sleep in the same blankets, perhaps because he feared a somewhat less polite refusal.

"There's a fight not too far off," Fergis said. He kept his voice low, in order not to wake the whole camp.

"Speak up," Lysinka said, uncoiling from her sleeping cocoon. She wore tunic and trousers, not trusting

Grolin's men to follow the rules of her own band concerning lack of clothing.

"Oh, of course," Fergis said. He shot her a look which said plainly that *he* did not care if Grolin thought the report was not for his ears.

Sometimes Lysinka wished likewise. But as long as the Soul of Thanza was a prize that only the united bands could seek, she had to be gracious toward Grolin. It was the only way she could repay the debt she owed to her band, for having given her life, honor, reputation, and such wealth as she possessed.

Grolin was not fully awake until Fergis had finished his tale, so the baron naturally insisted on the bandit repeating himself. Fergis looked as if he would rather have wrestled a she-bear but obeyed Grolin's request and the look in his chieftain's eyes.

When Fergis was done for the second time, Grolin was sitting up.

"Can I believe this? Who sent this tale?"

"The Village Brothers," Fergis said. "And what they tell, you can take as if sent by the gods."

"The gods send more lies than truths, in my experience," Grolin snapped, which made the pious Fergis look pleadingly at Lysinka. She motioned him to silence.

"In truth, Lord Grolin, the Village Brothers are soul-kin, I think, to the forest spirits. What can be seen, they see. What can be heard, they hear. And if they were blind, deaf, and still in the forest, they might tell you much by what they scented."

Unexpectedly, Grolin made a gesture of aversion. "Wolf blood?"

Lysinka had not thought of that old tale. She shook her head. "Only being woodwise since first they could walk, or perhaps while their mother carried them.

They are twins only she could tell apart, so perhaps that gives them some power."

"As long as it gives them no power that will anger the Soul of Thanza," Grolin said. "Otherwise, you might do well to send them away."

Lysinka bristled like a wet cat. "We none of us know what will please or anger the Soul of Thanza. We do know that the Village Brothers are the best among us at finding common foes before they find us. I will abandon this quest before I abandon them."

"I have heard better ideas," Grolin muttered.

"So have we," Fergis said. "What if the brothers have found the Aquilonian levies—those who dare call themselves the 'Thanza Rangers'—before the levies found us? Where I came from, lords gave silver to such men!"

"Plainly they gave none to you or you would not be here in the Thanzas following Lysinka," Grolin said.

Lysinka put a hand on Fergis's shoulder. Her companion looked ready to leap over the campfire and drag Grolin back through it, feet first and facedown.

"Enough insults," Lysinka said to both men. "With the Village Brothers watching, no enemy can move against us without our being fully warned. I suggest the best use for the rest of the night is sleep. The closer the foe, the sooner the battle, and the better rested we must be."

Grolin and Fergis both grumbled but saw Lysinka's wisdom clearly enough to take her counsel.

The Thanza Rangers spent the remainder of the night in untroubled sleep, save for those whom duty or restlessness kept awake.

Conan was not among the sleepers. He was making

the rounds of the sentry posts, while Tharmis Rog saw to the healing of the injured mules.

The Cimmerian had just left the last sentry post and was returning to his sleeping place when he saw a slim shadow leaning against a tree on the path. Enough moonlight crept through the branches above to reveal Klarnides's features.

"Hail, Sellus," the captain said. "That was well done at the mule lines."

"You mean my tumble arse over ear?" Conan said with a guffaw. "A carnival dancer can do better than that, believe me." He trusted that Klarnides would take no offense at his light tone. If the man did, he was captain over the wrong men in the wrong place.

Klarnides laughed. "I wasn't thinking of that, but I admit it was also well done. I feared you were going to dash out your brains against a tree trunk."

Conan snorted with laughter. "Captain, don't you know I'm a northerner? We're solid bone from the neck up!"

"So the tales run, I admit," Klarnides said. "But I wonder how much truth they hold. My uncle was with the Gundermen who founded Venarium. He was not among those who came home, after the Cimmerians burned it. They made it plain that we were not welcome in the northland, let me tell you."

Having himself been one of the horde who stormed over the stockaded walls of the frontier outpost and put the Gundermen to the sword, Conan needed no telling. But he held his peace about his own history.

Klarnides seemed in a talkative mood. "I—this was the first time I ever killed a man who was trying to kill me. Or anybody else. I thought—I knew I was good with a sword. Else my arms teacher cheated my father, and the count was no safe man to cheat.

"It's different when the steel goes into living flesh, and the blood comes out and gets on you. It—well, I'm sure your own first battle was so long ago that you have no understanding of what I say."

"But, I do," Conan said. "Believe me, Captain, that is something no man ever forgets. Or if he does, then he stops being a man."

Klarnides shuddered. "The gods spare me that, at least."

Conan did not much believe in the gods answering prayers, having been brought up to honor Crom, who did no such thing. But he hoped Klarnides would be spared long enough to either become a soldier or find another way of living that suited him. Had Conan wed at the usual age in Cimmeria, his eldest son might not be much younger than Klarnides seemed to be, wearing his first sword and perhaps talking to his father of *his* first battle.

The night seemed briefly darker and less friendly as Conan made his way back to find what sleep the remainder of the night might allow him.

Grolin's and Lysinka's united bands had marched at dawn. Now they were enjoying their midmorning halt.

The lord of Thanza stepped aside into the trees. He had given up hope that any of Lysinka's women would disrobe and bathe in the streams. Some of his men had not, but Lysinka and her women could do as they pleased with such fools. Both the world and his band would fare better without such.

It was only as the minutes passed that Grolin became aware of the sensation of being watched. Even then it was some while longer before he dared turn and study the forest around him for some sign of the watcher. A prickling up and down his spine had told him from the first that his visitor might be friendly but was not of nature, so he expected to seé nothing.

At first, that was so. Then he saw a face forming on, or perhaps *in*, the bole of the largest birch tree he had ever seen. It was a face full of persuasively lifelike details—long, with a high-arched nose and an under-sized, pointed chin, adorned with a small beard.

At first it looked old, then it showed color and Grolin saw a healthy flush to the skin. Finally the eyes took form—and Grolin decided not to even think about the face's age. The eyes looking at him had seen either everything or nothing; the face was either eternal or newly born.

Regardless, it was also a face that a prudent man allowed the first word. Grolin bowed, hoping this would convey his intent.

The lips moved. The voice reached Grolin's ears—and also his throat. He found himself hearing the words in both another's voice—a man's, he thought—and his own.

It was something other than a pleasure.

"You seek the Soul of Thanza." It was not a question.

"I do." Grolin thought an affirmation was needed.

"You have chosen the wrong companion."

The tone in both voices stung Grolin to irritation. At least he still commanded his own heart and mind.

"You are free with advice."

"Only to those who seek the Soul, and need it."

"Who is this 'wrong companion'?"

"Need I say?"

After a moment, Grolin decided that it was not a proven fact. Lysinka commanded thirty woodwise fighters, equal to twice their number from lesser bands or Aquilonian levies. The face's opinion weighed little against that.

"Who is the proper companion for this quest?" Grolin asked. "You?"

"Of course. I know where the Soul is."

"Oh. You know the Mountain of Skulls?"

"It is my home. It is from there that I sent the spell to the Soul, that brought it home."

Grolin's mouth was suddenly dry. The voices carried conviction—and certainly the owner of the face commanded some potent spells to thus travel abroad with such messages.

"Can you offer—?"

"Proof? It is not my custom to offer proof to those who doubt."

"Then you must find few willing to seek the Soul."

"Indeed. Too few. It needs a human being to become the Death Lord, before its true power is released upon the world."

Grolin's mouth was open, more in surprise than with intent to speak, when the face vanished. He stepped up to the birch and touched the curled white bark where the face had been. It felt unharmed, not even warm.

The lord of Thanza realized that he had perhaps just met one who deserved that title better than he. However, there were human friends and foes to deal with first.

Grolin rinsed the dryness from his mouth with the aid of his water bottle and returned to the column.

Six

Grolin returned to the marching column with a look on his face that Lysinka had never seen before. From the way his own folk stared at him, neither had they.

"We must move to strike the Aquilonians," he said, with the same finality as he would have said, *The sun will set this evening*.

"Can we reach a good place for surprising them and settle into it in time?" she said. "I was thinking of letting them pass by and attacking from the rear."

"That might let them come between us and the Mountain of Skulls or my citadel. Speak not so lightly of being so cut off, when your home is in no danger."

Lysinka had not thought she was speaking lightly, merely prudently. The Thanza Rangers were not an enemy who needed to be fought to the death. A dozen dead, and the rest would flee, to be picked off at leisure.

"Can we speak of being cut off from the mountain, when we still seek it?"

Grolin's hard look told her that she had challenged his authority in front of both bands, something that she had vowed (at least to herself) not to do. She spread her hands.

"Very well. Let us march swiftly, then, and if possible silently as well."

"It shall be so."

As the bands moved out, Grolin fell back to walk beside Lysinka, even daring to rest an arm lightly on her shoulder. She did not shrug it off, having no wish to add lesser offenses when he had forgiven a greater.

"Be sure of this, my dear lady," he whispered. "The men would not forgive me for turning away from a battle when we are this close to a sworn enemy. My power over them would weaken, and soon your band would be prey, not friend."

Lysinka thought that an empty threat, unless Grolin's men were such fools that they would fight rival bandits when the Aquilonian levies were practically upon their doorstep. If they were, she was not sure questing in their company was altogether wise.

But the work was begun; let them see it through to the end. Besides, *she* had no fear of losing authority over her folk, whether they fought the Aquilonians, evaded them, or flew over them and dropped pinecones on their heads!

It takes time, skill, and luck to hide an ambush from the war-wisdom of a Conan or a Tharmis Rog. Grolin and Lysinka lacked all three.

So it came about that Conan, marching at the head of the Rangers, suddenly spoke out of the side of his mouth to a man marching beside him.

"Take my place. Slow the advance but otherwise

act as if there's nothing wrong. I have to speak to the captains."

The man, who looked to be a mixture of Shemite, Bossonian, and hardened cutpurse, frowned. "Is there anything wrong?"

"There will be, and with you, if you question my next order."

Conan barely spoke above a whisper, but the look in the ice-blue northern eyes would have silenced an entire temple chorus in full song. The man jerked his head as Conan stepped out of line and appeared to seek the shelter of the trees.

Instead, he waited until the march of the column brought Klarnides and Nestorinus abreast of him. Then he emerged and fell into step beside the two captains.

"I've seen signs of an ambush ahead. Up there, where the trail turns to the right, around that brush-grown spur. They are waiting for us atop the spur."

"There?" Nestorinus raised an arm. The Cimmerian pulled it brusquely down. The captain glared.

"How dare you touch a—?"

"Assert your true birth some other time," Klarnides snapped. He looked as if he wanted to ask Conan, what to do but dared not, in the presence of Nestorinus.

"Keep on. They've likely chosen a worse spot for themselves than for us," the Cimmerian said. "If they're few, we can charge them, and I'll lead. If they're many, we've cover to the right."

"And if they're on both sides?" Nestorinus sneered.

"Then we charge to the left, as before, only *you* can lead," Conan said. His grin was wholly mirthless, and Nestorinus seemed to be holding his hand only because Klarnides had a firm grip on the other captain's swordarm.

The message ran up and down the column. Conan

saw several men look dubiously for safe paths of flight, find none, and apparently decide that safety lay with their comrades. That was a good beginning for the Rangers today. If it was enough to bring victory, there would be time to teach them the rest of a warrior's skills.

"They are two to our one, and we strike only one flank," Fergis said. "Is Grolin—?"

Lysinka put a finger to her lips, then her lips to her comrade's ear. "Grolin seems to fear a rival among his men. He would neither refuse battle nor attack from the rear."

"Then why should we—?"

"Because he has seen something of which he will not speak, but which has put him in fear."

Fergis made a gesture of aversion. "The magic of the Soul of Thanza?"

"Or something very nearly as potent."

"If he cannot hurl it at us—"

"Perhaps he can. Nor can we depart now without dishonor, as well as sleeping lightly ever afterward until Grolin and his last man are dead. Do you wish to court both, and lose the Soul into the bargain?"

Fergis muttered something about her body being worth ten Souls, but Lysinka chose to ignore it.

In the next moment, she had to ignore Fergis, as battle flamed across the slope below.

What ignited the flame was a chance arrow, shot up the slope with little discipline and less aim, by one of the Rangers' handful of archers. Tharmis Rog howled in fury at the archer's folly—then somebody above the slope let out another kind of howl, as the arrow found its mark.

A man clad in a rawhide tunic and fur leggings leaped up from behind a bush, the arrow jutting from his chest. He spun in a circle, lifted unseeing eyes to the gray sky, then plunged blindly downhill.

He covered perhaps twenty paces before the arrow in his chest bled vitality out of him. He fell on his face, then rolled downhill.

As if he were a magnet drawing iron filings, he drew his comrades out of cover.

Suddenly twenty men were charging down the brush-grown spur, howling, throwing stones, and waving spears and swords. None were archers, and if any still hid above, they seemed chary of shooting for fear of striking comrades.

The Rangers' archers had no such problem. None of them were masters of the bow, but they had plenty of targets coming straight at them and were well-supplied with arrows. They put down three or four men in the first moments of the charge.

Then Conan, having studied the forest to his right to be sure it held no enemies, led the countercharge.

Birds did not drop dead from the sky nor trees splinter and topple at the Cimmerian's war cry, as men told their children in later years. But it was a blood-freezing roar, that echoed around the rocks and trees, and it told everyone within hearing that the battle had suddenly become far more deadly for this man's foes.

Conan stormed up the slope with the speed only a born hillman could have managed, sword in right hand, dagger in left. He wore no more armor than a helmet and corselet, so little slowed his feet.

He struck the first rank of the charging bandits like a maul striking a wooden piling. All the men in that rank visibly recoiled, and two of them went down at the same moment. One was dead from a dagger in the throat, the other dying from a sword-gashed thigh.

The second rank came up, and now archers up the slope were shooting back. Arrows flew over Conan and his opponents, to plunge into the ranks of the Rangers with a force that only Bossonian longbows could manage.

Then the combined ranks of the bandits lapped around Conan like a flood around a hill, and he could see nothing farther than the end of his steel. Nor could his comrades see him.

The thought of leaving Conan to die amidst the ranks of bandits seemed to spur a dozen men up the slope in the Cimmerian's wake. None of them were as surefooted on slopes as was the man they followed, but they had the edge over the bandits in armor and weapons.

So some of them fell and not all of these rose again, but the rest came to close quarters, and the bandits around Conan suddenly found themselves pressed inward. At the same time, the Cimmerian was hewing his way out from within the circle. Blood flew, and once a severed arm; and now still other Rangers were coming up from below.

Seeing that Conan needed no help, these newcomers charged straight at the hidden archers. They knew this much about fighting: at close quarters a swordsman has the edge over an archer. The trick was to live to get to close quarters, and the Bossonian longbows saw to it that not all of the Rangers who began the climb finished it.

It was Klarnides who found the wits to rally the Rangers' archers. He bid them find a place on the flank of the enemy's bowmen and shoot as fast as they could nock and draw.

"We'll have the field when this is done!" he shouted. "You'll have your arrows back and theirs too!"

As he fought his way out of the circle of bandits, Conan heard Klarnides's shout and raised another battle cry of his own in answer. He hoped the young Aquilonian was not tempting fate by such optimism. He also knew that worse lies had been told to hearten better soldiers than the Thanza Rangers!

Now Tharmis Rog was bringing up more men, and Conan knew that he hardly needed to fear laggards among the Rangers this day. The battle was going their way, and nothing turned green soldiers into seasoned veterans faster than a victory.

But as Tharmis Rog came up, a slim figure in gray and green darted down from above and met the master-at-arms. He was not a slow man, yet he seemed helpless as a baited bear before the newcomer. In a moment Rog was on the ground, helpless with a bloody leg and a bloodier arm.

Conan strode forward, to stand over his friend; and for the first time, he realized that the slim figure was a woman. From out of a tanned face too thin for beauty but too fine to forget, stared eyes the exact hue of his own.

Conan raised his sword. "Ho, north-eyed lady! Have you a name? I sing for chiefs I kill."

"I am called Lysinka of Mertyos," the woman said. "But do not put it into a song even if you live to sing it. I'm sure you crack stones and make cows go dry when you sing."

Her voice was low and rough, not one Conan would have expected to move him, yet it did. He heard in it a rare quality—a willingness to die rather than flee that matched his own.

"I do not sing for soldiers I kill," she said. "But honor demands that I know your name."

Conan started to say, "Sellus," then decided that this woman deserved the truth in her last moments of life.

"I am Conan, a Cimmerian."

"That name is not unknown to me. But why does a wolf run with the Aquilonian dogs?" she asked. All the while her light broadsword was describing gentle circles in the air close to one booted foot. Conan remained aware of it every moment, even as he met the woman's eyes. He had seen how swiftly that blade could move.

"Because I swore an oath, and these men need me to bring them safely out of the forest."

"You swore yourself in bondage to babies?" The scorn in her voice would have cut a lesser man like a whiplash.

"Who have you sworn oath to?" Conan asked. "You do not look like one to desert your followers either. So why do we not do our duty to them and settle this?"

Lysinka replied with her blade. It leaped up so fast that even Conan's eyes barely followed it. He needed all his speed to leap aside from her thrust without trampling the prostrate Tharmis Rog. Conan struck down at her lunging blade, but she swept it clear in time. She followed through into spinning completely around so swiftly that she was facing the Cimmerian before he could even think of striking at her back.

As she came out of the spin, however, Conan had more to worry about than his opponent's honor. She had a dagger in her hand; and as Conan moved to parry a thrust, she tossed it and threw.

It was aimed at his throat, and only neck muscles as tough as the Cimmerian's could have deflected the steel enough to save him from a mortal wound. As it was, he felt blood trickle, but none of the weakness that would have come from a vital wound. He advanced on Lysinka, and she laughed and gave ground before him.

The two fighters circled each other three times before they closed in again. Conan thought that his back was safe, because his own men were there, and also because Lysinka did not seem the sort to allow treachery.

For his own part, he called back any Ranger who seemed ready to strike at Lysinka from behind. He was aware that arrows were still flying in both directions, that steel was clashing, men shouting and dying, and blood flowing.

None of it mattered in the least, if he could not gain honorable victory over this formidable woman.

The end came more swiftly than perhaps either expected. Certainly those watching could not afterward recount what they saw.

Conan, however, would remember the climax of the fight to his dying day, even among all the other battles of his long and war-filled life.

Lysinka came at him, thrusting. Her swordpoint raked his arm from wrist to elbow. A spasm of his hand let his sword fall. His unslowed feet shifted him so that his dagger was in position to lock Lysinka's sword. She drew a second dagger and thrust at his thigh. He rode the blow, but that unlocked her sword.

It also brought the Cimmerian within easy reach of a fallen spear. He dove for it and came up holding it like a quarterstaff, while with one foot he kicked upward. He was aiming at Lysinka's stomach or knee, but as she thrust again on a low line, his boot crashed into her wrist. Her sword in its turn clattered on the ground.

Conan kicked again, this time sending Lysinka's fallen blade skittering out of both fighters' reach. Lysinka dove, to rearm herself with the Aquilonian's heavier blade. Conan reached it first, slamming a heavy foot on it. The woman thrust again at his thigh with her dagger, this time from below.

Conan reversed the spear and thrust down hard with the butt end. He caught Lysinka's forearm; her fingers went limp and the dagger joined the sword on the ground. Before she could withdraw this time, Conan was on top of her, bearing her to the ground with his weight, kneeling with one leg to either side of her, and pressing the spear firmly against her throat.

"Well, Lysinka of Mertyos," Conan said. "I have won, but perhaps you need not lose. We can sing the song of this battle together."

The thin face twisted in what might have been an attempt at a smile. "My voice is no better than yours, Conan. We would drive all life from the forest."

"The Rangers are here only to drive bandits back into peaceful lives. There are pardons for those who wish them."

"*After* we've rotted in stinking cells on rations of slop and mold for years, so that none of us are fit to do more than beg," Lysinka snapped. "Pardons these days go only to those with gold."

Conan had heard as much, so he could not find words to convince Lysinka otherwise. He prudently changed the subject to one closer to his heart. He knew that neither Aquilonian law nor Klarnides had given him authority to negotiate, but here was a golden moment that would not wait on anyone else's permission.

"We've halved your strength at least, and we can do the same again any time we please," he said, in his harshest voice. It would have frightened most men and even some gods, save for Crom.

Lysinka laughed. "Have I not persuaded you that we would rather rot here in our forest than in Numedides's dungeons?"

"Can I persuade you to another choice? A truce, so that we can each gather up our dead and wounded. Meanwhile, you can speak with your comrades and learn what they think."

She laughed again but softly. "Why do you think I would listen to my followers?"

"Because you look like a leader with sense, and such listen to those they've led into battle. Otherwise they've been known to find a spear in their back in some night brangle. Then they rot, without grave or honor, where they fall."

"Cimmerian, may I call you more longheaded than most?"

"Call me what you please, but the truce is all I can offer. I'll have to speak to my captains while you speak to your men for anything more."

"Very well. Let me stand and take back my weapons, then we shall call truce. I will bring you an answer from my men as soon as they give it."

"So be it."

Conan descended the slope to find a number of ugly sights, beyond the normal litter of dead and dying men of both sides—and a few women bandits as well.

"None of them fought like that she-cat you bested," Tharmis Rog said, "and for that my thanks. But they were none of them to be taken lightly, either, even the small ones with naught but daggers."

Tharmis Rog was one of the ugly sights. He was sitting up, arm and leg swathed in strips of cloth that had mostly already turned red. Conan hoped his friend's wounds looked worse than they felt.

Rog seemed to read the Cimmerian's thoughts. "Oh, I've taken worse in tavern brawls." He spat. "That she-cat was playing with me, I'd wager. A good piece of work, that, you teaching her not to do so too often."

The master-at-arms lowered his voice. "Best watch your back. Nestorinus is down and Klarnides looks more than a bit restless over your proclaiming truce without his leave."

Conan said nothing of what Klarnides could do with his leave. It would be a waste to say it to anyone but the captain. He gripped Rog's hand, then continued downhill.

He came to the second ugly sight almost at once. Nestorinus lay on his side, wounds gaping in back and belly from a spear thrust completely through him. Conan looked at the wounds a second time and realized that the spear had entered from behind.

"He was advancing so boldly that a foe came up behind him unnoticed and did this," a high-pitched voice said from behind the Cimmerian. "Let that and only that be said of his death."

Conan turned, to see a Klarnides who looked ten years older than he had this morning, for all that his voice once more sounded like a eunuch's. But the blood and grime, not to mention the hacked sword blade, told plainly enough that he had played the part of a man in today's fight.

"As you wish," Conan said.

"I do not *wish*," Klarnides snapped, then swallowed. When he spoke again, his voice was both lower and softer. "I command. I also command that you explain that truce, which you called without my leave."

"Simple enough. It was that or kill Lysinka. Kill her, and every man of hers would try to kill us or die trying. We'd do well if a score of us saw sunset today, or any of us left the forest alive."

"How do you come to know so much about the bandits of Thanza, Conan of Cimmeria?"

Conan's hand tightened on his sword. Klarnides stood, bloody arms crossed on his chest, the smile of an older and wiser man on his grimy boy's face.

"So I enlisted under a false name," Conan growled. "Punish me for that, and you'll have to punish two Rangers out of three. Also, you'll have people talking about how Nestorinus really died, and I doubt his kin will thank you for that!"

For a moment, Conan feared he might be at sword's point with Klarnides, a man whom he wanted to kill even less than he had Lysinka. He carefully kept his hands away from the hilts of his blades, trusting that his speed and longer reach would save him when Klarnides struck first.

Instead, the captain thrust his sword into its scabbard, worked his mouth, and finally spat on the bloody ground.

"That for your threats, Conan. I wasn't going to turn you over to thief-catchers or Ophireans. I wanted to see if you knew more than swordplay.

"I wouldn't yield the command of the Rangers to a stranger called Sellus the Northerner. Conan the Cimmerian is another man entirely. One I would follow, if it gave us victory and brought the Rangers home."

Conan had perhaps the time of three heartbeats to consider Klarnides's offer. Then the captain's mouth opened. Before the shout of warning left it, Conan heard stealthy footfalls behind him.

Then a hot iron seemed to sear his left side, granite boulders fell on him from the sky.

Conan went down under the impact, but managed to twist so that his head struck none of the rocks littering the hillside. He rolled—and his attacker punched him savagely in the throat.

For a moment the world faded around the Cimmerian, almost to black. It remained gray for another moment, but he had the strength to grope for his opponent and grapple the first thing that came to hand.

That turned out to be the man's jaw. The attacker howled as Conan dislocated it, and he tried to bite the Cimmerian's fingers. Conan jerked his hands clear, and with his vision returning, smashed both fists against the man's nose. A riposte took him in the stomach, and once again the Cimmerian's breath left him.

But Conan could roll again, even if he could not stand; and when he was clear of his opponent, he saw the man's blood on his fists. Now the man lurched to his knees, his face a bloody mask as more blood dripped from his mouth. The attacker lunged for the fallen knife that was coated with the Cimmerian's gore.

The lunge fell short, as Conan slammed one fist down on the man's wrist. Bone cracked, and the man screamed. Then the Cimmerian's other hand smashed into his opponent's stomach. The man flew backward, and when he fell, his head found a rock. The life was out of his eyes by the time Conan was able to kneel beside him.

"Mitra have mercy," Klarnides exclaimed, as he unwound his sash. "Here, Conan. That gash in your side is going to bleed you on to a pallet if it's not stanched."

"Do as you please," Conan said. The wound was beginning to hurt, and he felt enough blood flowing to suspect that Klarnides was right. But there were more important matters to settle first, before he lay down and let Klarnides fuss over him like a woman.

"Lysinka!" Conan roared. The shout was almost as loud as his battle cry. Again echoes rolled around the hillside.

"Lysinka! Come down here and explain this truce-breaking or there is no truce! Come down now!"

Then he added, quite as loudly, "If any man so much as frowns at her when she comes, I'll kill the whoreson with my own two hands!"

"You'll kill nobody but yourself, Conan, if you don't let me dress that wound!" Klarnides snapped. "You haven't taken up the command yet. I can still give you an order; and by Erlik, you will obey it!"

"Yes, my lord," Conan said, with an elaborate bow that sent pain like a fire up and down his side. He cursed. "But be quick about it."

Conan was roughly dressed by the time Lysinka came down. He thought her eyes were wider than before, but she seemed otherwise unchanged. Then Conan saw that she wore no knives, that her sword was roughly peace-bonded into its scabbard with rawhide thongs, and that she carried herself rather more like a prisoner going to the block than a war leader coming to negotiate.

"The truce is broken," she said, before either Ranger captain could say a word. "But I ask that if you wish vengeance, it fall on me alone, and only after I have spoken."

"Speak, then," Klarnides said. "Conan praises your honor. Show it and I may do likewise."

The two men listened to Lysinka's explanation of how the Rangers had fought two bands, hers and a self-named lord of Thanza's. Grolin's men had done most of the attacking, although hers had provided most of the archery.

"That swine"—she pointed at Conan's dead assailant—"was one of Grolin's men."

"Did you tell him of the truce?" Conan asked.

"My most trusted man went to him. Grolin knows that Fergis speaks with my voice."

Grolin seemed like a man not apt to listen to any voice save his own ambition, but Conan held his peace. Before either he or Klarnides could find words for a reply, another shout came from the hilltop.

"Lysinka! Grolin's men have cut and run! Come back to us now!"

Lysinka cupped her hands. "Fergis, don't be a fool! I'm safe enough—"

"If you're safe, I'm a Stygian! If you won't come up, then we'll come down and fight—"

"No, curse you!" Lysinka screamed. "If anyone steps one pace this way, he'll be foresworn and I'll have his blood!"

"And I'll help you," Conan added, so quietly that only Lysinka could hear. "Friend—if I can call you that—you've been betrayed. You and yours can die with honor—or live with it."

"How mean you?"

"You owe Grolin nothing. Help us bring him to earth, and you can have either a pardon or a free path back to the forest, my life on it."

One pair of ice-blue eyes sought the truth in another and found it. Lysinka rested a hand on Conan's shoulder, and he realized that she did not have to reach up very far to do this. Nor would he have to bend very far to find her lips.

"I will surrender to the Thanza Rangers, not to the

crown of Aquilonia," Lysinka said. "I cannot promise more from my people."

"We need not ask more," Conan said, "Need we, Captain Klarnides?" As the command had not yet actually passed to the Cimmerian, they had to play out the comedy.

. Klarnides nodded so vigorously that Conan was reminded of a puppet on strings, and half-expected the captain's head to fall off. That would be a pity, now that the man had proved his head was of some use.

"By the authority of my warrant as captain over the Thanza Rangers," Klarnides said, "I accept the surrender of the band of Lysinka of Mertyos. This on condition that they prove their lawful intent by aiding in the pursuit and arrest of one Grolin, self-named lord of Thanza."

Then Klarnides blew out all his remaining breath in a long sigh, and both Conan and Lysinka laughed.

Seven

Lord Grolin had ordered his men to charge in a disciplined manner, not like a pack of howling savages. He had, after all, been trained in civilized warfare. It had been his intention that his men hold Conan's advance so that the Rangers could become the target for Lysinka's archers.

Instead, his men charged madly, and died under Conan's blade or from the steel of men they might otherwise have bested. In less time than it took to eat a venison pasty, Grolin had lost half his fighting strength.

Lysinka was in better case, but instead of continuing the fight, what had she done? Made a truce for both of them without asking his consent!

Hope rose afresh in Grolin's agile mind when Dimaskor made his desperate attempt on the big northerner's life. But his plan died again with Dimaskor. Grolin then looked down on the battlefield and knew there was only one thing to be done. Flee, and do so before Lysinka and her new friends made common cause against him.

With his dozen men remaining, Grolin set a good pace. By noon they outdistanced even the possibility of pursuit. They had taken a route away from the baron's citadel, knowing that their enemies were already across the path toward it. If they avoided the trails where their enemies could lay an ambush, they might find a safe way home.

Only—what would Grolin's band do when they reached home? They had too few men to hold their position against assault or if the enemy discovered the hidden way to the citadel. They certainly lacked the strength to break a siege, and their friends from Nemedia might not care to challenge besiegers who were under Aquilonian command.

For the moment there was peace between the two realms, and many on both sides wished this happy condition to continue. They would not find in Grolin sufficient cause for changing their minds.

The baron considered all these aspects of his problem, then walked off into the forest. He was not sure why, where he was going to stop, or whether he would stop at all before nightfall or exhaustion brought him to a halt.

Perhaps his surviving men could make their peace with Lysinka and the Aquilonians, if he were dead; and they could blame the truce-breaking on him.

"Cease thinking of leaving your men, Grolin. Those with you are the best you had, certain to endure with you, and sufficient for the task."

The face seemed perched amidst a large clump of ferns. The ferns lent a distinctly greenish hue to its complexion at first. Even when its colors took on their final form, Grolin noticed a fern leaf seemingly protruding from the face's left nostril.

He did not dare to laugh at this, but it somewhat eased his mind. It was impossible to be terrified of a sorcerer who sprouted fern leaves.

"Do you wish me to prove how terrible I can be?" the face's voice boomed in Grolin's mind. For a moment his skull felt like a vast cave in which someone had just struck hammer to anvil.

When his ears and brain had stopped ringing, Grolin frowned. "If you prove it by frightening either me or my men witless, you will have none of the human help you say you need."

"I have already proved it. I entered the minds of your weaker men, driving them into that mad charge. Then I thrust myself into Dimaskor's already failing wits, and turned him into a berserker truce-breaker.

"You know that Dimaskor would have been a leader rallying others against you, had your band remained strong enough to survive. He was not one to deal with potent magic but rather to grovel to old wives' tales and priests' teachings."

The words chilled Grolin, as if he had tumbled into an icy mountain stream. It was an uncannily accurate description of Dimaskor. Was the rest perhaps also the truth?

Had the sorcerer proved his power as friend or foe, so that Grolin had two choices—become the sorcerer's human ally or to die—and his men with him?

Experience told Grolin to wait. The tone of the face's voice told him that waiting would be fatal.

And if the sorcerer truly needed a human ally for the Soul of Thanza, he might do more for Grolin than Lysinka ever could have done, even if she had remained faithful.

"I am at your service," Grolin said. "But if you slay any more of my men on a whim, I will free them from all duty to me. They may depart, whether I allow it or not."

The face laughed aloud. "Let them try to flee, and watch how far they travel," it said. Grolin could not mistake notes of both mockery and menace in the words.

"If there is no Soul, they will be better off dying as free men rather than living as your slaves."

"Oh, but there is a Soul of Thanza. Soon you will know the truth. Then you will regret ever having doubted."

The face vanished before Grolin could begin to think of a reply to that threat. He backed away from the ferns, so intent on keeping them under his eye that he backed into one of his men.

"Lord, who was that you spoke to?" the man asked. Grolin noted that the man was sweating in spite of the cool air of the forest, and pale in spite of his weathered skin and rough beard.

"Myself," Grolin said. "We must see to finding new strength, to take vengeance on that treacherous bitch. I was practicing what I might say to our friends in Nemedia."

"Aye, that would be well," the man said. He sounded polite and respectful rather than convinced. "Where do we go from here, being as how we've shaken off pursuit?"

"We go around Kringus Hill and from there along Bluesand Creek back to the citadel. We do not wish to leave anyone or anything there as easy prey for Lysinka."

How Grolin's men, those with him and those at the

citadel, were going to evacuate their quarters in time
was a question that the baron could not answer.

He could, however, hope that the sorcerer—whose
name he ought to ask, even if he received no reply—
would have something useful to say about the matter.

Grolin's men fled from a pursuit that in fact the
Thanza Rangers and their new allies were not even
attempting.

The united bands had a number of tasks to accom-
plish before any of them took a single step off the
battlefield. They had wounded to succour and dead to
bury. They had to formally invest Conan with the
command of the Thanza Rangers—or as formally as
one could expect from an oath-taking witnessed by
a handful of young captains and otherwise only by
the gods.

Then all the men and women of the two newly
joined bands had to swear peace while on the quest for
Grolin and the Soul of Thanza. The Rangers had to
swear to abide by Lysinka's laws for the women, and
Lysinka's folk swore to obey Conan, Klarnides, and
Tharmis Rog as they would obey Lysinka herself.

A few of the Rangers looked at the women in a way
Conan did not much care for, and Lysinka even less.
The Cimmerian met with Klarnides and Tharmis Rog
once the oath-taking was done to settle that little
matter.

"One man's hand in the wrong place on a woman
and we'd be at blood-feud while facing sorcery, perhaps, or at least some desperate men," Conan said. "I
took command to lead the Rangers to victory, not have
them killed off faster!"

Klarnides flushed. "What about dividing the Rangers and Lysinka's band? We both of us have wounded

unfit to travel and needing rest and care. So why not leave some of both bands at the nearest good campsite with water, wood, and game? We can be sure that any bad apples stay in this barrel, instead of rotting on the trail."

Conan nodded. "Yes, but that means we must leave behind a captain all will obey." He looked at Tharmis Rog. "What about you, my friend?"

The master-at-arms swore so eloquently that he gained the attention of most of both bands. Had they not also been under close scrutiny, Conan and Klarnides would have collapsed laughing.

Finally Tharmis Rog ran out of breath, shrugged, winced, and raised his good hand in a placating gesture. "Can you both swear that you did not plan this to keep me out of the fight?"

"No," Conan replied. "But can you swear that your arm will let you fight, or your leg let you walk, let alone march?"

"No," Rog said in turn, sounding rather like a small boy who has to confess to a roaring stomachache after eating too many honey cakes. "But I heal quickly, and I don't see your hide entirely whole either. That gash in your side—"

"I can walk," Conan interjected. "I can wield a sword. I can—"

"—be a northerner, more stubborn than any Aquilonian ever whelped," Klarnides said with a sigh. "Give over, Tharmis Rog. You've had your share of fighting, and you'll have your share of anything we bring home from this quest.

"If we bring ourselves home, that is," the captain added, in a lowered voice.

*　*　*

Three of Lysinka's wounded who remained behind were women. However, the least hurt among them was also something of a wise-woman, who knew a good many poultices and febrifuges that could be made from common plants. Some of her knowledge she had passed on to trusted comrades, including Lysinka and Fergis, so neither band would lack for healing.

"And besides, the Rangers have several among them who can at least bind wounds and set broken bones," Lysinka added, in facing down the woman's protests. "Against what men can do, we shall fare well enough."

That was the truth, as far as it went. She doubted that Grolin had more than twenty-five fighting men left to face the sixty she and the Aquilonians were planning to take against him. She also doubted that his strength was any longer entirely in human form.

"The Soul?" Conan asked when she broached this matter to him.

"I think not. But those men of his who charged—I do not believe they were in control of their senses. Something had maddened them."

"I've marched within reach of more than a few sorcerers," the Cimmerian said. "I've marched out again too, which is more than can be said of them.

"If the Soul is only magic then let's see that Grolin doesn't command it. If it's more—well, I'll believe that when I see it."

This was as far as she could make Conan declare himself. Under his iron exterior, she thought she detected the same distrust of sorcery that she herself felt.

Did this make him a better man to march with, seeking the Soul of Thanza? It might. Although Conan could be destroyed by magic; he was not one to be tempted to possess it for his own.

In Grolin, that temptation had seemingly turned into lust, and might yet turn into madness even without the help of whatever spells the Soul held. Life and death—and the big Cimmerian with the eyes so akin to her own would be upholding life. If the gods existed, Lysinka decided, they had a taste for grim jests.

She laid a hand on Conan's arm. He almost jerked it away.

"Your wound?" she asked.

"It's more than a flybite, I'll admit that much."

"It looks clean enough for the march. It's only one day's good traveling to the citadel, and I've seen axe-root for the poultices growing at the foot of the cliffs."

Conan raised a hand. "You missed your calling, Lysinka. You should have been a healer or even a priestess."

He did not quite touch her, but that huge, scarred hand was only a hair's breadth from her skin. She vividly imagined his touch, half-hoping that wishing would bring the hand across the last bit of distance.

Then she shook her head. "I wasn't one to remain a maiden. I once thought that would give me an easy life, but I soon learned otherwise. This life's not easy, but I'm at no one's bidding either."

She stood without moving away. It was the Cimmerian who rose and stepped back.

"Best we be at our work," he said. "Or the stay-behinds will snatch up the choicest rations and gear and squall like catamounts when we take them back!"

Eight

To Lord Grolin, the dark forest seemed to be holding its breath. He wished his men would do likewise. In this silent darkness, even a cough seemed ready to float through the trees and warn their enemies.

"They are all intent on the citadel." No need to ask whose voice that was.

"Why should they be otherwise?" Grolin replied, whispering to help the words form themselves clearly. "There is nothing to keep them out of my home—mine and that of my men for six good years. They will enter and learn all its secrets."

"They will learn nothing," the voice said. (No face now, nothing to break the darkness.) "They may not even enter."

"What is to prevent them?"

"Do not waste your breath asking. Wait and see."

Grolin waited until the silence of the night seemed like frozen velvet, stifling him and chilling him at the same time. He took a few steps out from behind his sheltering tree to have a better view of the citadel.

It was only a silhouette against the starlit sky. He had never seen so many stars from deep in the forest, only in the clear air atop the citadel.

A man stumbled over something, probably another man, because two voices cursed, one challenging the other.

"Silence!" Grolin snapped. Something in his voice demanded instant obedience.

Then he saw that above the citadel, the stars wavered, as if he were seeing them through water.

The gap Conan found in the rocks had clearly been nature's creation at a time so long ago that even the gods had been young and Atlantis not yet risen from the sea.

Grolin's masons, however, had done their work cunningly. When one pushed aside two cleverly balanced rocks, a broad opening gaped ahead—broad enough for pack trains or men two or three abreast.

The back door to Lord Grolin's citadel lay open.

"How could this be safe, if we found and opened it so easily?" Klarnides asked.

"It's a cursed sight easier to find something you know exists and are looking for," Conan replied. "Also, I'd wager it was normally watched from somewhere up there." He pointed at the crags looming black against the stars. "I confess this was easier than I expected—and I dislike it more than a little."

Lysinka's eyes met his. She seemed to know his thoughts, on war and perhaps on other things, better than Klarnides.

"A trap?" she said.

Conan nodded. "Best we pick a few men, to go up and spring it."

Klarnides protested. "Conan, we've been roaming among these rocks all day because you said not to divide our strength! Why do it now?"

"Because dividing our strength down here would have tempted Grolin to attack us," Conan snapped. The day had been long enough and the climbing rough enough even for a hillman to lend an edge to the Cimmerian's voice. He took a deep breath and continued more politely.

"Up there, our being together is the temptation. If evil is waiting, we don't want all of us to be within its reach when it pounces."

Even in the darkness, Klarnides's grim face told Conan that he might have chosen his words a trifle better. Then the captain shrugged. "Very well, Conan. I will go with you."

Lysinka shook her head. "No. We need Conan for his climbing skill. He needs a second captain who has been up there. That means me. Klarnides, you and Fergis must keep the men down here under cover until we return—and lead them away, if we do not."

Fergis muttered a much ruder word than the pious bandit commonly used. But he nodded, and after a moment so did Klarnides.

Twelve fighters went through the gap and started to climb the slope toward the citadel. Conan went first; Lysinka brought up the rear; and between them walked ten men, the five best climbers from each band. Each was fully armed, and each had a white triangle chalked on his forehead and his back. In a night battle, telling friend from foe could be the edge that promised victory. If there were any foe up there—any human one, that is.

Conan thought that the citadel was either abandoned or else held the best-laid ambush that he had ever faced. Or both might be true, if the ambush was not in human hands.

Conan looked up. The stars seemed brighter, more numerous, and less friendly than usual, more so even than the cold sky of his native land. The wind was still, not even the usual faint piping of small creatures among the rocks reaching his ears.

He drew his sword, and the rasp of freed steel was a homely, earthly noise that briefly gave him comfort.

"I think we turn right here," he whispered to the man behind him. The message vanished into the night as the marchers repeated it down the line to Lysinka.

High above in the citadel, some of the stars briefly wavered, unseen by the climbing band.

From his vantage point, Lord Grolin saw the stars do more than waver. Some of them were extinguished. Not as if the clouds had swept across them but as if they were candles suddenly plunged into water. He almost heard the hiss of extinguished flames.

Then he heard real hisses. They sounded so much like serpents' warnings that he started to draw his sword, until he realized that it was already in his hand. He searched the ground on all sides of him, saw nothing, then heard the hisses again.

Fear clawed at his chest, sweat dripped from his forehead. Suddenly the fear vanished like clouds driven by the wind. Instead of dripping sweat, his face flushed hot with embarrassment.

It was his own men whom he'd heard, breath hissing between their teeth as they watched the stars vanishing. His own fevered imagination had done the rest.

But what was that blackness? Potent sorcery, to be sure; but that told him little. It did not even say whether it would help or harm him among his enemies.

Then he heard it—not within his ears, or even within his mind, but someplace deeper. If Grolin had thought he had a soul, he would have said that the crying voices were within his soul, calling out to it in their loss and pain.

"Can you put a name to *that*, O Lord of Thanza?"

This time the voice came from within his mind. So came his reply.

"The Spider Wind." Then he dared to ask:

"Do you command the Spider Wind, O Master of the Soul of Thanza who will not give your name?"

Silence answered, within and without. No, not complete silence. Faintly in the night, the crying of the Spider Wind reached across the forest.

To those climbing toward the citadel, the Spider Wind gave scant warning. Conan heard a man scream, looked around him for signs of attack, then saw heads bent back and wide eyes staring at the sky.

Or rather, they were staring at where the sky had been. A hideous black maw seemed to have swallowed a patch of the blazing stars, and more were vanishing every moment. At the same time Conan felt gossamer fingers of wind trailing across his face, and heard a thin, distant cry.

At the cry, he knew what the climbers faced. Lysinka had described it as vividly as any talespinner by a northern fire. Conan remembered the chill he'd felt at the name of the Spider Wind.

One of Lysinka's people cried out the name at that same moment. Then the wind became a gale, the Cimmerian had to brace himself against a rock to stay on his feet, and one of Lysinka's men rose into the air.

The man hung suspended in midair, his feet kicking frantically a spear's length above the highest rocks. Conan expected the wind to carry him to the edge of a cliff and fling him to his doom.

Instead, the wind began to crush the life out of the man, like a gigantic snake, invisible but of immeasurable power. The man's eyes bulged from their sockets; his hands flailed at emptiness; blood dripped from his mouth.

Choking on his own blood, the breath driven from his lungs, the man still screamed.

"Captain Conan! Someone! In Mitra's name! Kill me!"

Grolin heard only two sounds now. One was the distant cry of the Spider Wind. He was sure it was the wind. He had to believe it was the wind, not living men about to die, crying out like ghosts in the night.

The other was the receding footfalls of his men. The idea of lingering close to where someone was *commanding* the Spider Wind, bidding it attack where he wished, had snapped the remains of their courage.

Grolin wondered if his dignity allowed him to join them. He could see little good that might come of remaining here, a chief without a band to follow him.

He might indeed become only a dead lord, instead of the Death Lord.

Grolin began to laugh at his own modest wit, but the laughter rang false on his ears, like that of a madman. He swallowed his laughter and nearly his tongue as well; then listened in silence to the Spider Wind sowing agony and terror in his old home.

* * *

If it had been one of his own Rangers, Conan might not have hesitated to deliver the death stroke. But his hand balked at shedding the blood of one of Lysinka's people, despite the man's mortal agony.

In the last moments of Conan's hesitation, Lysinka moved. She snatched a spear from one of the Rangers, lifted it, and threw.

The point drove deep into the man's chest. A last cry burst from his mouth, along with a gush of blood. His writhing ceased, and his eyes now stared lifeless into the blackness above.

The next moment, a scream that made the man's agony seem like a babe's cooing tore at everyone's ears. It was a sound that mountains might have made, or even gods, dying in anguish for which there were no words in any human tongue. The death of every animal that Conan had ever witnessed seemed to be part of the cry. Men, women, and children of every race of Man, and even unnatural beings such as dragons and *chakans* repeated the sound.

The scream went on, as if the world itself were dying horribly—but looking up, Conan saw part of the blackness shredding like cheap cloth. Stars wavered into sight, brightened, and shone steadily once more, as they had before the Spider Wind's maw swallowed them.

A war cry reached Conan's ears, piercing the Spider Wind's screaming. Then more cries, of rage this time, made the Cimmerian whirl.

The Spider Wind had plucked Lysinka up off her feet. But she had a firm grip on a rock, and one of her men had an even firmer grip upon her legs.

"Conan! If the Spider Wind's prey is slain in its grip—the Wind can be slain too!"

The man holding Lysinka's legs blanched. Conan

wondered to what color his own face had turned, under the scars and weathering. The idea of slaying Lysinka to destroy the Spider Wind froze not merely his sword arm, but almost his soul.

Yet Conan's will drove his muscles into action, and Lysinka and the Spider Wind might have died together save for the courage of the man holding Lysinka's legs. He heaved so fiercely that he broke her grip on the rock and the Wind's grip on her.

Then he leaped forward. From the top of the rock, he flung himself into the air. He did not fall, for the Wind caught him. Nor did he die in agony.

The moment she saw that the Wind held the man, Lysinka struck. Her sword pierced his side. He seemed to smile then, before an archer put an arrow through his throat from a safe distance.

Life left the man without his making a sound—or at least no sound that any human ear could discern. Not so was the unearthly agony of the Spider Wind. It was as if death itself was dying, raving in agony and rage at meeting the fate it had dealt so often to others.

Abruptly silence returned, for a moment as tangible and overwhelming as had been the sound of the Spider Wind. Overhead, the blackness did not shred, it shattered like glass. Conan half-expected to hear the tinkle and crash of blackness falling into the rocks of the citadel.

To his amazement the stars returned, all of them, all as bright as before. The silence ran on, broken only by the thud of the man's dead body falling onto the rocks and the thud of Lysinka's boots as she ran to kneel beside the faithful follower who gave his life for her.

"Are you all right?" Conan asked, after Lysinka's tears abated.

"Oh—yes. Yes. That Wind—it barely touched me. I—I was only frightened."

Conan put a hand on her shoulder, thinking she might welcome the human touch in her sorrow. She did not draw away, but he felt her trembling.

The Cimmerian's respect for Lysinka rose several notches. She had retained command of herself in spite of fear that would have frozen most men or women into statues—and she could admit her sorrow openly. It spoke highly of the respect in which her folk held her, that she need not appear perfect or fearless to them.

As if to herself, Lysinka now went on. "He was the guide who led us the day we sought the chest. We did not know that the chest held the Soul of Thanza. If we had reached the road in time, we might have taken it that day."

"Or it might have taken you," Conan ventured. "That kind of magic's a chancy affair at best."

Lysinka nodded. "So you saved us twice, my friend." She was addressing the dead man now. "Once that day, by chance; once tonight, when you gave your life. And all I can offer you is a cairn of rocks to keep off the carrion birds."

She looked ready to weep again, which accorded her no shame but would waste time Conan thought they had best not spend here in the open. He lifted her gently.

"We can sing a song for him or at least create it and have others with more pleasant voices sing it. But that and everything else must wait until we are safe inside the citadel."

"Safe?" He was pleased to hear the wryness in her voice again.

"Well, my lady. If this rockpile holds worse than the Spider Wind, we're dead, but we might as well die standing up. If that death-glutted Wind was the worst, and we've fought it off, we should be fit to do the same with any lesser foe."

"As I said, Conan, you have a longheaded way of looking at war."

"It's either that or be dead, when you're a wanderer like me." He turned and raised his voice. "A messenger needs to go back, to tell the others of this fight and have our men start looking for a way to bring the mules up. I don't know about you, but *I* feel like sleeping on something softer than a rock tonight!"

The sky was gray before the last of Grolin's men returned.

The lord of Thanza (whose title now seemed but a rude jest) counted them. He had eighteen men left to him, with ample food, weapons, and other supplies for fighting and surviving. If all he had intended to do was to resume his career as a bandit chief somewhere else, he would not have been so ill-furnished as he had feared.

"But you intend more than that, do you not?" rang a familiar voice in Grolin's mind.

"I do. Guide us to the Soul of Thanza, and I doubt that we shall have a quarrel."

"No, not until then." The sorcerer's face was now dimly visible, almost a wraith, amidst a large clump of fungus. Perhaps it was only a sleepless night he faced, but it seemed to Grolin that the face had taken on some of the pallid hue of its host.

Was the sorcerer in his mind at all times, or only when they spoke, or even not at all? Grolin wondered if the face's pallor came from the death of the Spider Wind in last night's battle.

If so the sorcerer was not invincible. It followed,

therefore, that not even a man who gave him total obedience and served the Soul as well would become invincible.

So Grolin would seek another way to the power he now knew must be his alone. He could never again allow himself to be vulnerable through the weakness of lesser men—or sorcerers, or even gods.

Anything less than absolute power was to him no different from death.

Above the citadel, the sky had turned pink in the east and the gray was fading to blue overhead. Only the last few stars still glimmered in the west, sinking with the moon toward the rock-fringed horizon.

From below, Conan heard the mules braying. They would warn the whole forest that the citadel was occupied, but somehow he doubted that anyone cared. Grolin and his men were gone, so was the Spider Wind, and archers commanded both routes by which anyone else might approach the citadel.

What the Cimmerian wanted now was a change of dressings for his wounded side, which had begun to ache insistently. Then he wanted a long drink of anything cold, and finally, sleep.

Grolin and his men had largely stripped the citadel of anything useful, but the Rangers had been hauling rations and bedding up from below since the stars began to fade. Water he could find at any one of three live springs that fed basins carved into the rock.

Searching for the spring, he also found Lysinka, sitting by one of the basins, absently trailing her long fingers through the water. As he bent to drink, Conan saw that her fingers were scraped raw, from her fierce grip on the rock, and two of the nails were missing.

"I was going to ask you to change my dressing,"

he said when his mouth and throat no longer felt dust-caked. "But I think your hands need dressing themselves."

"Perhaps we can do for each other," Lysinka said. She fumbled in her belt pouch. "Oh, plague! I've the herbs but no more dressings." She looked downcast for a moment, then grinned.

"Perhaps this will do." She pulled her green leather tunic off over her head. Under it she wore a shirt of soft pale gray linen. She pulled that off too, baring herself to the waist, save for scars and gooseflesh from the chill morning air.

Conan felt his blood heating. He had thought Lysinka a trifle thin-flanked. Now he had good reason to think otherwise.

"You will be cold, Lysinka."

"Not for the little while it will take to rip this up for dressings," she said, tearing off one sleeve of her shirt. "There is a bowl in my pouch. Fill it with water and hand it to me."

Conan obeyed without taking his eyes off Lysinka. The heat of his blood was reaching a point where he feared Lysinka would sense it. However, he would abide by the laws of her band, as all the Rangers had sworn to do.

This did not keep him from thinking that a woman like this was sadly wasted on a chaste existence as a bandit chieftain.

Lysinka steeped the crumbled herbs in the bowl, then soaked the shirt sleeve in the herb-water. Finally, she poured the rest of the water over Conan's old dressing, softening it until it came off with hardly a twinge of pain.

"You've good-healing flesh," she said. "No bad thing for a soldier." Her fingers probed the wound.

Conan saw her jaw set, and remembered that her fingers must be giving her as much pain as his wound gave him.

Now her fingers were not so much probing as caressing. Conan assured himself that this was merely the work of applying the new dressing. He sniffed the faintly acrid, faintly woody scent of the herbs joining the smell of the smoke from the cookfires.

"Thank you," Conan said at last, when the warm trail of those fingers on his flesh was about to make him lift Lysinka's battered hands to his lips. "Now, what about your hands?"

"Ah—we need a fresh bowl of herb water," Lysinka said. "And—Conan, I am still cold." Her tongue crept out over her lower lip.

Conan lifted both hands and stroked her bare shoulders and breasts until he was caressing her throat. "Then perhaps I can warm you, Lysinka of Mertyos."

She had finished disrobing by the time Conan had spread blankets and furs. She gripped him with hunger and fierce joy; and when she cried out, the echoes from the rocks made sweet listening.

Nine

That first morning, Conan and Lysinka enjoyed only a short embrace in each other's arms. There was too much to do, even without sending a single fighter outside the citadel.

The first task was a thorough search of Grolin's citadel, to discover what or who he might have left behind. Human spies were most likely but also least feared. A hand's-breadth of well-honed steel could silence them forever. Magical perils were another matter.

When the citadel was pronounced clear of at least all recognizable dangers and sentries were posted, the mules remained. They had to be brought safely higher, unpacked, fed, watered, tethered, and then persuaded that they should not retaliate for all these indignities by kicking their handlers off the nearest cliff.

Some of Lysinka's folk kept peace between man and mule with some effort, much sweat, and enough cursing to crack boulders. Between bursts of cursing the mules, they congratulated Conan.

"Not much of a secret, is it?" the Cimmerian said with a wry smile.

"Don't remember that you were trying to keep it," one replied. "Most of her people, by the way, think it's high time she had a man of her own."

"If I want your opinions, I'll ask them," the Cimmerian muttered. "And if I don't like them, I may just have to break a few heads."

"Just be sure you don't break any skulls Lysinka thinks are hers to break," the man said. "Otherwise she'll break something of yours, and I much doubt it will be your head!"

The search of the citadel did reveal some dry chambers and caves sheltered from the wind, and into one of these Lysinka and Conan moved their bedding. They also retired to that bedding earlier than they had the previous night, and were asleep in time to rise before dawn and inspect the sentries.

The third morning, Conan awoke to feel a brisk wind rising, then long firm fingers gripping his ankle.

"Must you rise so soon, Conan?" The pleading contrived to be both real and mocking at the same time.

"What, does three nights with a man turn you into a clinging girl?" the Cimmerian growled, with the same note in his voice.

"No," Lysinka said. She sat up, wearing only a fold of blanket over her loins. Conan turned to admire her, as any man with eyes in his head would have done.

"I do not cling," Lysinka added with dignity. "But I had all but forgotten that shared furs are warmer than sleeping alone. Come back and warm me up before we have to face a stormy day."

They warmed each other so thoroughly that by the time Conan next rose, half a gale was blowing over the citadel. He sent a messenger to the patrol he was about to lead in exploring the area around the citadel more thoroughly. They would depart when the storm passed, not now when the wind could blow them off cliffs or mask the approach of enemies.

With no duties, Conan and Lysinka found themselves warming to each other yet again. They lay in contentment afterward, until the angry roar of the wind had diminished to a distant and discontented muttering.

At last, as they both rose, Conan remembered another time he had thus spent a morning. Remembering was not all pleasure, for the long ago morning had been spent with the pirate lady Bêlit.

But the Cimmerian had no wish to be free of memories, even those that brought no joy, if it meant forgetting Bêlit altogether. Indeed, Lysinka had much in common with the late queen of the Black Coast, being also lithe, deadly, and the unquestioned leader of a band of cutthroats. The bandit chieftain was fairer of skin, and those ice-blue eyes said that some of her blood flowed from the north, not from the land of Shem like Bêlit's.

All of which might mean much, little, or even nothing whatsoever; and meanwhile Conan had to cram a day's scouting into what remained of daylight. Grolin seemed to have fled the area. Or else, be cunningly hidden. Regardless, other bandit companies might have wandered in, drawn by the uproar at the citadel and hoping for easy pickings.

Conan had no intention of giving them any opportunities by allowing himself to be trapped outside the citadel with only a handful of men. When he marched on Grolin's trail, he and Lysinka would lead a stout band.

* * *

Conan's scouts numbered twelve, all picked for archery or spear-throwing, clear eyes, climbing skills, and stout boots. This meant that Lysinka's band gave Conan eight and the Thanza Rangers only four scouts; but one of the Rangers was the sharpest-eyed man in either band.

Dutulus was in fact keener of sight than either of the Village Brothers or even Conan himself. The man had done most of his climbing up walls to ladies' windows and down again to escape jealous husbands; but those days were behind him—or so he said.

Dutulus was the first to sight the approaching pack train. Conan sent the men to cover and remained on watch with his lookout. As the pack train ambled closer, Conan grew more certain that it could not contain Grolin. Even as a most desperate form of disguise, the lord of Thanza would hardly saunter up to his old citadel in the full light of day, encumbered with some twenty-odd pack animals.

"Some caravan that hasn't heard of bandits?" Dutulus asked. His tone held wonderment that any people so witless could be alive and breathing.

"The men look harder than most of your caravan guards," Conan said. "And their armor's Nemedian style, or I'm a Khitan."

The Cimmerian remembered what Lysinka had said, of Grolin's boasting about friends or at least allies in both neighboring kingdoms. It looked as if one set of friends intended to pay a visit to the departed lord of Thanza.

Conan bound his long hair up in a rough pigtail, the style favored by a good many of Lysinka's men.

"What in Mitra's name—?" Dutulus began.

"Mitra will stand well clear of this, if he's wise," Conan said. "You stay up here and keep a lookout for any friends these folk may have. I'm going down to see if I can accept their loads in Lord Grolin's name."

Dutulus's mouth opened, then closed and formed a smile as he took Conan's meaning.

The Cimmerian nodded. "You may yet live to die in your own wife's bed. Don't let anyone so much as nock an arrow unless you see me attacked."

Conan then ambled down the slope, with the easy carelessness of a man walking his dog in his own garden. If he were wrong about these men being Grolin's friends, his own life might be near its end. But they could never cross half a league of rugged mountains to the citadel in time to catch its occupants unaware.

Crom did not much care for men's prayers, even for their battle luck. All Crom asked was that a warrior do his best and accept what came with no outcry. Conan was one who would have done this whether he worshipped all gods or none.

It still sobered the Cimmerian a trifle, to think that for the first time in a long while, he might be leaving behind a woman ready to mourn him.

By the time Conan had settled this in his mind, the men below had noticed him. One of them blew a horn that sent the caravan's guards into a circle, with drawn steel. A guard broke out of the circle and mounted the slope toward Conan.

"Hola! How fares the lord of Thanza?" the man called.

"Well enough," Conan said.

"Hunh," the man said, after another dozen paces. "You're a new face in Grolin's band. What do you here?"

"I won't be the only one, when you reach the citadel," Conan said. "Grolin's made a pact with

Lysinka of Mertyos. That gives each of them two camps and near double the fighting strength."

Conan would rather be flayed alive than deal in magic or court the Soul of Thanza. Nonetheless, the man below studied the Cimmerian intensely, as if trying to read some deep secrets in the battle-hardened face above.

His efforts were in vain. Conan now smiled more than he had in his younger days. He could also more skillfully make his countenance as unreadable as a granite boulder.

"You look like a canny fighter," the man finally said. "Did you come with Lysinka?"

Conan shook his head. "Deserted from the Aquilonian host. I've sworn nothing to Lysinka."

"Good. Then let me just say it'll be worth your while not to. Men in Nemedia will see to that."

Conan refused to be drawn into what was doubtless some intrigue among Grolin's Nemedian friends. Instead, he played the honest warrior.

"I'll worry about my reward when I've done something to earn it. For now, we'd all best worry about making a safe way to the citadel. If it comes on to blow again, we'll not be there before nightfall, and that's no healthy fate hereabouts.

"I name no names," Conan went on, "but there've been tales of new bands of the brothers of the hills moving in. Some think they want to join, some think they want the price on Lysinka's head—"

The other man's face showed that Conan's random shot had struck home.

"—and none of them are yet friends enough with Grolin to resist a fat pack train. So let's be off. I've a few good fellows with me, and we know the land. Give us the word, and you've scouts in plenty."

That arrangement, if the man accepted it, should

allow Conan to march with the visitors and listen to what they said in unguarded moments. Meanwhile, his own men would be hiding their strength and staying well ahead, to spy out ambushes or deliver one themselves, as necessary.

The man seemed about to answer, when a wild cry from above made Conan whirl.

Dutulus was standing on a boulder, waving his arms as if beset by angry bees. Vaguely Conan made out that he was shouting something. Then Dutulus pointed off to the northeast, behind Conan.

The Cimmerian turned, his eyes grew colder still, and without a word to the man or the other guards, he drew his sword.

So black that they stood out even against the gray sky, so glossy that they seemed to glow, the pack of flying snakes swept down on the prey offered to them as if tethered at the stake.

At least, "flying snake" was the name that first came to Conan's mind. Legless, they had fanged heads, long sinuous bodies ten paces long and seemingly covered with scales, and two pairs of broad, leathery wings. He also saw that they seemed to know exactly where they were going, and he doubted that their intentions once they reached their destination were friendly.

"Archers!" Conan bellowed. His voice not only raised echoes, it brought the archers of the pack train to the alert and the archers of his own band out of their hiding places.

The man facing Conan looked at the Cimmerian, then uphill. His look turned into a glare, and his hand went to his sword hilt.

Before he could draw, three of the pack train's archers let fly. The man had to duck to keep the arrows from parting his hair. By then Conan had grappled him and was shaking him as if to shake his sword out of its scabbard or some wits into his head.

"Those creatures are no friends of ours! If you see treachery where it isn't, you're a bigger fool than I thought a man could be. Draw, but not on me, if you don't want to be snake fodder!"

The man drew, but not in time to avoid that fate. One of the snakes flew directly overhead, then tipped up and plummeted vertically to the man. Its fanged jaws sank into his shoulder, blood spurted, and a throat-tearing scream burst from the man's lungs. When Conan saw his eyes rolling up in his head, and turning green as they did so—the Cimmerian swung his sword with both hands.

The blade caught the serpent between the two pairs of wings, and nearly sheared through its body in a single stroke. The fanged jaws opened, leaving a bloody wound surrounded by greenish ichor that was rapidly turning black. Then the half-severed serpent thudded to the ground.

Conan's sword descended again, on the neck. Scale-armored as it was and thick as Conan's arm, the neck parted at the blow. It was not just the Cimmerian's imagination, however, that the head went on snapping its fangs for a moment after the sword cut it off, nor that more of the greenish ichor flowed from the poison glands—nor that where the ichor touched the ground, it *smoked*.

Conan leaped back, coughing from the merest whiff of that smoke, and looked about for other foes.

One that he faced immediately was human, one of the pack train guards who was convinced that the snakes were Conan's friends. The Cimmerian wasted no breath in argument, but struck the man's sword out of his hand. He was trying to grapple the fool, to twist a knife out of his grip, when a snake swooped down and tried to engulf the man's head in a single bite.

The man was not much shorter than Conan, and he wore a helmet over a mail coif as well as a corselet. The fangs scraped futilely on the man's armor, giving Conan time to snatch his dagger free and thrust it over the man's shoulder into the snake's eye.

The creature let out something more than a hiss and less than a scream, and released its hold. Before it could try for another grip, the man whirled, and stabbed deep into its belly. Conan finished off the writhing creature with a blow that split the skull.

"Your pardon, northerner," the man said, stamping hard on the snake to end its final twitching. "Where *did* those—?"

A scream that made all cries before seem like the mewing of kittens half-deafened the Cimmerian. It came from one of the mules, who had two of the snakes attached to it, one tearing at its muzzle, the other at its belly. The creature kicked and bucked frantically, but blood was already flowing and poison working its way deep into the mule's body.

At last the mule toppled, with a jingling of harness and packsaddle, and the snakes stooped to feed. That was their last mistake. Conan and his former opponent advanced on them, the guard with his recovered sword raised. The fellow chopped through the spine of one snake; Conan, with his longer reach, tore the other's head off its neck.

But it was too late. The sight and sound of their mate dying had panicked the other mules. They reared, lashing with hooves and teeth and stretching two of their handlers senseless on the ground. Before any others could regain a grip on harness or bridle, the mules clattered off in all directions.

Two surviving snakes seemed to turn end for end in midair to follow the mules. This left them all but hanging within bowshot of archers above and below. The creatures' scales were as good as a corselet, but enough arrows flew to find vital spots. One serpent crashed to earth almost on top of Conan, a second managed to fly a few-score paces before its strength departed and aborted its flight.

By the time Conan had made sure that all of the fallen men were indeed beyond help and all the dead snakes needed no finishing strokes, most of the pack train's guards had followed the mules. Conan looked at the man who'd fought at his side, and the man looked down at his dead captain, then spat on the ground.

"So much for promises of an easy month's pay," he said, mouth twisted. "And I reckon my wife's a widow by sunset. But if you'll let me march with you, I can at least go out fighting."

If the man expected to find Grolin or any of the baron's friends at the citadel, he would be sadly disappointed. But Conan warmed to the man's determination. He would have wished the same under like circumstances.

"You can join us," he said. "But one word of warning. Whatever you see or hear, keep it to yourself, and not so much as a harsh look at Lysinka. I reckon there's a bigger price on her head in Nemedia than on this side of the border. But we need her head on her shoulders more than you need its price in your purse. And if you don't understand that, best follow your friends while *your* head still sits where the gods put it."

The man swore that he was innocent of any ill intention toward Lysinka of Mertyos. He swore this in the name of several gods and two noble houses in Nemedia. He also swore that he would obey Lysinka in all things until he had avenged his comrades.

The man, who called himself Regius Panon, claimed kinship with both of the noble houses he had invoked in his oath. Conan did not care if he claimed descent from the royal house of Atlantis, as long as he kept his oaths and did his share of the work.

Of work, there was more than enough for twice the men present. A messenger was dispatched to the citadel, with an escort in case some of the Nemedians had regained enough courage to lie in wait. As much of the mules' loads as possible had to be retrieved, for Conan had guessed truly: the beasts had borne food, weapons, and other supplies for Grolin.

"Indeed, it's known that Grolin has been sent enough to fight a small war," Panon said. "But don't be asking me against whom he was to fight, for I do not know."

"I also doubt you'd tell me if you did," Conan added dryly. "Never fear, it's no part of your oath to me to commit treason. But watch your tongue and your back, for there will be those within hearing more curious than I am as to why Nemedia intrigues with bandits in Aquilonia."

"If this is Aquilonia," Panon said impudently. "All the maps I saw when I learned soldiering showed this to be Nemedian territory."

"Maps are drawn mostly by men who've never walked the ground they draw," Conan said with a shrug. "Most of these go in fear of their lives if their maps don't uphold some potentate's claim to the Bottomless Swamp of Glur or the like."

"Indeed," Panon said. "You've clearly been a soldier long enough to make a fine cynic."

It was then that Dutulus scrambled down from his perch so fast that he stumbled twice and reached Conan bruised, bloody, and dust-covered.

"I've spotted the nest of the snakes," he gasped. Conan handed him a water bottle. The Ranger drank, then repeated his message in more detail.

Conan looked off in the direction where Dutulus pointed. "You can't see them from here, but they were circling a peak less than a league away," Dutulus said. "That may not be their nest, but it's some place where they seem ready to perch."

Conan clapped his hands together, in both signal and triumph. "Good work, Dutulus. We can learn a trifle more about these pests before nightfall if we work fast."

The Cimmerian quickly divided his party. All the men volunteered to go with him to seek the lair of the flying snakes, but he only chose six, Dutulus among them. The rest he commanded to return to the citadel, bringing down a party large enough to defend itself while it searched for the fallen and any scattered booty.

Conan planned to send Panon back to the citadel, when the Nemedian unexpectedly volunteered to go snake-hunting.

"I know this land, and this is the first time I've seen or heard of such creatures," Panon said. "I won't be a burden, and I've a duty to learn if Grolin's about anything in the way of magic."

"Grolin, or any new friends he may have made of late," Conan said. He decided that the secret of the Soul of Thanza could wait until Panon proved himself further.

"Do your duty as you please," the Cimmerian went on. "Just remember we stop for no laggards, and this is no safe land for a man benighted alone."

"I'll keep up, northerner," Panon snapped. "I've not spent my years of manhood play-soldiering with wine on the table and a wench on my lap."

Several sets of eyebrows rose, Conan's among them. Panon shook his head emphatically. "You would not believe what wine costs in Nemedia, since the last two grape harvests failed. And my wife would break my head if she caught me fondling another woman."

"Then let's make sure to send you home with a story that will make her fondle you," Dutulus shouted, sparking a chorus of bawdy laughter.

The twin-peaked mountain Dutulus had pointed out was a single league away only if one flew like a bird or like one of the monsters they sought. On the ground, it was nearly half again that far, and much of the ground was steep with jagged slopes.

Fortunately Lysinka's men were among the toughest and hardiest Conan had ever met. Even the Thanza Rangers had sweated to stay on their feet over the rough ground. Fortunately, the sun came out—but the clouds had fled only before a brisk wind that held a biting chill.

Conan remembered travelers' tales, which spoke of some peaks in the Border Range not too far north of the Thanzas, which remained snowcapped half the summer. Right now, the wind felt as if it had blown across a glacier just beyond the next crest. Even with his northern blood, Conan was happy to be well-clad.

The wind, however, did not slow the scouting party's march. It was still daylight as they approached the peak. No snakes or birds were to be seen, either flying or perched.

A cave mouth gaped black against yellow-gray rock, atop a near-vertical cliff rising at least three hundred paces. No one was surprised to find that the snakes sought a lofty perch—

"—lest the catamounts and bears make an end of them," Panon said. No one cared to mention what everyone thought, that the flying snakes might be creations of magic who had no need to fear the common wild beasts.

Conan pointed aloft, toward the northern edge of the cliff face. "There's something very like a trail going up and around. It passes out of sight halfway up, but I'd wager it goes on around to the far side of the mountain. I've never met a flesh-eater who didn't have a back way out of his lair. I'd wager a gold arm ring that's where we'll find another way to attack the snakes."

Even Lysinka's hill-wise fighters looked askance at the climb Conan was promising. "Better we scout the mountain from down here," someone said, keeping his back turned toward the Cimmerian.

Conan recognized men who had been led as far as they would go. Keeping his voice light, he said, "True, there's no need for us all to go. But we need a man aloft, to see if there are any small caves we can't see from down here. The rest can go roundabout, but—"

"I'll go with you, Conan," Dutulus said.

"And I," Regius Panon joined in.

Conan glowered at both of them. "What makes you think I was going?"

Dutulus made a parody of a deep, courtly bow. "Your pardon, Lord Conan. I had not thought you so fond of sitting by the fire."

"Nor I," Panon said. "Besides, if you can't walk, it will take two of us to carry you down."

The scouts split, three to climb aloft and three to circle the base of the mountain. The climbers lightened their loads and tied themselves together with ropes around their waists. Conan doubted that the rope could hold his weight, but it might break a fall long enough to let him find a handhold.

The cave high aloft remained as deserted as before, as the three climbers made their way up the rough trail. It had clearly been man-made but so long ago that the men might have carved it with stone hammers or bronze chisels. Below, the scouts on the ground shrank steadily, and Conan saw Panon turning pale.

"Are you fit to go on?"

"Hardly a choice, is there? I just remembered that as a boy I was always queasy about heights."

Panon remained pale, and once Dutulus had to stop to empty his stomach. But they climbed on as gamely as if hill-bred, seldom forcing even the iron-limbed Cimmerian to slow his pace to accommodate them.

They were now nearly at the edge of the face, and the daylight was beginning to fade. For all they could see and hear, the flying snakes might have been creatures of fantasy, but their noses told them otherwise.

When the breeze blew from the caves above, a pungent odor of ichor and carrion wafted down to them.

The path did not round the edge of the cliff face. Instead it came to an abrupt end in front of an opening in the rock that might once have been a doorway. Eons of weathering had left it as gaping and shapeless as any natural cave.

Conan stepped forward cautiously, testing the footing with his boots and the chill breeze from the dark opening with his nose.

"It reaches the snakes' lair, just as sure as jewels glitter," Conan said. "I had another good whiff of their stink just now."

"What if they're waiting for us?" Dutulus said.

"We came up here to find their lair, and we've

probably found it, and now you want to go back without being sure?" asked Panon.

"Here now, you son of a Nemedian—!"

Conan put a large hand on each man's shoulder. "Uncoil another rope; tie one end to my waist and the other to this outcropping. I've better night-sight than most, so I'm the best one to go in without a torch. Light would just wake up our scaly friends, and I'm for cutting their throats as they sleep."

Panon and Dutulus, forced allies, looked at each other. Then they looked at the sky, as if hoping the gods would heal the Cimmerian's apparent madness. At last they began uncoiling the rope.

Nothing except the carrion stench drifted out of the doorway as the scouts prepared for Conan's entrance. Nothing else drifted down from above either. Panon tried shouting a message to the men below, but the wind blew his words away or drowned them with unearthly moans as it curled around the rocks.

"An uncanny land, this," Conan muttered. "If Grolin has any sense, he'll have a friendly sorcerer conjure him up a flying chariot to take him somewhere else."

"There," Dutulus said and grunted as he tugged on the tethered end of Conan's line. "Much tighter and the rock edges will chafe it through. You've two hundred paces to play with. If the serpents do take you, we'll ask them to return the uneaten rope—along with your bones for proper rites."

"I've no need for rites," Conan grunted. "Just find a safe hilltop and tell the sky that Conan of Cimmeria died like a warrior. Crom may hear, and if no others do, that's their loss."

Again the other two men stared at each other, as if still further persuaded that they were in the presence of a madman.

Conan walked to the entrance, wrinkled his nose at a particularly raw blast of the carrion odor, and took a cautious step into the shadows. Then he took a second.

On the third step, he felt rather than heard rock giving way. He took no fourth step, either forward or backward. Instead the rock underfoot cracked across, wobbled uncertainly for a moment, then plunged down into blackness.

The moment was a heartbeat too short for even the Cimmerian to find a handhold. He ended up dangling on the rope, his breath jerked out of him as it tightened, and no handholds anywhere within reach.

Then the rope jerked again, and Conan felt himself sag. A desperate wail sounded from outside, echoing through the blackness. Conan thought the snakes were attacking, and tried to gain enough breath to tell his friends to let him go and save themselves.

"The rope's cut!" Panon's voice shouted. Then both the Cimmerian's comrades appeared, struggling with the severed end, trying to pull it back and Conan with it.

"Wait—!" Conan shouted. He cursed himself for not remembering that within the cave, sheltered from wind and rain, rock edges might be sharp as swords.

It was too late. A second sharp edge deftly slit the rope. Dutulus made a desperate grab for the vanishing end, overbalanced, and with a wild scream fell after Conan.

The Cimmerian's last sight as he plummeted into blackness was Panon's horror-stricken face staring over the crumbling edge. His last thought was to hope that Panon would not stand there gaping until either the snakes woke up or the rest of the ledge brought him down to join his comrades.

Ten

Lysinka was taking a sentry's watch herself at the citadel when the flying snakes attacked. She intended to prove to both bands that her bedding Conan had not made her slothful.

It was also a good way of studying the land about the citadel and adding more details to the map she already carried in her mind. With two few fighters to guard every possible road of attack even by human foes, she had to make sure which were the most likely, (and therefore probably unused by an opponent with the wits of Grolin) and the least likely (which Grolin might be shrewd enough to use).

The actual battle against foolish Nemedians and ferocious flying snakes was too far within a steep-walled valley for Lysinka to see clearly. But she knew that something had swooped down behind a ridge, and something else—rather smaller—had soared up from behind the same ridge not long afterward.

If that was an attack on Conan and his men, she

almost felt sorry for the attackers. She looked forward to resting her head on the Cimmerian's shoulder—a place that had in only three nights become familiar and friendly to her.

Idly, she wondered how many of his tales of war were the truth. More than many other wanderers', she would wager. His own prowess she had seen for herself, and indeed the bruises she had taken from it were still healing. Nor would she doubt for a moment that he had faced more than his share of formidable foes.

The world held potent enemies enough and to spare. Not all of them wore stinking furs and came at you with steel either. Some wore silk and delicate linen, and they had no weapons but honeyed words, to persuade you that if you gave them all they asked they would return the favor.

Lies, all of that. But she did not fear lies with Conan. Whether he swore eternal fidelity to a friend or eternal vengeance against an enemy, he would not be foresworn while there was breath in his body.

It was toward the end of her watch that Lysinka felt the ground quiver underfoot. It was only a single shock, and it felt to her not at all like an earthquake. It reminded her instead of a time when she had been standing atop a fallen tree, and a bear denning underneath it crawled out, shaking the tree.

That time she had saved herself by climbing high up the next standing tree for the bear. But there were no trees close to hand in this alien wilderness of rock, for which she had abandoned her familiar forests. She wished briefly that Grolin and the Soul of Thanza would both fall into a cave that would then collapse upon them, grinding them both to dust and removing them from the memory of men.

But wishes led no bands of warriors. Her watch was

done; and she had much to do before daylight faded and night brought Conan's return.

Conan awoke slowly, in what at first seemed complete darkness. Gradually he became aware of a grayish twilight that seemed to envelop him like water. He also became aware of pain in several parts of his body and saw that he was lying on a bed of fine sand.

This was as well, because he felt no great urge to rise or move about. No bones seemed broken, and he could breath and move every part of his body without unendurable pain. But plainly he had taken such a fall that even for him rest would be prudent.

Before resting however, he sat up. This sent pain ringing like a gong through more of his body than before. It also showed him his surroundings.

The dim light came from patches of grayish moss on the walls and on boulders jutting from the sand. It was enough to reveal the bottom of a vertical shaft, that shot up to vanish in darkness far above.

Conan's wits were returning. Plainly the ledge that moved under him at the top of the shaft, and a cave lay at the bottom. How far he had fallen, he did not dare to think about. The bed of sand rose at a sharp angle, fit to break a man's fall and leave him merely stunned rather than dead—if he were fortunate enough to strike only sand.

Dutulus had not been so lucky. A patch of blood showed where he had struck a boulder. As if that blow had been insufficient, he had *bounced*, like a child's ball, to strike another. He now lay across the second boulder, his blood smearing the moss into a grisly paste, his half-crushed head lolling and his back bent far beyond any angle imaginable for a living man.

To test his strength, Conan forced himself to his feet

and walked over to Dutulus. If he took one step at a time, he could walk without too much pain. He suspected that it would be some time before he could fight or run.

So he knelt beside Dutulus and told Crom that here was a brave man who deserved his attention, and that any help he gave in avenging the man's death would not come amiss. The Cimmerian was not a man for death rituals, and in any case he did not know whether Dutulus's folk buried, burned, or exposed to the sky their honored dead.

A shadowy opening in the wall beyond Dutulus revealed a faint glimmering and enlarged the sound of rushing water. As underground rivers were not uncommon in this land Conan saw that he need not fear thirst.

Rest and water should make him fighting-fit long before either friend or foe came searching for him. Conan returned to his first resting place, lay down in the sand, scooped out a shallow nest like a dog lying down in high grass, and fell swiftly asleep.

Lord Grolin was so weary after the day's march that he was asleep almost the moment he sat down. He thought briefly that he should see to the cookfires and the sentries, as a captain's duty required. But he decided that discipline of his dwindling band of followers would survive their chief's inattention for a single night. Indeed, it might solve many problems if he did not awake.

When Grolin did awake, it was fully dark, except for an area immediately before him. What he saw at first made him believe that he had indeed died and gone to some particularly unpleasant afterworld.

A maw gaped before him. It was not the mere

incorporeal blackness he had seen above the citadel but the mouth of a gigantic serpent. The creature seemed to stretch from the stars to the earth, and all around it jutted gleaming teeth longer than a man.

Above the maw shone two red eyes that might have been ruby-colored. But Grolin would have happily thrown any ruby of that hue into the nearest fire, although it was worth a king's ransom.

He wanted to scream. He knew he would, if he said nothing. So once more he articulated the first words that came to his lips:

"Cease these jests, friend sorcerer. If you have come for serious matters, speak of them. If not, depart and let me sleep."

The gigantic maw shrank down to the size of a large melon. Grolin saw that it belonged to a real creature, a snake easily twenty paces long, covered with glossy black scales, and sporting two pairs of leathery wings.

It hissed twice, then closed its mouth. As the fangs vanished, the sorcerer's long face appeared where the snake's head had been. It held no expression.

"How are we going to speak?" Grolin whispered.

"Briefly, as you wished," the sorcerer replied. If human words could describe creations of magic, Grolin would have said that the sorcerer seemed uneasy. Grolin spoke first:

"Enemies are closer to the Soul of Thanza than we are. I tried to drive them away, but they would not be driven. Some have entered the Mountain of the Skull."

"If one of the enemies you tried to drive forth was that Cimmerian, it does not surprise me that he would not go save where he wished. You may slay that man, but do not expect to frighten him."

"Indeed. That is why I do not seek to make him the

Death Lord of Thanza. You, one may dream of guiding. The Cimmerian, never."

Grolin decided that he had not been insulted, only described. He also decided that Conan would be a poor choice for other reasons. Many northerners loathed even lawful sorcery, and he would also have been giving ear to Lysinka.

So Conan would instead be implacably on Grolin's trail, and nothing would save the baron except becoming the Death Lord. He propped himself up on one elbow.

"Do we seek the Mountain of the Skull now, or will morning suffice?"

"You dare much, Grolin. Without my guidance, you will be too long in finding the mountain."

"Without my presence, you lack a human to become the Death Lord. Without my men, you will not have my presence. I will fight neither Cimmerians nor any other being with men so weary they can barely stand, let alone wield a sword."

Grolin thought this defiance might be a death sentence. He hardly cared. He and his men would rather be dead than to undertake a night march.

The sorcerer's face shimmered so brightly for a moment, in rich amber hues, that Grolin blinked, then looked about to see if any of his men were awake and alarmed. None seem to be stirring.

Then the sorcerer spoke in Grolin's mind. "Very well. Please yourself. But do not presume on such friendship as I bear you."

The face vanished. The snake reared upright until an impossible portion of its length rose like a tree. The two pairs of wings beat three times, and with a *whusssh* of torn air the creature soared out of sight.

"My lord!" called a sentry. "Was there a bear in the camp just now?"

"Hardly that," Grolin replied. "I saw something too, but I think it was just a trick of light and shadow."

"Aye, my lord."

As before, the man sounded willing to obey rather than believe. Grolin wondered how often he would lie to the men about the sorcerer before they ceased to believe him in this matter—or in others.

Once more, he knew that the only real power was one that he held absolutely and alone, needing no aid from either men or sorcerers.

Conan's sleep greatly refreshed him. His robust frame also healed quickly. When he awoke a second time, he hardly felt pain, and sprang up nearly as limber as before.

Exploring beyond the opening revealed that an underground river indeed flowed through the caves. It was not much more than two spear-lengths wide but of a depth he could not plumb. It was cold enough to freeze not merely a man's flesh but also his bones.

Withal, it likewise seemed the only way out of these caves for an unassisted man. Conan looked briefly up the shaft, to be assured that it was indeed vertical. It was of height he could not even guess.

He had been very fortunate to survive his recent fall; he could not hope for such luck a second time. Nor did the smooth walls of the shaft offer any hand- or foothold to keep him from that second fall.

Waiting for help to come went against Conan's nature, and moreover seemed less than prudent. Regius Panon might not have escaped to spread the news of Conan's fall. Even if he had, it could be days before Conan's friends came in search of him; days more before they found him. Meanwhile he would be growing weaker from lack of food, and friends were not all who might come seeking him.

Somewhere above him laired the flying snakes. Whether they were newly come by magic or were ancient dwellers in this land, Conan could think of only one reason for their presence. They were here to defend the Soul of Thanza.

If so, those scaly creatures were about to start earning their keep!

Conan stripped off his boots, sword, and most of his clothes. Then he bundled them up inside his oiled-leather cloak. With the weight of the sword, the bundle would barely float, but tied to Conan's waist, it did well enough that he would have both hands free.

That he would need. He could hold his breath longer than most men, save only the pearl divers of Vendhya, but he could not know how far the river ran between caves. He would be swimming for his life the moment he entered the river, with little chance of retracing his course against the current before he ran out of breath.

So be it. He hoped that if the gods did care anything for men, they would be kind to Dutulus and also give Lysinka either victory or a fleet pair of heels, if he could not be found at her side.

Then he slipped into the stream, gritting his teeth at the bite of the cold and vanished into the bowels of the mountain.

The scouts who had not climbed the mountain with Conan brought Regius Panon to Lysinka the moment they returned to the citadel.

Shaken as he was, he had kept his wits about him, and neither told the tale of Conan's vanishing nor allowed the other scouts to do so. Luckily there had been no further sign of the flying snakes.

Of them he spoke freely, with Lysinka's approval. The men would have to defend themselves against this new menace; they had the right to know. Keeping such a secret from them would sow distrust between captains and fighters, and if that came to the citadel, they would have no need for other enemies.

Reluctantly, Klarnides agreed with her on that matter. Still more reluctantly, he agreed to follow her as he would Conan.

"A divided command is worse than none at all, which is what we might otherwise have," Klarnides said. "Curse that Cimmerian! I trusted him not to fling himself off cliffs or whatever else he's contrived to do!"

"War is the realm of chance," Lysinka murmured.

"You need not quote scribes to me," Klarnides said, his voice as sour as his face. "Just as long as you can make the Rangers follow you, that will be enough."

"I can probably do better by the Rangers than you could with my folk," Lysinka said with a thin smile. "They are all bandits, and we have neither Conan nor Tharmis Rog with us to keep them within lawful bounds."

"Again, tell me what I do not already know, which is not as little as you think," Klarnides said. "For example, I know that we must guard the mountain where Conan vanished even before we seek him within it.

"The guards must be able to send messages to the citadel faster than a man can walk. I know the Aquilonian host's torch signals. Shall I teach a few of them to our men?"

"With my blessing, for what that is worth," Lysinka

said. She tried to hide the fact that Klarnides's loyalty truly moved her, surly and reluctant as it might be.

"Your blessing might not be worth much in Tarantia or Shamar," Klarnides said. "Here in your homeland, it earns my deepest gratitude." Now he did not sound surly at all.

Eleven

Conan's head rose and bumped the roof of the cave. It barely deserved the name—but as long as it held enough air to let him fill his lungs . . .

Five times the Cimmerian's lungs had been near to bursting before he found air above him. Three other times he had an easy passage. After one of these he had found a cave so large it might have been worth exploring. But the luminous moss that grew so abundantly elsewhere was scanty in that cave, shedding just enough light to hint of its size without revealing more.

Conan did not hope for much after groping blindly in the dark. The cave offered no better chance of escape and hardly less peril than riding the river. The only thing the cave offered him was a brief respite from the chill water.

Then he plunged in again and now was in his ninth (or was it tenth?) breathing space. Another round won in this deadly game he was playing with the river, the darkness, and the mountain.

It was a game with the gods themselves perhaps throwing dice to determine the Cimmerian's fate, as he had heard some irreverent souls suggest late at night when much wine had gone around. The notion made as much sense to the Cimmerian as anything else he had heard said of the gods, who surely gave less thought to men than the priests would have fools believe.

Meanwhile, Conan's lungs were filled again, and his vision cleared of the sparks of gold and silver fire that broke the blackness when his breath grew short. He turned in a circle, treading water as best he could in the current while he studied what he could see.

In three directions that was little enough. At its highest point, this cave rose barely an arm's length above the water. But downstream, a faint arc of light broke the darkness.

It had the same pallid, dubious quality as the glow from the moss in other caves, although it was much brighter. Conan did not dare hope it was daylight, unless he had been within the mountain so long that he was about to be carried out of it into the dawn.

The force of the current saved him much swimming. Soon he could see that the arch was too low above the water to allow him to remain on the surface. He braced himself against the rock, sucked in air until his head swam, then dove and began thrashing his way downstream once more.

The passage between the low cave and the next one was among the shortest of Conan's underground journey. He had barely dived when the water above turned distinctly lighter in hue. It was not an agreeable color. It reminded Conan of a singularly foul stew he had once choked down while on campaign with the hosts of Turan. But it was light, and where there was light there would be air.

Conan burst to the surface. The splash alone raised echoes, which informed the barbarian that he was in the largest cave yet. Unlike the previous large caves, however, this cave was not lost in impenetrable shadows that might hide any sort of menace.

. The floor of this cave was a broad pool, in which the swift current of the underground river slowed perceptibly. On one side lay only a narrow ledge. On the other stood a broader shelf, stretching away into shadows as the roof lowered. As best Conan could judge, at the far end of the shelf a low archway, too regular to be natural, led into a further cave. The archway seemed to be partly blocked on either side by piles of white stones.

The edge of the shelf appeared to be scored in two or three places as if by a giant's chisel. Conan also saw what seemed to be scattered bones around each of these scorings. The bones did not look like fish bones: sheep or goats would have been the Cimmerian's guess.

Cautiously, taking care to use steady, even strokes without breaking the water's surface or making any other avoidable noise, the Cimmerian swam toward the shelf. He remembered now that he had not seen a single fish, skeletal or living, since he had entered the river for the first time.

The experienced wariness of both warrior and hunter painted an unpleasant picture for the Cimmerian. Add the absence of fish to those scorings in the rocks and the littered bones of animals who had tumbled through crevices into the depths of the mountains . . .

Add these together and the sum suggested that a large flesh-eater was living in the river, perhaps sharing the pool with Conan at this very moment.

The Cimmerian did not alter his stroke in the least, save to reach down to make sure that his dagger was still in his belt and his bag still towing behind him. Fifty paces to the shelf, forty, thirty—

Something rose from the depths behind the Cimmerian. He felt the wake of its passage against his skin. Then he felt a sharp tug at his waist as the intruder seized the bag.

The water dragon that inhabited the underground river had been hatched as a pet of the last Death Lord of Thanza. That was in the days when the magic of Acheron and other powers that had justly earned equally vile reputations clung to the Thanzas, like a swarm of flies circling a dunghill.

This made the water dragon one of the oldest of its kind yet living in Hyborean lands. Yet in its early days, the magic surrounding it had so thoroughly strengthened it that it hardly noticed at first when the magic departed.

Centuries passed, the Death Lords became tales told to frighten children, and still the water dragon swam blithely through the dark waters. At times decent, warm-blooded prey, some with two legs and some with four, found its way into the subterranean warrens. Then the dragon fed its body, if not its essence.

But the essence needed feeding too, and for that it needed magic that was nowhere to be found. So like others of its kind, the dragon at last fell into a profound sleep, which lasted for hundreds of years.

When the dragon fell asleep, the land of Aquilonia had not yet earned the title of "kingdom." When it awoke, it was because of the flight of the Soul of Thanza from the caravan and the magical storm this raised.

The storm passed, the dragon awoke, and both its body and its essence hungered. There was enough magic to give the essence vitality for a while, but as for food, it faced a different fate.

It could not climb the shafts within the mountain to raid the nests of the flying snakes. Many of those shafts in any case had crumbled over the centuries, so that fewer animals found their way below ground. Those beasts and all the fish in the river under the mountain were not enough to feed its body.

The water dragon's body began feeding on itself. Yet, dim as its mind was, it knew enough not to flee beyond the Mountain of Skulls. Then the magic that fed its essence would no longer reach it, and the essence would begin to devour the dragon's flesh to sustain itself.

The dragon grew famished, likewise savage of temper. It also grew cunning, so that in spite of its hunger it did not at once fling itself upon the mortal who swam into its home water.

It waited, instead, until the mortal was close to the imagined safety of the rock, and had all its attention turned ahead.

Then the dragon struck from behind.

Had the dragon not been dim-eyed from age and hungry in both body and essence, Conan would have died the moment after it struck.

As it was, the dragon's jaws slammed shut on the bag floating behind him. Those jaws were also weakened and missing more than a few teeth, but they were nearly as long and as broad as the Cimmerian's torso, and still strong enough to snap rope like thread.

The bag, however, was too large to be swallowed in one gulp. The dragon shifted its grip on this unexpectedly awkward prey, and bit down again. This time its upper jaw encountered the point of the Cimmerian's sword.

As Conan scrambled on to the rocky shelf, the dragon's head broke water. Its bellow mingled pain, rage, frustration, and hunger. The mouth gaped, showing Conan an array of yellowed, broken, and missing teeth. The gape also revealed the barbarian's sword rammed deep into the creature's upper jaw.

Conan supposed that it might do him some good there, although he would much rather have held it in his hand. At the moment, it seemed only to enrage a creature who needed no help in this matter.

Conan drew his dagger, then held himself as motionless as a statue, even making his breathing shallow. Movement could well be the only thing the water dragon could sense. If its rheumy yellow eyes saw nothing moving—

But the water dragon was craftier than the barbarian expected. Somewhere within the reptilian brain, a thought formed: the bag was unfit to eat and dangerous beside. But there had been a second prey swimming with the bag, who might now be resting on the shelf.

The dragon sank out of sight. Conan remained motionless. The dragon might be swimming off to free its mouth of his sword. Its departure might also be a ruse—

Ten paces from where Conan stood, the water dragon lunged out of the pool. It lunged so hard and so accurately that its rough-scaled snout grazed the Cimmerian's ankle.

He still did not move, even as the scales ripped skin from flesh. Blood flowed—practically in front of the dragon's nose. Its powers of scent had declined along with everything else, but it could still smell fresh blood.

Its tail lashed, driving more of its body out of the water. Conan had to move now, before those jaws clamped on his ankle in a grip not to be broken even by the Cimmerian's strength.

Instead of moving back, he moved forward. The water dragon saw something vast and dark looming up in its vision and jerked its head aside. A dagger thrust meant to drive through to the dragon's brain took only one eye.

The dragon, howled, screamed, and hissed so furiously that Conan half expected the cave to collapse and bury him under the rubble. The creature thrashed about so wildly that Conan had to retreat farther to avoid the swinging tail.

Then head, tail, and all four clawed legs were flailing about, driving the dragon up the shelf. Conan had no choice but to move toward the opening at the rear of the shelf. It was partly blocked, which might not keep the creature from passing through but would certainly slow it enough to let the Cimmerian strike a few telling blows.

He might even be lucky enough to regain his sword before the dragon's jaws bent it double!

Then Conan had a clear look at the archway—and that look shook not only his confidence but his very soul.

The archway was partly blocked on either side by skeletons. Human skeletons, standing erect like soldiers of a royal guard on palace duty. Each had armor and weapons piled at its feet, but wore only a crumbling leather belt.

Conan counted close to thirty skeleton guards in the archway alone. Beyond them, in the passage, he saw more, too many to count as they faded away into the shadows.

His retreat lay past an army of skeletons.

The Cimmerian did not hesitate. It was either retreat past the skeletons, or stand a good chance of making his last journey down the water dragon's maw. Those skeletons had to be nothing except brittle bone; one good lunge by the dragon would reduce them to dust.

But the passage did narrow beyond the archway. He could still fight there at more of an advantage than out here. Step by step, Conan withdrew, moving as much as possible, waving his arms, shouting, even darting in to kick the dragon in the muzzle and darting back out of reach before the jaws crashed shut where his foot had been.

He was careful to avoid the skeletons. Flesh and spirit alike had long fled them, but Conan would no more dishonor the unknown dead than he would have poisoned a well in the desert. The dragon would do enough damage when it finally charged.

Conan was now bleeding in several places. He had scraped a hand and an arm on the dragon's scales, and the wound in his side was oozing blood again, although without much pain. Still, if this turned into a battle of endurance, the Cimmerian could not be entirely hopeful of victory.

He gave more ground, and in so doing brushed his bleeding hand against the outermost skeleton on the left. The skeleton quivered all over, then seemed to fall apart into its component bones in the space of a single breath.

Conan's oaths almost outechoed the dragon's roarings and hissings. Whether this was a good omen or not, he could not say. But he now knew he had to make his stand before the skeletons, and keep the dragon from ravaging them, or die without honor.

The Cimmerian crouched, ready for a leap on to the dragon's back. If he could take it from behind, blinding it, he might then start drawing it away from the skeletons. He would be slow in such a deadly dance but so would the dragon, and the Cimmerian would stand between it and the water if it tried to flee.

Then dust rose from the fallen skeleton. Bones scraped on rock, but it was the rock that yielded. Before the Cimmerian's widening eyes, leg bones joined above and below knee caps, and legs set themselves into hip sockets while feet settled in at the other end. Ribs, spine, arms, skull—all skittered across the floor or rose into the air, and somehow all found their proper place.

In the time a hungry man takes to gnaw the meat from a chicken leg, a pile of bones was a complete skeleton—but no longer standing stiffly on guard. It moved as freely as any living man of flesh and blood. Conan thought he had seen everything ... then the skeleton bent, rummaged through the pile at its feet, and came up with a short spear.

The skull-face turned toward Conan and the jaws—still furnished with a full set of strong white teeth—clacked twice. Then bones rattled, and incredibly the skull wore something very like a smile.

By sheer force of will, the Cimmerian cudgeled his wits into order and pointed at the dragon. The skeleton nodded.

The dragon hissed. Conan raised echoes with a Cimmerian war cry. The skeleton clattered the spear against its ribs, as a living warrior might have struck his spear against his shield.

Then living Cimmerian and skeletal warrior advanced against the dragon.

Conan might have hoped that the dragon's exertions had wearied it or that his sword had cost it blood as well as temper. Except that "hope" was not a word he allowed himself to use when facing mortal combat.

Also, the evidence of his senses was somewhat against the dragon being weakened at all. He thought it showed admirable courage on the part of the skeleton to match its frail bone against the armored flesh of the dragon. He also suspected that he would be fighting alone again within moments.

Nonetheless, the skeleton seemed to know that when two men faced a single opponent, they should separate so as to force it to choose which one it would attack. The skeleton *ran* out to the left while Conan moved to the right.

Perhaps Conan was now more familiar to the dragon. Perhaps his living flesh gave him a scent it could detect. Perhaps he made more noise—although since the skeleton sounded rather like several carpenters all hammering at once, Conan doubted this last.

For whatever reason, the dragon grated around on its belly—which was scoring new marks in the rock—and charged the Cimmerian. With ample room, Conan now gave ground nimbly, seeking to place himself between the dragon and the water. His swift movements drew the dragon's entire attention, and the Cimmerian himself was too busy keeping a safe distance between him and the beast, so that neither paid much attention to the skeleton.

That was the dragon's final mistake. So swiftly that

Conan saw the skeleton only in midleap, the ancient warrior sprang on to the dragon's back. It braced itself on both bony feet, and with terrible strength in its bony arms thrust the spear down.

The shaft of the spear was wood, but seemed as limber as the day it was carved. The point looked to Conan like iron or perhaps some alloy of iron and unknown metals, although there were precious few such alloys he could not recognize. Certainly it was as rustless as bronze or newly forged iron, and also as sharp.

The spearhead drove between the scales, then through a gap in the skull plates of the dragon. Sharp metal reached the dragon's brain; it bellowed and spasmed. The warrior flew off like a slingstone, and Conan commended his spirit to a safe journey. Then the Cimmerian rushed in on the dragon's blind side, reached in, and thrust his dagger hard into the remaining eye.

The dragon's last spasm was more of a twitch, but still violent enough to send Conan sprawling. It also brought the dragon's tail down with an echoing crash on top of the skeleton. Conan listened for the sound of bones crumbling, but heard only the dragon's last gasping breaths.

The dragon's body hid the fallen remains of the skeleton warrior from the Cimmerian. Conan gave the beast a wide berth as he walked around, knowing from hard experience the tenacity of reptilian life. Indeed, the creature was still bleeding, which meant that somewhere in that scaly mass the heart still beat.

Then Conan stopped, and only an iron will kept him from gaping like a boy at his first woman. The skeleton he had expected to be reduced to dust was sitting up, and flexing all of its limbs. The gestures were exactly those of a living man who had been thrown down, bruised, and grazed, seeing if anything had been broken.

Conan stared, bemused. He wondered if he was still in the real world, or if not, where. Then he decided that perhaps he did not want to know.

The skeleton finished its self-examination by leaping up and down several times. That solved part of the mystery for the Cimmerian. As the skeleton's feet came down, he heard, not the clatter of bone on rock, but the sharper impact of stone on stone.

Whatever magic had given the skeleton its power to reanimate, had also turned it from ancient, desiccated bone into something very like the rock of the cave where it had stood sentinel for so long.

The skeleton promptly scrambled on top of the dragon, gripped its spear with both hands, and pulled. The spear came free so suddenly the skeleton nearly fell, but this time turned the tumble into a leap. It looked at the blood on the spearhead and the blood oozing from the wound, then turned and practically ran toward the line of skeletons.

Again, it wore something very like a smile—if one could use human terms to describe the expressions of a face without flesh. It wore that smile as it struck the bloody spearhead against the ribs of one skeleton, the thighbone of another, the skull of a third.

All three skeletons fell into pieces, then began reknitting themselves. Conan was not even surprised when all at once three skeletons stood again at attention.

Now each bore a weapon—a broadsword, a short sword, and a long-shafted spear—and each had its free hand over where its heart would have been, in an archaic form of the salute of honor.

As Conan watched, he also saw that the bloodstain

on the first skeleton had vanished, and that the blood-stains on the other three were also fading. It was as if the skeletons drew the blood into themselves, like desert sand swallowing water.

Conan told himself firmly that these beings were magical but not hostile. The first one owed his animation to the Cimmerian's blood, and had fought beside him.

The Cimmerian therefore believed that he had nothing to fear. Still, he was careful retrieving his sword and bag from the dragon's maw. Clothed again, albeit in sodden garments, and with a sword (slightly bent) in his hand, he felt more fit to deal with the skeletons.

How he was to fight beings of stone with no flesh or vital organs for steel to sunder was another matter. Meanwhile, he stood close to the wall, his hands near to weapons' hilts, and watched the army of skeletons take shape.

The dragon went on bleeding long enough to animate half the skeletons. The first four carved several more wounds in the carcase, to speed the process.

After that it seemed that animating the rest needed more than a smear of blood from the point of a weapon. The thirty-odd skeletons now formed into pairs, and each delicately lifted a comrade, and carried him intact to the dragon. There they dipped a foot, a hand, or sometimes a skull into the congealing blood, set the skeleton down, and stepped back to await results.

At last it seemed that the blood was no longer fresh enough to reanimate skeletons. The last few merely fell apart, one as it was being carried. The bones quivered and twitched, and a few of them knit, but remained more a pile than a completed skeleton.

By this time there were more than fifty-odd rock-boned skeletons roaming about the shelf. Conan judged that all had been good-sized men, probably in the prime of life as befitted picked soldiers.

He had no time for further study. A few of the skeletons had put their skulls together in a circle, close to the water's edge. Now they broke out of that circle and advanced toward the wall—and Conan.

Others joined them as they moved—no, *marched*, for Conan saw that they kept in step as they approached. At last more than half the skeletons were gathered in a half-circle around the Cimmerian. They could not get at his back, against the solid wall—nor could he break out of that circle without a clash he did not wish.

He would have liked to be able to say that the skeletons had the same peaceful wish. But the way the fleshless bones held themselves and their weapons gave him cause to doubt.

Twelve

Lysinka could not sleep. Nor was it because Conan was not there to warm her and their sleeping cocoon. She had not allowed any man to mean that much to her in years and if the gods were kind would never do so again. The price of doing otherwise had proved too high.

So she was making the rounds of the sentry posts, to seem to be doing something useful while she waited for the night to pass or for sleep to come. She feared that sleep would come only with daylight, when it would be time to lead scouts to the mountain where Conan had disappeared, and mount guard on it until he reappeared or something else became more urgent than finding him.

Lysinka passed the third sentry post with a cursory glance and a brief exchange of polite remarks on the weather. She noted that this post held Rasha, one of her women, and a Thanza Ranger with a head too large for his body and too much hair and beard even for his head.

She was halfway to the next post, approaching a deep-shadowed flight of crumbling stairs, when she heard footsteps behind her. She did not turn, nor even quicken her pace. Her sword and other blades were always well-placed for a quick draw, and she was wearing a light mail shirt under her tunic—

"Countess," came a soft whisper.

She smiled, and replied as quietly, "I did not know you were so light-footed, Fergis."

"Oh, my skills are without number. My hearing is also keen. Tonight has taught me things I would rather not have learned."

Telling Fergis not to talk in riddles would be futile. When the mood was upon him, he would ask a riddle of an opponent in mortal combat—some said he had won several fights this way, by thoroughly distracting his foes.

"Our people are uneasy about Conan's disappearance," Lysinka said.

"Indeed," Fergis said, sounding rather cast down at being understood so easily. "They say they will not go to the Mountain of the Skull tomorrow."

"We do not know that it is the Mountain of the Skull or any other part of the legend of the Soul of Thanza. And who are 'they'?"

Before Fergis could even begin a reply, a shrill scream echoed around the rocks. It was a woman's scream, seeming to come from the sentry post Lysinka had just left.

She thought briefly that it might be a trap, to lure her and Fergis into an ambush. But her feet were already moving of their own will as that thought passed through her mind. By the time it was gone, she was back in sight of the sentry post, with Fergis close behind her. .

Both had drawn their swords, and this was well, for

the Thanza Ranger was standing over Rasha. Blood smeared the rocks about her head, and he was bending to collect her weapons.

Lysinka ran at the man with sword drawn. He promptly put his own blade's point at Rasha's throat. Lysinka halted abruptly, but did not sheathe her sword.

"We'll none of us stay up here as prey for the snakes just to save your bedmate," the Ranger muttered. "Not your folk, not the Rangers."

Lysinka was about to reply, knowing that she needed most of all to give Fergis time for some stratagem. For all his piety, his wits worked more swiftly than most people's, nor did fear of the gods ever make him accept folly or villainy—and this was both.

The words never came out. A large rock flew seemingly from nowhere, striking the man in the forehead. He went limp all over, the sword falling from insensible hands, as he toppled.

Unfortunately, he toppled sideways, landing where the rock dropped sharply away. A single roll, the rattle of dislodged pebbles, and the senseless Ranger plummeted into the night. Lysinka stood as if transfixed, until a distant thump told of the Ranger's reaching the bottom of the cliff.

The chieftain now found her voice in muttered curses. The night was ill begun and worse continued, with one of her women dead and her slayer also gone, so that none could tell the tale and some might doubt that the Ranger was truly guilty—

The woman sat up.

"Rasha?" Fergis said, his jaw dropping to his boottops.

"Aye," the woman replied. She felt her bloody hair and did not try to stand.

Lysinka instead knelt and examined Rasha's

wound. "Just my scalp," the other said. "I rode with that bastard's blow. The blood was enough to make him think I was dead. I reckoned there was no cause to make him think otherwise until he turned his back. Sorry that I screamed, though."

"You had to draw our attention somehow," Fergis said. "So never mind that. What did he say?"

The Ranger had claimed to know of six men who were going to raid the recovered Nemedian supplies then flee. He had thought that they might accept him too, if he brought a woman.

"And he asked you?" Lysinka said.

"Aye."

The chieftain spat over the cliff. She hoped she struck the dead Ranger below. His death still would raise more suspicion than she liked, but the gods knew it was well deserved!

"Did he give names?"

"No."

This was *not* well done. She could double the guards on the stores, but how to be sure that she was not setting wolves to guard the sheep? Or she could divide up all the supplies tonight, so that everyone could guard their own.

Either way might encourage desertion, and not just of the weaklings that the band could spare. Enough of those otherwise brave and shrewd might look to their own safety, to ruin the band and leave both Conan and the Soul of Thanza to their fates.

Lysinka had just reached the point of a short prayer for good sense among her followers when a war cry broke in on her thoughts. Then the night breeze carried another, with a background of confused shouting— and unmistakably, the clash of arms.

Lysinka was already nearly out of sight before Fergis and Rasha began to run.

"Grolin. Grolin! Do you wake?"

Lord Grolin did not know where the voice was. He only knew that he heard those words and no others. He also doubted that it would be useful or prudent to guess at this latest of the sorcerer's mystifying tricks.

He sat up, threw off his dew-dampened blankets (praise Mitra for the tall trees that had kept rains from turning the forest floor into a bog!), and stood.

"Turn right, and walk until you are out of sight of the camp," came the voice.

Grolin obeyed, first looking at the sentries to make sure they were alert enough to notice his departure. At least one of them was. He hoped the man was not also a waggle-tongue. Rumors were already skittering about, like dry leaves in the autumn wind, of the baron's mysterious conversations with the empty air and mysterious nighttime walks.

The sorcerer's instructions should have been: "Walk until you have bumped into seven trees." The canopy overhead kept off the rain but also kept out even the faintest starlight. Beyond the reach of the watchfire, the blackness was what one might expect to find at the heart of the universe.

This time the sorcerer appeared in one of the trees again, but only his body. The glow was amber; and as his robe was of the same hue, it was hard to learn much of the man's size or build.

"I am here," Grolin said. "Bruised and weary, but here. Speak, and I shall listen."

A greenish glow appeared in the heart of the amber, where the head would have been. The green glow wavered, took a spherical form, and developed features. At last it became a face—and Grolin wanted to strike at it with his sword, or even his bare fist.

Although green light still shimmered around the face, it was unmistakably the face of one of the flying snakes.

Fergis and Rasha caught up with Lysinka halfway to the fight. The three of them pelted together into the open courtyard of the citadel.

The courtyard was almost full; every man and woman of both the bandits and the Rangers seemed to be present. All eyes were on the entrance to the store-room, where lay not only the day's Nemedian spoils but everything brought to the citadel.

One man stood with a blazing torch before the open archway of the storeroom. Five others made a half-circle in front of him. Lysinka recognized four Rangers and two of her men, including the one holding the torch. His name was Horkas, and he was a doughty fighter of uncertain temper and still more uncertain ancestry.

It was, Lysinka supposed, a monument to Conan's work at binding the Rangers and the bandits that they were willing to mutiny together. She also hoped that the Cimmerian would have a better monument, or best of all, no monument at all for many years to come.

Now she stared hard at Horkas. He had always acted upon impulse and might change from mutineer to sup-pliant as quickly as he had gone from loyalty to mutiny.

Before Lysinka could speak, Horkas waved the torch. "Hear me! We six are going out of this cursed land, with anyone who will join us and follow me."

This drew some murmurs of agreement but more laughter, a few curses, and several bawdy jests about why anyone should want to get *behind* Horkas other than to avoid looking at his face.

None of this pleased Horkas. It was a while before

he went on. In that time, several of the more trust-worthy men of both bands slipped in behind or beside Lysinka and whispered that they stood with her.

She would have been happier if they had shouted it aloud so that all could hear them. No doubt they were being cautious, waiting to see which way the wind blew.

The silence was drawing on unreasonably. Lysinka cupped her hands and shouted:

"So this land is cursed? Likewise are oathbreakers! If we do not punish you, the gods will. Why should we let you go?"

"If I throw a torch into the storeroom, everything will burn," Horkas replied. "All of us, all of you, must alike flee. Flee, or starve unless you can eat rocks!"

Lysinka was not the only one who gasped. Trying to flee a real danger might be no worse than cowardly. Threatening to doom your sworn comrades if they did not allow you to flee was not merely accursed, it was disgusting.

It was also a potent threat. Lysinka was certain that a fair number of both bands thought it no great matter to lose six fools and even their share of the food and weapons.

Lysinka knew she had to halt that thought before it swept away all good sense. What six fools would do today, ten might do tomorrow, and twenty the day after that.

Mutiny would kill the band and perhaps also Conan, leaving the world at the mercy of the Soul of Thanza whether in Grolin's hands or another's. Kill swift, kill slow, but death was certain.

Lysinka shouldered her way through the crowd. Several followed her, but they were barely more than shadows seen dimly from the corner of her eye. The moon was up, but the only other light in the courtyard was Horkas's torch.

She stepped out into the open.

"Horkas! I have a better idea. You have the right of challenge for the leadership of my band. Fight me, and if you win, then you may give a lawful order that all must obey. Are you——?"

"Hold!" came Klarnides's voice from behind. "*I* swore no oath of friendship with any leader of Lysinka's band except Lysinka herself. Change leaders, warriors of Lysinka of Mertyos, and the Thanza Rangers will march alone!"

"Big windy words, from a little captain whose own men won't follow him!" Horkas sneered. "Did Conan's favor make you think you were worth something?"

Except that "favor" was not the word Horkas used. It was something far more obscene—and Klarnides lost what little remained of his temper.

He strode out into the open, sword drawn. Too late to halt the Aquilonian, Lysinka saw that one of the mutineers had a bow. He nocked an arrow and started to draw.

"No, fool! No!" came from several voices. The archer hesitated.

"I have offered myself," Lysinka shouted. "Fear the gods' wrath, if you shoot at anyone but me."

The next moment, she realized that these words were hardly wiser than Klarnides's. Horkas clutched the archer's arm, turning him. The point of the arrow suddenly seemed to Lysinka as large as Conan's face when he pinned her to the ground after their duel.

And two shadow figures suddenly became solid flesh so that Lysinka's feet went out from under her, and she crashed to the ground. Both solid men were on top of her, and she thought she heard Fergis using most unaccustomed oaths.

Then somebody screamed, a scream that ended in choking. Warm, salty wetness ran over Lysinka. With frantic strength she heaved herself upright.

Fergis went sprawling, but sat up at once. The other man did not. He would never rise again.

Regius Panon lay on his side, the arrow meant for Lysinka protruding from his chest. Blood had already pooled beneath his chest and was trickling from his mouth to form another pool beneath his head.

"You have a low taste in jests," Grolin said, to the snake-headed image of the sorcerer. "You offend the eye, as those who speak such jests offend the ear."

"Your dignity is the least of my concerns," the sorcerer replied. For the first time, Grolin detected a note of impatience in the sorcerer's normally even, almost inhuman voice.

It would be as well to not offend the fellow—one had to call him "man," as he had surely been human at some time since the birth of the world. It was most necessary for Grolin to know about anything capable of making the sorcerer sound impatient.

Knowledge, others besides scribes said, was power. All spoken truly. Grolin sought power, therefore he would not turn away knowledge.

"I am sure that from where you stand, that is so," Grolin said. "But I do not know enough of our road toward the Soul of Thanza, to know what *are* your greatest concerns. Speak, then—and if I must beg, I shall."

For a moment, the reptilian countenance seemed to hesitate, as though the sorcerer were considering taking Grolin's offer seriously. Then what had to be laughter (although it sounded more like files on rusty iron) hammered through the baron's skull.

"You would know, then? Well, you may learn if you look where you see the stars."

Grolin started to look upward. Then the snake-face opened its mouth. Framed in fang and scale was a pit of blackness, in which stars, or at least starlike sparkles, swirled and glimmered.

"Stand close," said the sorcerer. "Look deep within the darkness where the stars dance. Deep within, and do not turn your eyes away no matter what your senses bid you do."

Grolin's senses were urging him to flee and bid his men to do the same. More immediately, the stench of rotten carrion from the serpent's maw was real enough to make him gag.

Knowledge would lead him to freedom, Grolin told himself firmly.

When he had done so three times, he had the courage to thrust his face into the maw. As he did, the stars faded and the blackness began to turn gray, with dim shapes slowly taking form in the grayness.

In the moments it took for the crowded courtyard to realize what had happened, only one man seemed able to move. Klarnides's rage had not entirely driven out his wits.

With a steady, even pace, Klarnides walked toward the semi-circle. He kept his eyes fixed on something invisible just above the heads of the men, rather than asking a challenge with a stare. Only Lysinka saw that his knuckles were white and sweat had broken out along the line of his jaw.

The man and the warrior were breaking out from the shell of the youth within which they had hidden.

Lysinka would have given years of her life if Conan could see how well he had done his work on Klarnides—he and Tharmis Rog.

The archer threw down his bow and flung himself on his knees in the pose of a suppliant. Klarnides ignored him.

Not so Horkas. The man looked wildly about, snatched a dagger from his belt with his free hand, brandished it wildly, then flung the torch into the storeroom.

Lysinka would have given even more years of her life for a bow, to shoot down Horkas before he closed the door on himself and the flames. Doomed, he looked a man determined to doom as many others as he could.

But Lysinka had nothing to hurl except a dagger that would never carry this far. The other archers either lacked bows, wits, or a clear shot without risk of hitting Klarnides.

In the end it made no difference. Klarnides seemed to spring forward like a leopard. He knocked the archer to one side, another kneeling man the other way. Horkas whirled to face him, stabbing with desperate strength and deadly speed.

Klarnides seemed to dance away from the dagger thrust. He had only his short sword at a bad angle for thrusting. But his strength was also that of desperation. His slash looked wild . . . but went where it was aimed.

Horkas screamed, dropped his dagger, and clutched a blood-spouting arm. His lips moved. They had not quite shaped themselves into a plea for mercy when Klarnides's sword thrust into Horkas's belly, chest, and throat in three strokes that seemed to be a continuous motion, so swiftly did one follow upon another.

Then Klarnides turned and screamed, sounding like a eunuch with his leg in a bear trap:

"In Mitra's name! Come and put out the fire before it reaches the oil!"

So many rushed forward that they trampled Horkas's body, nearly trampled Klarnides and the surviving mutineers, and would have trampled out the fire if they had all been able to get through the door. Some made it through, others jammed, and there was much pushing, cursing, and shouting before order reigned again.

Lysinka was one of those who helped to restore it. She had not been among those who rushed forward at once. Instead she had knelt beside Regius Panon, closed his eyes, then draped her cloak over him.

Only then did she join the reunited bands in putting out the fire.

The shapes in the black snake's maw ceased to waver. Then they coalesced into a single shape.

It was a roughly carved (or perhaps vastly ancient and weathered) stone head. It seemed raw mountain rock, the only color fragments of jewels partly filling the eye sockets.

It stood upright on a cracked marble slab within a high, narrow cave dimly lit by the ubiquitous moss of the Thanzas. He saw a crack in one wall and a thin sliver of starlit sky beyond it.

"You ask me to believe that this piece of rubble is important?" Grolin said.

"It is the Soul of Thanza," the sorcerer said.

To that, Grolin had no reply. He did not quite dare to call the sorcerer a liar, but nothing else came to his mind.

The sorcerer continued. "You may need to recognize it once you are within the mountain, for all the guidance I can give you on the way."

"You cannot enter the Mountain of the Skull?"

"Perhaps not in the face of the new magic that may be unleashed within it before we reach it. Or should I say, old magic newly unleashed?"

Grolin's thoughts must have told the sorcerer that he had no patience left with riddles. Suddenly the image of the Soul was gone, and another, far larger cave filled Grolin's vision.

He saw the bloody carcase of something vast and reptilian, likewise without wings. He saw a man standing amid a half-circle of opponents and recognized the man.

"Conan *is* within the Mountain of the Skull."

"Did you expect me to lie to you?"

Grolin chose polite words. "Some sorcerers have been known to do so."

"They may do as they please. I do as I please, which is to tell my allies the truth, or as much of it as merely human minds can face."

Grolin heard only some of those words, for he had seen what the Cimmerian faced. Not who—that was still a mystery—but *what*.

Armed, animate skeletons—a score of them or more in the half-circle, others standing about at random. More bones on the floor, that might have been skeletons or might become skeletons when the right magic was applied.

"Did you do this?" Grolin asked, finding his voice at last.

"Not I, nor has Conan turned sorcerer," the reply came.

The two truths balanced each other. The Cimmerian was no more potent than before—but within the Mountain of the Skull lay magic enough to make skeletons walk.

Grolin was suddenly prepared to believe in his ally's weaknesses.

* * *

The fire in the storeroom was out in hardly more than moments. It was another fire that burned the next morning, staining the sky above the citadel as Lysinka led out what everyone called the "war party."

It was Regius Panon's funeral pyre, assembled at some cost in time and labor, but no one begrudged either. The Nemedian's death had not perhaps thunderstruck the fighters into virtue or loyalty, but it had certainly done much to drive folly from their minds.

Forty fighters marched with Lysinka. The others remained in the citadel under Fergis. After Conan's disappearance, it seemed unwise to leave the citadel unprotected in their rear.

Fergis turned as red as the coals on the pyre when Lysinka asked him to respect her wishes. He turned even redder after he agreed and she sealed the agreement with a long, public kiss, that made bawdy cheers echo around the rocks.

"A finer sound than death-cries, I suppose," Fergis grumbled, wiping his face as if she had smeared it with ashes.

"The sound of fighters who will win or die," Lysinka said, then signaled to the trumpeter to blow for the assembly.

She could not speak for all those who would march under her. For herself, she knew that she would return with a living Conan and Lord Grolin's head, or failing that, with the knowledge of their fate.

If she achieved neither, she would be beyond the world of men—and she would then accost the gods and inquire of *them* what had befallen Conan and Grolin until they answered her or sent her back to the world to learn for herself!

Thirteen

Conan had faced stranger and deadlier opponents than the company of skeleton warriors. He had met the former without fear and outfought the latter without mortal hurt, although not without scars.

The skeletons, however, were enemies that he had not only never faced but also not even imagined that he could face. The intentness with which they looked upon him was disquieting—if one could say that eye sockets without eyes "looked" at anything.

He felt a chill down his spine that had nothing to do with the cold roughness of the stone against which he stood. He wondered, not altogether idly, how long his final combat would last, faced with opponents who might be impervious to the edge of his sword.

The Cimmerian had known swords that could cut stone, and smiths capable of forging them. Even his father might have been able to conjure such a blade out of the charcoal and bog iron that were the smith's raw materials in Cimmeria.

Conan doubted, however, that his present blade was equal to the task of chopping through stone ribs, skulls, and limbs. It had not even survived unscathed its combat with the river dragon.

He therefore left the blade sheathed. He saw no bows or throwing weapons among his opponents. They would have to close in on foot, and he could draw steel long before they came within reach.

Meanwhile, not baring his steel first might be taken as a peaceful overture. He had fought side by side with one of these stone warriors. Through both his own blood and that of the dragon he had slain, he had been the instrument of bringing them back from—where they *had* been—to where they were now. (He would not use the words "death" and "life." For not the first time, he was in a place where these ideas had small meaning.)

All that he had wrought for them should be worth something. Whether it would be worth enough to make them forsake his blood, the blood they doubtless needed to revive their remaining comrades—

Now the skeleton warriors were looking at one another. One whom Conan thought was his battle comrade stepped up to the half-circle around Conan, and put his skull close to that of one in the circle. The two leaders seemed to be discussing what to do next, even though they made no sound that Conan could hear nor opened lips that he could see moving.

No lips moved, but in the next moment the skeletons did. The half-circle opened outward, like a blooming flower, to make a space in the middle, directly in front of Conan. The skeletons by the wall remained where they stood, some now standing straighter than others.

Conan smiled. He would have laughed, except that

a living sound seemed an intrusion here where only the click of stone on stone broke the silence.

It was still irresistibly funny to see how the soldiers who had in life slumped in ranks and the ones who had held themselves like spears, still retained their stance eons after their flesh had perished. Suddenly the leader caught sight of the slumpers, snatched a spear from the nearest skeleton in the circle, and slammed the butt on the rock.

Echoes danced about the cave, almost drowning the Cimmerian's gusty laughter. He could not help it. The more slovenly skeletons had suddenly snapped upright, like newly-recruited Thanza Rangers when Tharmis Rog roared at them. He wondered how the master-at-arms was faring, commanding the encampment of cripples and he wondered also what Rog would have made of this underground encampment of the dead.

Probably he'd have them practicing forming squares before the day was done, the Cimmerian decided. Rog was a soldier to his fingertips, even if there had once seemed to be more bone than brain between his ears.

For a moment, the gap in the half-circle in front of Conan was large enough to allow his escape—if he could swerve fast enough to escape the leader and his companions, who stood just beyond the gap. The Cimmerian took the space of three heartbeats to consider that alternative, then foreswore it.

He did not know how fast the skeleton warriors could run, nor did he care to learn. Being pursued through the dark warren of caves below this mountain by living bones seeking one's flesh with ancient steel was a death too gruesome and too lacking in dignity for the Cimmerian to contemplate without a shudder.

What might come to him from these skeletons, he would face here and now.

Instead of ordering an attack, the leader now held the same spear overhead in both hands, then raised and lowered it three times. The other skeletons—his "men," Conan had begun to call them in his mind—quickly formed a broader half-circle, with only a single narrow gap in front of the leader.

Then the leader stepped into the gap, knelt with some grace if not without the grating of stone on stone, and laid his spear on the rock at his feet.

Conan nearly drew his sword at that unexpected gesture, until wisdom overcame instinct in time to prevent such folly. Just as well—for now all the skeleton warriors were laying down their weapons at their feet.

Then they rose, all standing as straight as if Tharmis Rog's eye was searching each of them for a twitching muscle or a strap out of place, and joined hands. Conan held back laughter with difficulty at the sight of these whitened bones imitating children at a festival. He half-expected them to start dancing or putting mushrooms in their ear holes instead of chaplets of flowers around their heads!

Instead, he heard a faint droning. It quickly ceased to be faint, but never became loud. Instead, it began to waver. Conan knew several battle languages; he wondered if he was hearing one.

Then the random wavering turned into a regular rhythm. The rhythm steadied, and Conan now heard sounds that with a little imagination might have been words.

Then he no longer needed imagination. Joined together, the skeletons were speaking.

Their first intelligible words were:

"Are you an enemy to the Death Lord of Thanza?"

* * *

Lysinka and Klarnides had agreed not to divide the men they were leading in search of Conan—or of any other secrets these mountains might hide.

As for those secrets, Klarnides wanted to ferret them all out. Lysinka was more inclined to find Conan and go home, whether he wished to go there with her or not. Klarnides was thinking of his duty to Numedides. She was now hardly thinking beyond her duties to her band and to her comrade of battle and bed.

If a Death Lord of Thanza was dangerous to him or them, she would fight the lord, even at the cost of her own life. If a Death Lord would pass by her and hers, then he could do so, if not with her blessing, at least without her armed opposition.

She said nothing of this to Klarnides, however. There was still enough of the prickly boy within the newly fledged warrior and man to make matters difficult if he began to mistrust her.

They swung wide to the east of the mountain where Conan had vanished without seeing any signs of the flying serpents, the Cimmerian, or anything else they sought. (Or which might be seeking them, Lysinka reminded herself.)

One thing she and several others with sharp eyes did see: an alternative route up to the summit of the mountain. It was broader, easier for those not hillborn, and allowed both advance and retreat elsewhere than the actual trail.

Altogether, it seemed such a gift from the gods that Lysinka and Klarnides agreed that others must have seen it the same way.

"If there are any others about, besides Grolin's men."

"Best be safe," Klarnides suggested. "We know about the flying serpents. Perhaps they have gorged themselves into ten days' slumber and perhaps not. With room to fight, we are fitter to stand against foes with fangs or hands."

The chieftain looked at Klarnides with new respect. Apart from his courage, he was now uttering words that might have come from far more seasoned warriors, even though his teachers were both absent.

But then, much in fighting and war was merely good sense. She wondered if Klarnides was newly come to good sense, or had merely hidden it until good teachers and necessity (also a teacher, of sorts) brought it out.

"Very well," she said. "We rest and water here for . . . oh, half a candle. Then we go up."

And you be there in some other form than serpent-gnawed bones, my Cimmerian friend.

Conan knew that he was in the presence of magic, ancient, potent, mysterious (but then most magic was such to him, and he was as glad to leave matters thus).

He was not certain it was evil.

Had he been certain, he would have shattered the skeletons or his own bones in a fight to the finish—he could not say "to the death" when his foes were already dead!

But the magic that animated these warriors of bone-turned-stone had left with them something of the humanity they had possessed when they were flesh and blood. Perhaps they had enough of it left that he and they could find a common ground, one that did not leave either him or them in pieces on the cave floor.

It might even be one that would help their still-inanimate comrades, and allow him to escape these caves and continue his search for Grolin and the Soul of Thanza.

Certainly their first question had hinted of the right direction.

"There is no living Death Lord of Thanza," Conan said. He spoke slowly, trying to make every syllable ring like a blacksmith's hammer. It was hard to read expressions on fleshless faces, but he thought he succeeded.

He knew disappointment when he saw it, even in skeletons. Shoulders slumped and heads turned to look at one another.

Conan sensed deep grief, that a long sleep should have ended in a purposeless waking. He grinned mirthlessly. This was the first time that his telling someone evil sorcery was abroad in their land would be called good news!

"There is a man named Grolin, who seeks the Soul of Thanza," the Cimmerian said. "I think he has the aid of evil magic. Will this make him evil, if he finds the Soul of Thanza and becomes the Death Lord?"

"All Death Lords are evil," the skeletons said. "If they were not before they joined with the Soul, they become so afterward. We are vowed to destroy all Death Lords, until the power of the Soul is exhausted and there can be no more."

Conan forebore to point out that they might not be equal to the task or they would not have waited so long as bony skeletons instead of living men. Before he could choose words for a reply, the skeletons continued.

"It also is possible that the sorcerer might become the Death Lord. If he is evil, he will become more so through the Soul. We must fight him as well as the man you call Grolin. Has the sorcerer a name?"

Conan replied that he was tolerably sure of the sorcerer's existence, but knew nothing else about him.

"Then it is time and past time for us to march to end

the menace of the Death Lords of Thanza," the skeletons said. Or rather, intoned. Each time they spoke, they sounded more like a chorus of priests chanting the praises of some obscure god.

"We need three things for the fight," they went on.

"One is a leader of flesh and blood. Will you be he?"

"You might do better with someone else—" Conan began, with a wry twist to his mouth.

"There is no one else," the skeletons replied. "There has been no one else for all the time we have been here. There will be no one else in time to fight Grolin and the sorcerer. You will lead us."

Conan was tempted to reply to this command with one of the salutes he had learned. He decided against it. The skeletons might be a trifle lacking in humor.

"The second thing we need is all our strength. As many more of us as you see here remain afar from the world. When we all move together, we are mighty. As we are now, we are not. The Death Lord will come again."

That made sense. No captain worth the price of his helmet straps went willingly into battle with less than his full strength. Books were filled with the names of those who had done otherwise—and Conan had seen too many battlefields littered with the bodies of their men.

"The third thing we need is blood. Blood gives movement. Movement gives strength. Strength gives victory. Victory saves the world from the Death Lord of Thanza."

"Blood," Conan mused. He remembered how he had put all this in motion when his scraped and bleeding flesh touched the first skeleton. Then the work had gone on, with the blood of the water dragon.

"The water dragon's blood has lost its power," he said.

"There is strong blood here," the skeletons replied. "It will give our comrades movement. Movement will give strength. Strength will give . . ."

Conan was not listening. He was looking at the skeletons. All of them were looking back, in a way that left him in no doubt whose "strong blood" they wanted to revive their comrades.

He had stepped away from the wall while he was talking to the skeletons. Now he withdrew three paces, until once again his shoulders were against the stone.

Then he drew his sword.

In the wounded camp, Tharmis Rog had just hobbled back from the burying ground when Sergeant Julilius accosted him.

"We finally made that deserter from Grolin's band fit to talk," he said. "I doubt me he'll last out the day, but he's said enough to earn himself a peaceful end."

Rog sat down on a stump. He could walk with a stick now, but running or marching with a heavy pack would be well beyond him for days. A small voice whispered at the back of his mind, hinting that his soldiering days were over for good.

As often as the voice whispered, he told it to be silent. At this moment, he felt like doing the same to the sergeant. Rog was just back from seeing to the burial of another Ranger, the fourth to die of his wounds since the company divided.

Lysinka's healer was a hard-bitten, hard-handed, but soft-hearted woman, without whose help there might have been twice as many dead. But she was only a skilled healer, not a worker of miracles. After the inward festering began in Lopetas's belly, he was doomed, and now another boy who had never been a man was gone.

Rog considered whether he had seen this too often in his many years of war. By Mitra, he'd been a soldier longer than the Cimmerian had lived, and Conan was no green youth! If the voice started whispering that he did not want to see any more boys die, maybe he would listen to it.

Meanwhile, he would listen to Jululius.

"So what did the man say?"

It seemed that Grolin was now obsessed with something called the Mountain of the Skull, where the Soul of Thanza was supposed to reside. A sorcerer might or might not be helping him turn that obsessive dream into stark reality.

Meanwhile, Conan, Lysinka, and Klarnides held Grolin's old citadel with a firm grip. They too seemed to be in search of the Mountain of the Skull. How far either side had gone on their quest, the man did not know.

He was quite sure that he wanted to be far away when either of them found what they sought. Unfortunately, while he had begun his escape in good time, an ill-tempered bear had delayed him, and perhaps ended his journeys in this world.

"Hard way to go, even for a bad man," Rog said finally. "See that the healer gives him a good stiff dose of her green draught tonight."

"She's making up the red draught now," Jululius said. "Threatened to dose Cartos with it the next time he patted her bottom."

"He must be healing faster than we thought," Rog said. "I'll remind him that worse than a red-draught flux will afflict him if he does that again." The healer's red draught was a potent purgative.

Both men looked at the sky to the north, as if they hoped to see what the deserter had not said written in the clouds. The clouds being blank as always, they turned away after a moment.

"No," Conan said.

The skeletons continued to stare at him. He found the eyeless stares more uncanny with each passing moment. Perhaps the skeleton warriors' dead stares had some power over the minds of the living?

Or perhaps they were just confused? Conan suspected that he would be too, if he had slept as long as these men and then wakened with only bones and weapons to hold his spirit, if he had one.

Best do more to end the confusion.

"No, you may not have my blood, however strong it is," he said.

"It is very strong blood," the leader replied. "Never had we dreamed of such strong blood. Blood gives movement. Movement gives—"

Conan raised his sword. "The next one of you who chants that again, I will chop to pieces. Then I will pick up his fallen bones and use them to smash his comrades until I collapse.

"Maybe you can take my blood then. But it won't be as strong. There won't be as many of you. And I might just throw myself into the pool before I die, so that none of you or your friends will have anything from me except being killed all over again.

"I can be a fair bit more dangerous than any Death Lord, if you cross me."

Conan's anger had been said to terrify demons. While no one could say that the skeleton warriors were frightened, certainly they now looked more at one another than at Conan, and they neither picked up their weapons nor advanced.

At last the leader stepped forward, crossing his arms over his ribs with a marvelously human gesture. It hinted of a man who had been brave and shrewd when he had flesh and blood on his bones.

"It seems that we need of you two things, Cimmerian, and you can give us one or the other. We need you to lead us. We also need strong blood, that all of us may be prepared to lead. Do you swear by all that you hold sacred, you cannot give us both?

Conan ran through the names of all the gods he knew, except Crom. Some of these he had never held sacred or even accorded much respect, but the names seemed to impress the skeletons. As living men, they had doubtless come from many lands and worshipped many gods.

"It's not that I would refuse to do what you're asking if I could," Conan finished. "A good leader is always ready to shed his blood for the men he leads. But if you need a leader, you need him with all his blood intact and all his strength. Strong blood makes movement, in living men as well as in bony ones."

"I thought we were not going to chant that again," the leader said. It was impossible to doubt that had he been a living man, he would have smiled.

Conan felt a strong urge to do something to lead these warriors out of their dilemma. No good soldier liked to leave comrades out of a battle, any more than a good leader liked to be weakened.

An idea glimmered in Conan's mind—far off and dim, like a single candle in a cave no larger than this.

"Must strong blood be human?" he asked.

The others looked about, their gaze finally resting

on the water dragon's remains. Their leader slowly shook his head.

"Human blood is best. But if the living creature is strong, it will create movement . . . and everything else."

"Good. Then let me lead as many of you as are willing, up inside the mountain to the caves above. Those caves shelter flying serpents. They are strong, fast, brave, and fierce. If their blood isn't strong enough, then I don't know what is!"

Conan would have sworn that the leader was frowning. "Are they . . . are they creatures of the Death Lord?"

"I said that there is no living Death Lord. But that may change, if we stand around here arguing while Grolin snatches the Soul above."

"You did not answer me."

"Then ask a question that I can understand well enough to answer!" Conan snapped. He had never been overfond of law courts, and the leader was beginning to sound more like a pleader than a warrior.

"Are the flying snakes creatures of magic?" the leader asked.

Conan frowned. He could at least try to answer that question.

"They could be. I've never seen anything like them elsewhere or before. But they can be killed. I've killed some with this sword. Does that make them fit to give you blood?"

The leader looked along the line of his followers. Conan saw some of them nod. Others shook their heads. More looked at the rock at their feet.

"I think you have given us hope, which is almost as great a gift as blood," the leader said. "We will not take your blood unless the serpents' blood is useless."

In his mind, Conan vowed that they would not take his blood at all, Death Lord or no Death Lord. Then inspiration came again.

"Can you carry your comrades up to the caves, the ones who cannot move?"

"We can, but that makes the fighting more dangerous to all of us."

"You wouldn't need to carry all of them. Just one will do, to see if his blood will serve. Then we can drop the dead serpents down here, before their blood weakens. If we leave some of your men here, they can wake up the others and lead them to us.

"Then we can go hunting whatever needs to be hunted."

The skeletons bent to pick up their weapons, and Conan raised his sword. But they were not attacking. They began to strike their steel rythmically on their ribs until the clang and crash hammered at Conan's ears.

At least for the moment, he had trustworthy allies and a place to go. With luck, his friends on the surface would not have to worry about the flying serpents much longer.

Then matters would go as the gods decreed, and Conan had not expected them to warn him about their wishes since he was a lad in Cimmeria!

Grolin was leading his men because the sorcerer had to guide them through this wilderness of rocks and would speak to no one else. Sometimes he did not even speak to Grolin, and then the baron would break into a chill sweat in spite of the mountain wind.

He could have sworn that the slope ahead looked different each time he studied it. Was that his imagination, which he knew to be working with greater vigor than usual? Or was it magic at work on this mountain-side, changing the shape of the land the way the sorcerer had changed his shape each time he appeared to Grolin?

"A profitless question," the baron heard in his mind. "I can guide you whether it is magic or only your fear that makes the rocks dance before your eyes."

Then, well below him and near the limits of his vision, Grolin saw something. It was not rock, and it was not dancing.

It was an armed party on his trail.

At first he thought it was Conan and whatever weird allies he might have discovered within the mountain. That idea made his blood run even colder than the wind.

Then he saw that there were too many. He also thought he recognized the lithe figure leading the party.

He fell back to the end of his own line, ordered it to halt and go to cover, and crouched beside a boulder. He ignored the sorcerer who was fussing at him in his mind. This was business for warriors, not for nameless wizards who hid in various guises from real dangers.

He did recognize the leader. Lysinka and her people were on his trail. Also some of the Thanza Rangers. Whatever else might have happened since Conan entered the Mountain of the Skull, the unlikely alliance of bandits and Aquilonian soldiers still held.

This meant Grolin had enemies of twice his own strength on his trail.

"Up!" he called to his men. Then he ran as fast as the slope allowed, back to the head of the line.

He said nothing to the sorcerer. But after a moment, he heard the voice in his mind again.

"Bear left, at that rock with the reddish streak down one side. The ground on the right side is too loose and crumbly for marching . . ."

There was no returning the way Conan had come. The skeletons could not swim, the Cimmerian could not face another water dragon, and the way led nowhere save to the bottom of the shaft down which he had fallen.

Fortunately the skeletons had some memories of the interior of this mountain. Sharing them with Conan, they enabled him to find a useful way upward from the cave where they stood. Time had little meaning in this endlessly-twilit underworld, but it could not have been more than a few hours before the Cimmerian hillman found himself climbing as he had never climbed before.

He had clambered up mountains, through mazes of caves, tunnels, and shafts. He had indeed done this many times, sometimes retreating, sometimes advancing to battle with stranger foes than flying serpents. But he had never advanced with twenty-odd armed skeleton warriors climbing behind him, making a din that would deafen a god.

Nor had he climbed with one of those warriors' comrades on his back, the skeleton disassembled into its individual bones and wrapped firmly into a bundle with thongs cut from the water dragon's hide. In spite of their stony composition, the bones were not too great a burden for the Cimmerian, even on the roughest ascent.

The burden would, however, slow him in a fight. He hoped the unknown warrior would not mind being brusquely put out of harm's way, when Conan and his strange company reached the caves of the flying serpents.

The serpents would surely be alert and ready to fight. The sound of the climb would not only deafen gods, it would awaken any creature with ears in its skull!

Fourteen

Lord Grolin thought at first he could simply outrun Lysinka's fighters. He had, after all, a considerable head start, as well as guidance from the sorcerer through the mysteries of the upper slopes. He even knew what the mouth of the cave looked like.

Unfortunately for him and his men, he had not reckoned on how hard Lysinka's rage was driving her—and how hard she and Klarnides were driving their men. Or pulling them along, or pushing them, or dragging them, or spurring them to undreamed-of efforts with nothing more powerful than the rough sides of their tongues.

In much less time than Grolin found agreeable, it had become plain that he was going to have to stop and fight. The ground ahead was growing steeper. This would slow his already-weary men—but it would also give them an advantage.

If they could gain a little help from the invisible and, for some while, silent sorcerer.

"A fight now was not part of my plan," the sorcerer said, in reply to Grolin's unspoken question.

"Welcome to the real world of the warrior." Grolin's voice would have been a dry-throated rasp had he not been speaking the words only in his mind. "To survive, a plan needs the cooperation of your enemy. Lysinka is not cooperating."

"Then I suppose you speak the truth. Lysinka and her people must be fought, if you are to come safely to the Soul and what it will give us."

Grolin did not say "Us?" even to himself. Had he done so, the sorcerer would have heard an edge of sarcasm. What work the sorcerer was doing that entitled him to a share in Grolin's gain, the baron did not know.

"I may need some help," Grolin thought. "Am I valuable enough to your plans that you will give that help?"

The sorcerer hesitated so long that Grolin guessed he would have drawn his sword against any living man within a reach of his steel.

The sorcerer must have read Grolin's thoughts. He sounded almost pleading when he spoke again.

"Do not be hasty, friend, or ask haste of me, or mistake my slowness for reluctance to aid you. I am merely studying the rocks, to see how I can best be of use to you."

"What about sending out your flying serpents?"

"They will soon have to defend their own nests."

"From Conan?"

No answer to that question came.

"Can you send magic within the mountain and halt—whoever menaces your snakes?"

"Within the mountain, I do not have such power as I would need." The sorcerer added hastily, "The serpents would be less useful than you think. They would attack moving flesh, your men's and Lysinka's."

That argument carried weight. Grolin was outnumbered already. The serpents could devour equal numbers of his men and Lysinka's and still leave her queen of the mountain.

Unless they devoured that bitch too! Grolin briefly imagined that pleasant spectacle and the sound of Lysinka's screams.

Except that she probably would not scream, because she would know that he anticipated hearing her cries. A man did not get much satisfaction from a woman like that, living in his bed or dying before his eyes!

The baron realized that the sorcerer was speaking again.

"Halt your men and send them into hiding. I can combine my power with that of nature to help you. Make sure you are ready to charge when I give the sign."

"Are you a god, to speak of giving signs?"

"No. The signs the gods give are often hard for men to read. Thus do fools come to believe that their gods do not exist, or else that they must listen to priests to understand the wishes of their gods. And thus do priests become rich and strike at anyone who threatens their wealth and power."

Grolin heard raw hatred in those last words. It was the first thing he had learned or at least reasonably suspected, about the sorcerer's life as a man on earth.

"What I am now is of no concern to you. I offer a promise of help and intend to honor it. Trust me with your life and those of your men, and I will repay that trust."

Something had the sorcerer approaching desperation,

Grolin thought. Those last words sounded almost like
a plea.

Grolin decided to give the sorcerer his chance. He
waved to his men, his hands signaling them to find
cover and halt.

He hoped they would not be so weary that once they
went to ground, they could not rise for the attack the
sorcerer said would be necessary. Even if the sorcerer
had not requested the attack, Grolin would have
wished to make it.

He wanted to make Lysinka, or at least her people,
bleed.

Other earth tremors that Lysinka had felt seemed
to rise from deep below the ground. This tremor felt
different.

She was no seer or sorcerer. All she had to judge by
was the soles of her feet and long experience in the
Thanzas. Her feet and her experience told her that this
tremor had been shallow.

Her eyes also told her that the earth was shaking
under her when she and her fighters (she called the
Thanza Rangers hers now, for they called her leader)
were directly downhill from a field of precariously
seated boulders. There seemed to be scores of them,
ranging from man- to horse-sized.

In Lysinka, two notions warred savagely.

She knew magic was at work, which meant she was
in the right place for finding Conan—or so near it that
those charged with defending the place were hurling
spells at her.

She also knew that if those spells forced the boulders down on her and her fighters, it would be chancy
for anyone to live long enough to rescue the barbarian.

She had always expected to die at the head of her

band, so that the survivors would at least remember
that she fell with her face to the enemy. Now she con-
templated the prospect of there being no survivors, to
remember how she died with her face crushed into the
earth as tons of boulders rolled over her.

She challenged that thought for possession of her
limbs and mind as she had challenged fear for ten
years. As she had for ten years, she won.

Lysinka had drawn sword and dagger, more to lend
authority to her gestures than to menace any foe, when
the boulders began to move.

Grolin had reached such a pitch of rage against
Lysinka that had he been promised her death in return
for giving up the Soul of Thanza, he might have
accepted the bargain. He wanted to see the entire hillside of boulders rolling down upon the chieftain and
hear her scream as she vanished under the crushing
weight of stone.

He would even be content if her screams were lost
in the roar of the rockslide, as long as he could find her
body afterward and know that she had died in agony
and fear, with all her comrades with her.

But instead of an entire hillside turned loose, only a
few boulders started to move. They heaved themselves
out of the ground like mired bullocks from the mud,
and at first they rolled so slowly that a walking man
could have kept pace with them.

But the slope was steep. The rocks were heavy.
They gained speed, and soon they were leaping and
crashing down the mountainside, toward Lysinka's
people.

Grolin saw the men scattering, with Lysinka leading
one way and that boy-warrior Klarnides the other. He
realized that his own men were going to have to take a

hand, weary as they were. The enemy would lose a few men and perhaps a trifle of courage.

They would also lose all their positions. While they were disordered, a smaller force could strike them hard. Grolin wondered how many of his own men would return uphill after such a stroke.

Lysinka counted eight boulders thundering down upon her people. Klarnides was leading the escape to the right; she led the one to the left. The slope offered too little room for them to scatter without dividing.

The chieftain could only pray that Klarnides's new-found shrewdness and quickness of wit would not desert him now.

Then she saw the boulders towering higher. One of them hit a firmly embedded rock and shattered into fragments, rattling off in a dozen directions. No fragment touched a man.

Another boulder also hit something solid at such a speed that it leaped into the air like a horse taking a fence. It rose so high that Lysinka could have stood upright under its arc without disordering a hair of her head.

Then the boulder crashed to the ground and split in three. Two pieces shot off harmlessly downhill. A third rolled inexorably toward one of the Rangers. At the last moment he tried to leap over it but in vain.

He could only scream before the boulder crushed the breath from his body and rolled on, leaving a bloody sack on the hard ground.

"Don't try to run. Lie down, heads upslope. If you see one coming at you, roll to either side. But *stay low*!"

That was Klarnides, and Lysinka thought she could not have done better herself.

A boulder loomed up, bearing down on her like a wounded bear. She waited until she was sure that only smooth ground lay between it and her. No bumps or rocks, to send it to either side or over her.

She rolled over a jutting root and felt her clothes and skin tear. She rolled over rocks and felt bruises that reached through garments to flesh and touched her bones. She rolled until she feared rolling out of the path of the first boulder into the path of another. She rolled until much work of healers' hands and simple remedies was undone, and old pains screamed anew.

The boulder crashed past her. She felt the wind of its passage as dust and gravel stung her skin and eyes. She heard a hideous scream, swiftly cut off, as someone's luck ran out.

Then at last she heard only boulders rolling away below her, while none rolled down from above. She raised her head—and immediately leaped to her feet.

Grolin was not leaving matters in the hands of whatever magic was allied with him. He was leading his men down to finish the battle hand-to-hand.

Grolin felt as if he could leap downhill like one of the boulders. Was it magic in the earth touching him, battle-fury strengthening him, or merely the act of going downhill instead of up that made his way easier?

Regardless, he wished that he could inflict as much harm as the boulders had done with as little effort. Out of more than forty fighters, Lysinka and Klarnides appeared to have five or six down and most of the rest scattered. Grolin had barely a dozen with him, but they were in a compact body.

They were also the strongest of his men and the longest-enduring. The gods willing, they would be the hardest to kill.

"Stay together!" Grolin shouted. "Strike when the odds are with you! A wound is enough!"

A bloodthirsty growl answered his last admonition. Grolin understood it. He felt as his men did. But wounded fighters on this slope were as useless in battle as dead ones. Worse, their comrades could not leave them behind. They would have to carry the injured out of reach of rolling boulders and other mountainside terrors.

Grolin drew his sword, sheathed it again, and unslung his old battleaxe. He had not used it in years; and before he removed it from the wall of his old family seat, no one had used it for generations. The weapon was heavy and needed a strong man to wield it for long.

But it gave satisfaction as no sword could, to feel the blade sunder flesh and crush bone. The screams it drew from those who died under it satisfied a warrior's soul. Life that departed under it *fled*. It did not simply ebb away like a receding tide.

Grolin whirled the axe overhead with both hands, and shouted his house's ancient war cry.

Lysinka saw Grolin charging down upon her tattered line, at the head of a compact wedge of his men. He was screaming and brandishing an axe. Was he mad? Or had he become the Death Lord already?

Lysinka's own cry rallied a handful of men around her. Klarnides had gathered twice as many and was running toward her. But some of his men bore hurts from the boulders; all were winded from the climb. They would not arrive soon enough.

The chieftain did not look behind her to see if her back was guarded. She would not show doubt now. If it was protected, she was safe. If it was not—well, Grolin or his men would have to find their way behind her before they could use her bare back to their advantage.

This time Lysinka gave no war cry. She merely screamed like a lost soul and rushed forward at Grolin.

Grolin knew no fear at the sight of Lysinka for all that she had been his master in combat the last time they met. Fear now seemed something that he had heard of, perhaps even seen, in other men.

It was no part of him.

So he met Lysinka without regard for his own safety, and with less studied weaponscraft than he might have used. Lysinka owed her life to that, for Grolin wielded the axe with blurring speed and terrifying strength.

Thrice it slashed only air where Lysinka's head had been a heartbeat before. Twice it struck where it would have sliced off the arm of a slower opponent. Once it struck sparks from the rocky ground, where Lysinka's bleeding foot might otherwise have lain.

Lysinka knew that she could, in theory, get in under the swing of that axe with sword and dagger. Even a less than mortal wound could slow Grolin enough to let her inflict more harm later. At least it might slow him enough so that she would not stumble or exhaust herself from the frantic speed she used to avoid the axe now.

Meanwhile, Grolin's own men were doing their share of harm. Two or three of them would charge one of Lysinka's people, slashing and stabbing with small regard for anything save drawing their opponent's blood. The moment the blood flowed, they would leave the first opponent and move on to another.

If this went on, Lysinka would have a band of the crippled and maimed to nurse downhill. Fortunately most of the wounded fighters were still on their feet, even if slowed, and still fighting, even if one-handed. The Thanzas bred hardy folk, or they made hardy those who came to them from elsewhere and survived long enough.

She spared a glance for Klarnides, whose men were approaching at the best pace they could manage. Was it her imagination, or had the ground before their feet suddenly grown steeper and rougher since she last looked upon it?

The ground beneath her feet seemed to grow cold. The chill made her miss a step—and in the next moment Grolin struck with the strength and fury of desperation.

Lysinka's sword seemed to fly up of its own accord. It broke across the handle of the descending axe, and a piece tore Lysinka's flesh. The axe handle smashed her across the shoulder and back, and pain roared through her.

She went down, but it was half a fall, half a roll, and she came up where Grolin could not easily see or strike at her. Before he could do either, she uncoiled like a striking serpent, and rammed her dagger up to its hilt in Grolin's belly.

Grolin knew both pain and terror as he felt the dagger sunder his flesh. He also felt rage. Failure was impossible, after all this. Lysinka would *not* defeat him. She could not.

Two of his men seemed less sanguine. One on either side, they gripped him and drew him back. Lysinka's second thrust missed. A third man cut at her, but she was cat-quick as before, and opened his throat halfway to his spine with a dagger slash.

The dying man reeled, then fell against Grolin. His

blood poured over the baron. The baron gagged at the stench—then felt as if something warm and soothing was growing in his belly.

Where the wound *had* been.

As Grolin looked down, he saw the blood cease flowing from his belly. He felt more than saw flesh and internal organs knit—although not without pain.

The man with the slashed throat was now all but dead. Grolin embraced him as he would a brother. Now, his senses all alert, the baron felt life leaving the other's body—and entering his.

In the last moments of the other's life, the baron's healing completed itself. His belly felt as if it had never been wounded. Moreover, it felt solid, like a wrestler's. He looked at his arms. They were no larger, but they seemed harder, as though he were a blacksmith or a tree feller who labored hard every day.

Grolin found himself reluctant to describe what was happening to him. As for asking why, he did not even care to guess.

The sorcerer was less accepting.

"This is not yet to be!" the voice came into his mind. "You have a power of the Death Lord already."

"Well, then plainly I am to be his successor," Grolin replied.

"Not without my laboring for you!" The sorcerer now blurted out his words. Grolin detected fear in the voice that spoke within his skull.

"I labor for myself," Grolin said. He bent down, picked up with one hand a stone that he could not hitherto have lifted at all, and flung it. It crushed the chest of the man to his left. The man sprawled on the ground, and Grolin knelt beside him. As both his hands pressed on the man's ruined ribcage, life again flowed out of another into Grolin.

This time when he rose, he felt as if he could lift mountains, swim oceans, or even fly. He doubted that this strength was as yet more than an illusion, perhaps even a trap.

He needed more life from others. He advanced on his companion, axe ready to strike as one of Lysinka's fighters leaped on him from behind. He stooped and flung the man over his shoulder. The man's dagger barely pierced his flesh, and the wound healed almost at once.

The man fell on his head, crushing his skull and breaking his neck. As Grolin knelt to absorb his life forces, the man who had served Grolin struck at the baron's skull with a heavy club.

The blow staggered Grolin. It seemed he was not wholly invulnerable nor did loyalty seem to weigh much in the face of what he had become. But still, the blow should have shattered his skull. It did not even give him a headache.

Grolin rose and swung his axe at the club wielder. The steel cut off the man's right arm. He screamed, turned, and tried to run. He had no more chance than a rabbit fleeing a wolf. Grolin was on him in moments, and this time he willed the life out of the man.

So fiercely did the baron will the life force from the man, that he was not only dead but crumbling into reeking brown powder in moments. It was that sight that broke the courage of the fighters on both sides. The baron's men ran uphill, fearing both Lysinka's followers and their former lord.

Lysinka's men ran downward. They might have gone on running a long while except that Klarnides faced them. His sword was out, and the look on his face would have stopped a pack of rabid jackals on the hunt, let alone mere men fleeing from magic they did not understand but feared to be near.

Klarnides did not even have to wield his sword. The men slowed from a run to a trot, from a trot to a walk, and at last stood still around him. He did not ask them to return uphill.

Instead he called Lysinka down to him.

As she went, the chieftain looked over her shoulder. She saw the last of Lord Grolin's men vanishing among the remaining boulders.

She also saw, far too high on the hill and moving far too fast for any human being, a running figure.

Lysinka went downhill with less reluctance than she usually felt at turning her back on an enemy. But when an enemy was death to face . . .

She also felt numb contemplating the deaths of so many fighters, hers and Grolin's. Even enemies did not deserve so fearful a death by magic.

The numbness lay not only in her wits. She had bruises and grazes all over, from her desperate efforts to stay clear of Grolin's axe. Her wounds were better than being a corpse unnaturally stripped of life, but she still hurt and knew that she would be slower than usual for days.

Rasha spread her cloak on the ground and motioned for Lysinka to lie down on it. "Let me see what I can do for you."

"If you can heal, there are others more in need than I."

"All are in need of you at our head, Lysinka. Do we have the time and you the strength to argue?"

Lysinka forced a smile and lay down. She did not even think of undressing, and this surprised her. Then she realized that if she undressed, she would be naked to more than Rasha's soothing hands and the eyes of those who had seen her bare more times than they had fingers and toes.

She would be naked in the presence of whatever evil power was loose on this mountain.

That thought chilled her, as if she was not only naked but also sprawled upon the ice of a Hyperborean glacier.

Lord Grolin had to exert himself to stay well ahead of his fleeing men. His newfound magical strength was vast but not infinite. He was sweating before he reached a safe hiding place, in the path of his men but invisible both to them and to Lysinka's fighters.

He felt a trifle more respect now for Klarnides, having seen the "boy" rally the fleeing Rangers and bandits. A pity that he had. All would now have to be killed, Klarnides first, and perhaps without Grolin's being able to absorb any of their life into his increasing strength.

But he already had many powers of the Death Lord. Soon he would *become* the Death Lord. A few lives more or less would make no difference.

Meanwhile, there were his own men to hunt down. If wounded men gave Grolin strength in dying, what might he not expect from the deaths of his unwounded men? He began circling uphill, moving from rock to rock, seeking to remain invisible until he was ready to strike.

He expected success. His men would be half out of their wits with fear, and he could move faster on this kind of ground than any mortal.

At this moment, the sorcerer's presence returned to Grolin's mind.

The baron had read of "shrill, small voices" in

poems. This voice would have been shrill had it been in his ears. It would not have been small. The sorcerer would have been shouting at the top of his lungs.

"What are you doing? What is this power in you? Where did it come from? The Soul of Thanza is mine, not yours. You must not take it for yourself!"

And much else to the same effect, without causing Lord Grolin to miss or even slow a step.

It was useful to have the discipline of mind to ignore the sorcerer. However, this discipline might work only against the powers the sorcerer was now exerting. If in a panic he invoked more potent magic—

The answer was simple.

The more life he drew from others, the more the baron could resist the sorcerer. In the end, there would be no contest over the Soul of Thanza. Grolin would simply be invincible.

As that thought passed, Grolin saw that one of his men had wandered a little farther uphill than his comrades. It might be possible for Grolin to take a first healthy life without being seen or having the victim put up a fight.

Just as well. Clearly he was already nearly invulnerable to mortal weapons. He would become still more so. Clearly it also cost him strength to heal himself from grave wounds. Moreover, some of his men had bows and could inflict such wounds from far beyond his reach.

Grolin settled down to stalking the man. He discovered that all his senses were now sharper than ever before. He could see eagles an hour's ride away, feel the ground beneath his feet as if he were barefoot, and smell small animals in their burrows.

For a moment he wondered why he was using this glorious new life to kill others. He could live content with his powers on this mountain for centuries, letting no one harm him but harming no other being.

The moment and the thought passed. Grolin snarled like a hungry wolf. That thought had to be the work of the sorcerer he had once thought an ally. The man had grown so desperate that he would abandon the powers of the Soul of Thanza if he could make Grolin do the same!

Grolin wanted not to snarl but to howl. He wanted to tear out his next victim's throat with his teeth and drink the man's blood. He—

Grolin heard the sorcerer's voice again. Now he was trying to drive Grolin into revealing himself, so that he might be killed from a distance.

Grolin willed himself to deadly silence, even in his mind. He left room for only two thoughts.

Kill the men below.

Take the Soul of Thanza and all its powers for himself.

He had not decided what to do with the sorcerer when his chosen victim appeared below. Grolin leaped down from a rock, landing on the man's back, and snapped his neck before the fellow had time to move or cry out.

Grolin found that he wanted to cry out, however. Cry out in exaltation as the man's life force flowed into him.

It took some time for Lysinka and Klarnides to gather all their people and divide them into three groups. Some were sound of wind and limb; some were wounded but still able to fend for themselves; and some were too badly hurt to be left alone.

In such situations in the past, other bandit chiefs had resorted to killing their wounded. One reason why

Lysinka was held in such honor was that she had never done this. Some of her wounded had slain themselves, rather than be a burden, but if a wounded fighter wished to remain with his comrades, he would be carried and cared for.

While this work was going on, an awful silence reigned above on the upper slopes of the mountain. Twice Lysinka heard it broken by something that might have been the howl of a wolf—if one could imagine wolves or any other natural beast in this wilderness.

Once an unmistakably human scream broke the silence. It sounded like a man in mortal agony. Lysinka saw fear twist faces all around her, and she and Klarnides were sharp-tongued for a while until the fear vanished. Neither of them wished to let their thoughts dwell on what might have made any man scream like that.

At last the walking wounded were left with the seriously wounded, and the able-bodied resumed the climb. They were no more than twenty now, and if Lysinka had not sworn an oath before the gods and on her honor to find Conan or die trying, she would have hazarded no more lives on this quest.

Klarnides seemed to be of the same mind. She was just about to ask him, when they came upon the first dead man.

Or rather, a dead thing that had been a man to the moment of its death. The skin was brown and crackling; a puff of wind would turn the body to mud-hued dust. The eyes were white blanks, the mouth clamped shut and twisted in a rictus for which there were no words in any sane language, and the hands had become blackened claws.

Lysinka and Klarnides stared at the horror at their

feet, then at their men, daring them to so much as breathe without orders. Then they looked at each other, and Klarnides spoke.

"I'm beginning to feel a trifle dead myself. But the more of this we see, the more we need to find who's doing it. No one will ever walk these hills in safety again if we do not. Every man who dies will lie upon our consciences."

Some of the fighters looked as if they would forego a clean conscience for a clean pair of heels that would keep them out of the ranks of the dead. Lysinka did not agree, but understood.

A simple quest to locate Conan and make her band safe had turned into something not even nightmares could match.

Grolin—he would not yet think of himself as the Death Lord, lest the Soul of Thanza grow angry—was careful to leave none of his men alive behind him. He might not need all the life in all of them for his own purpose. But it was necessary to be able to resist the sorcerer's increasingly frantic efforts to interfere.

Also, he would not leave behind anyone to be tortured by Lysinka. The men who had followed him so far and so faithfully did not deserve that fate. They also could not talk of what was happening on the mountain if they were dead.

The sorcerer or whoever had been shifting the landscape about foreswore that game before Grolin breasted the last few hundred paces to the summit. He recognized the cave mouth from two hundred paces off, and quickened his steps.

A hundred paces from the cave mouth, a living figure appeared, standing on a boulder. At first Grolin thought that one of his men had evaded him and was waiting with futile thoughts of revenge.

Then he recognized the sorcerer. Was the man finally presenting himself in the flesh, to fight Grolin more effectively? The sorcerer would learn that flesh was more vulnerable than a magically-presented image.

But first, Grolin must approach the Soul of Thanza. The sorcerer was between him and the cave, but that need not be a problem without solution. Not with Grolin's new strength.

The baron ran straight at the boulder. The sorcerer raised his hands. Lightning streamed from his fingertips, making the ground smoke and hurling gravel into the face of the running man.

Grolin did not miss a step. Like a schoolboy rushing a friend off his feet in a game, he slammed his shoulder into the sorcerer's perch. The rock was as large as a small hut, and pain shot through Grolin's shoulder.

But the rock split. Half of it rolled off downhill. The other half tottered, then toppled. The sorcerer, however, did not crash to the ground, because he caught himself with a spell of levitation.

That spell distracted him. Grolin was tempted to strike another blow at the sorcerer, perhaps finishing him off. He resisted the temptation, however, and ran toward the cave.

He plunged inside as another blast of magical lightning tore at the cave mouth. Stone cracked and crumbled, dust poured out, and looking behind him, Grolin saw the cave mouth collapsing.

Part of the roof followed, but he shrugged that off and ran on through the darkness. His eyes could

penetrate it now like a cat's, and soon he saw a skull
looming up.

What part of the skull was the true Soul of Thanza,
he had never thought to ask. But the mouth turned out
to be large enough to allow a man to enter the skull.
Grolin dashed up and flung himself into the mouth.

He landed on the open chest—or rather, on what lay
inside the chest. He had no clear sight of it, before
light poured out of it, as if it were a crucible of molten
metal, and something plastered itself across his chest.

For a moment Grolin knew pain as if his soul was
tearing through his body from chest to back, taking his
life with it. He had a brief thought, that in old tales
creations like the Soul of Thanza could reject and
destroy unworthy suitors.

Then the pain vanished. So did the light. He was in
darkness again but not as great as before. The skull
was gone, crumbled into pebbles, and dust was heaped
all about him. Several new cracks gaped in the rock,
revealing the sky outside. Through one such opening,
he could see black smoke spiraling into the air.

That had to be more enemies. But there was an old
enemy to deal with first, and his now being in the vulnerable flesh would make the task easy.

The Death Lord of Thanza focused his mind on the
rockfall behind him. He imagined pressing on it, with
a battering ram swung by giants. He imagined the ram
striking the stones—

The rockfall erupted outward. More of the ceiling
rock fell, but it also went flying, reduced to fragments.
Sharp-edged bits of rock scoured the slope.

Lysinka's band was too far below to be touched.

The sorcerer was not. He sensed what was coming,
and attempted to raise shields of lightning and
invisible force, the last and most potent spells at his

command. If they failed, he was doomed to death or at least to flight.

The shields might have sufficed, if they had been raised in time, but shards of rock tore into the sorcerer's flesh too quickly. Pain distracted him from completing the spells. He reeled until a larger rock fragment split his skull and ended pain, spells, and life all at once.

Within what had been a cave, now largely open to the sky, the Death Lord of Thanza laughed.

None who heard that laugh ever forgot it—or wittingly spoke of it to others.

Fifteen

About the time Grolin's men were taking their positions for the attack on Lysinka and Klarnides, Conan began to smell the serpents' nest. It was as putrid a reek of carrion as ever, now mingled with other stenches that might be brooding eggs or the gods alone knew what other foulness.

The Cimmerian felt certain that no sorcerer could be in or near the nest. None could have endured the stench. He himself had long since wrapped a spare headcloth over his nose and mouth, and found himself envying his skeletal comrades their lack of a sense of smell.

Soon Conan found himself also envying their lack of flesh. They could wedge their limbs into cracks that would have scraped the Cimmerian as fleshless as his comrades. They could grip with a ferocity that would have raised blisters on living fingers. They could survive falls that would have shattered living limbs.

Two of the skeleton warriors took violent falls.

They lay helpless and twitching for a moment, then crumbled into dust so fine that even the slight currents of air within the caves scattered their remains.

Each time one fell, his comrades halted, held their weapons point down, raised their heads, and gave vent to an indescribable moan. The first time he heard it, Conan wanted to make a similar sound, from the sheer horror of this song of the skeletons.

He remained silent. A warrior was a warrior, however he died or whatever his form. His life had most likely been hard, his death probably worse. Conan would not refuse him death honors. Indeed, the second time Conan joined the dirge—although the leader said afterward that the Cimmerian had the worst voice, living or dead, that the other had ever heard.

Conan feared that if the rattle and crash of the climbing skeletons had not warned the serpents, the dirge would have. But as the stench grew stronger, he heard no movement above. Either the serpents were asleep, gorged on recent meals, or perhaps they shared the poor hearing of their smaller, crawling kin.

Before much longer, the advancing warriors began to find scraps of offal and bits of bone on the floor of their tunnel. Then they came to loose scales, patches of discarded skin, and even the best part of one complete skeleton, from its size a new hatchling.

The leader shook his head at Conan's questioning look.

"There is no blood in any of this. Not strong, not fresh, not at all."

Conan laughed. "Then I suppose I'm spending this day as a vampire after all!"

"Better than our becoming vampires on you, or so you said," the leader replied.

"I do not unsay it either," Conan said. Then he halted, raising both hand and sword.

From ahead, he heard the scrape of scales on rock. Conan knew from much bloody experience the sound of a large serpent moving. They had come to the lower end of the nests.

He looked back, and every skeleton raised a weapon, two if they had them. They knew the meaning of his look: from here onward it would be a fight every pace of the way.

Conan kept the lead, advancing alone for a few paces. Even shod in boots, he could tread lighter and more quietly than the skeleton warriors. From what he remembered of serpents, their poor hearing was balanced by a keen ability to sense vibrations in the ground about them.

Moments after Conan began his stalking advance, the serpents became agitated. He heard hisses, louder scrapings, the flapping of wings, and the thump of flailing serpentine bodies.

He rounded the bend, both weapons in hand, to see a pair of the serpents entwined. They wriggled and writhed, flailed at each other with their wings and tails, and butted each other with their heads, mouths closed.

Conan could not tell if the serpents were mating, fighting, or merely having a friendly wrestling bout. What encouraged the Cimmerian was the fact that the serpents had all their attention on each other, with none to spare for whatever might come upon them from below.

Conan's stalk turned into a run. As his boots thumped on the rock, the serpents sensed his approach—but too late. One fanged head reared up, but Conan struck it from its neck before it could so much as open its mouth.

The other serpent coiled itself to strike. It would have done better to uncoil itself and flee, Conan thought. It was a poor sentry, human or animal, who neglected his duty and then allowed himself to be killed before he could warn his comrades.

Conan swiftly dealt that fate to the second serpent. He hacked at a wing to provoke the serpent into striking, then thrust at the gaping mouth with his dagger. The dagger pierced the lower jaw; the snake writhed and dripped venom. Conan slashed deep into its body just above the first pair of wings.

The Cimmerian did not quite sever the serpent's spine on the first slash, and he had to jerk his dagger free of the head to keep the venom from splattering his skin. Another backhanded gift from death to his comrades, he realized—their bones would not absorb the venom.

But the snake was half-mad with pain and struck wildly. It hammered its head into the wall so hard that for a moment it lay half-stunned. That was all the time Conan needed to slash again, this time wielding the sword with both hands. The spine parted under the battered blade, and the snake's writhings were now the last spasms before death embraced it.

Conan retrieved his dagger, discovering that its point was soaked in the snake's ichor, and signaled to his comrades. They came forward at a run, scrambling over the piled bodies of the serpents and spreading out beyond as the tunnel widened.

The Cimmerian held up his dagger and gestured at the skeleton on his back.

"Shall we try it?"

The leader looked at the greenish ichor, which was turning black upon exposure to the air. A human face would have shown doubt, distaste, and also skepticism about the Cimmerian.

"You knew they had this in their veins, and you still led us up here?"

Conan was briefly surprised to hear the leader speaking without being joined hand-to-hand with his comrades. Then he remembered hearing other skeleton warriors calling briefly to each other or cursing as they climbed.

It seemed that with time and activity, each individual skeleton warrior was recovering the powers of speech. Conan rejoiced. This would make commanding them easier, and improve the odds when battle was joined. A skeleton in danger could summon help; one seeing danger to a comrade could shout a warning.

Not that the skeletal voices would ever be pleasing to the ear. The leader's voice periodically broke into sounds that resembled stones scraping on one another, loud enough to set the Cimmerian's teeth on edge. But the leader had asked a question, and deserved an answer.

"I described the serpents to you, my friend," Conan said. "They are certainly everything I said they were. And I do not know what is blood to you and what is not."

The leader's eye-sockets held Conan's eyes for a moment. Then he shook his head.

"In truth, neither do I. It has been long since our bodies perished. Even in those days, many who knew the secrets of the magic that sent us to fight the Death Lord of Thanza had perished, leaving not even a bone.

"We will not thank you for leading us here if we

find no strong blood. But on my word of honor—you and your friends will not be harmed."

"Except by the Death Lord, if he has returned and no strong blood strengthens you."

"I was not going to say that, Cimmerian, but as you have said it yourself—"

Then a cacophony of hisses, scrapings, thudding, and the clash of weapons made it impossible for either skeleton or living warrior to make himself heard.

Plainly enough, the battle had been joined.

Conan and the leader ran past the dead serpents, the leader nearly stumbling over one outflung wing. They turned the bend in the tunnel to see daylight ahead.

The daylight, however, was half-blocked by a mass of fighting serpents and their skeleton opponents. One serpent was already pouring ichor on to the rock from three wounds. A hatchling was writhing with a broken spine, as a skeleton warrior trampled it underfoot.

But another skeleton warrior was gone, flung against the wall so hard that his skull had shattered. He was already half turned to dust. Another skeleton was struggling savagely in the coils of a particularly large serpent that was trying to grip his skull.

Conan saw smears of the serpentine ichor on several of the fighting skeletons. But that proved little. Clearly they needed only one dose of "strong blood" to animate them.

The Cimmerian and the leader advanced together on the enwrapped skeleton. The leader drew the serpent's attention, making it release the skeleton's skull to launch a strike. The leader dodged aside as nimbly as Conan himself could have, particularly on a floor no longer remotely dry.

Conan moved with more care, not wishing to test

the effect of that ichor on his boots. At least it seemed not to corrode sword blades.

The serpent's strike at the leader released part of its victim and tightened the remaining coils around the other.

Conan had just slashed at the coils when he heard something crack within them. The skeleton threw back its head, somehow managed to pull one arm free—then with terrifying strength tore one of the serpent's wings out by the roots.

The display of raw strength made the Cimmerian rejoice at his comrades' prowess—and be grateful that they were his comrades instead of his enemies. Leading them against the Death Lord would be an honor; fighting them would have been a quick death.

Conan's second slash ended the serpent's life, but too late for the skeleton warrior. As the coils writhed and spilled him out, he was already crumbling. Conan had barely time enough to notice the broken legs, when the last of the skeleton's bones crumbled to powder.

The next moment, the powder was scattered and mixed with ordure and offal, as a writhing mass of serpents and skeleton warriors rolled over it. Conan hastily gave ground, using his ability to move backward as fast and precisely as he could move forward.

He kept on moving backward until he came up against a niche in the rock. Hastily he undid the dragon-hide straps holding the skeleton to his back, while leaving those that bound it together intact. He shoved the whole bundle into the niche, as far back as it would go.

The skeleton might have a rough passage, if some serpent tried to hide in that niche. But it would have a rougher time and a harsher fate if it had to ride out the battle on Conan's back. It was also just heavy enough to slow the Cimmerian a trifle against foes who were as swift as any he'd ever fought and who gave no quarter—

"Behind you, Conan!" a grating voice cried.

Conan whirled, kicking with one foot and wielding sword and dagger more by instinct than by sight or design. His boot caught a serpent in the belly just below its first pair of wings. This diverted its strike, so that its fangs and teeth grated on the rocks. Conan stabbed with his dagger, the point nearly skittering off black scales before it penetrated.

The snake hissed and tried to turn to strike again, but the dagger slowed its movements. Conan brought his sword around, up and down across the back of the snake's neck, just below a head the size of a newborn calf.

The head did not fall. Instead it flopped about in a fashion so gruesome that even the Cimmerian's hardened stomach twitched. Then the writhing neck tossed the head straight into the niche where Conan had put the bundled skeleton.

The severed head vanished into the shadows with a hideous slithering and scraping of ichor-smeared scales against stone. Conan had no time to watch further, as he found himself in the middle of a triangle of three serpents, two half-grown and one a mere hatchling.

Conan imitated the skeleton warrior he'd seen earlier, stamping his boot down on the hatchling's back. It writhed underfoot but was too short to raise its head high enough to strike above Conan's boot.

The other two tried to rescue their nestmate. Conan chopped one in half with his sword, lopped a wing off the other with his dagger, then beheaded the pain-maddened serpent as it tried to strike him in the face.

As the half-grown creature fell, the other head flew out of the niche, as if hurled from a siege engine. It struck a skeleton warrior in the back, knocking him down. A comrade tripped over him and fell, but by then the first had regained his feet. The two stood back to back, one with a spear and the other with a battered sword with a heavy curved bronze blade. They fought that way long enough for three good gulps of wine before the battle drove them apart. Conan would have sworn that they were laughing as they fought.

The battle also drove Conan back until he could no longer view the niche clearly. He hoped the head would do nothing worse than plug the opening for the rest of the battle or even protect the skeleton within.

More serpents appeared, some with red wings or yellow bellies, others glossy black all over. Conan could not help wondering, between bouts of desperate swordwork, whence these creatures had sprung—and whose magic had conjured them, if they were not native to the Thanzas.

By now the fight had driven the serpents back far enough so that Conan caught a glimpse of the creatures' nests. They were vast, spongy masses of rotten straw, leaves, and twigs, with eggs the size of a child's head. Some nests were large enough for half a dozen men the size of Conan to sleep in, and they emitted an odor worse than anything he had encountered in the mountain thus far.

Then smoke began to trickle out of the niche. A moment later it poured forth. To Conan's eyes, it looked a virulent shade of green, but a closer inspection revealed that it held sparks of many colors. Most of them he could not name; he doubted they had names in any language spoken by lawful men under the sun.

The smoke seemed to have no odor, but it made Conan's breath come hard and short. It did not affect the skeletons, but the serpents plainly did not care for it. They began slithering out of the chamber where most of the fighting had taken place, seeking safety or at least fresh air.

The skeleton warriors pursued. The Cimmerian had no need to remind them that the serpents had to die. Alive, they could only help the Death Lord or at least hinder his enemies.

It also seemed to Conan that the sheer joy of their first battle in eons had animated the skeletons. They might have no hearts to beat faster with joy but delight was plainly in them nonetheless, wherever it had found its seat.

Conan started to shout a Cimmerian war cry—then the words died on his lips. *Something was crawling out of the niche.*

At first Conan thought matters had gone horribly awry with the skeleton. Then he realized that it was intact and more or less normally arranged. But it had reanimated from the serpent's ichor in the darkness and cramped quarters, and now apparently had to back out of the niche. Its feet waved in the air briefly—and a last serpent, thought long dead, reared up to snatch those feet from their ankles.

Conan crossed the cave so swiftly that his feet barely touched the ground. He came down with both boots on the snake's back, but the creature heaved so fiercely that he flew off. Still, Conan's attack gave the skeleton time to climb down, turn around, waver briefly—then grip the serpent's neck in both hands.

From where the serpent had flung him sprawling, the Cimmerian watched the newly animated skeleton squeeze the snake's neck until its writhing stopped.

Then he twisted hard until the serpent's head and body separated.

The fresh ichor that spattered on his hands seemed to give the skeleton new strength. Conan would have sworn he grew a hand's breadth in width and height.

The skeleton's voice squealed, grated, and moaned. Dust puffed from between his toothless jaws, then words trickled out.

"Whoever brought me here, my thanks. Are these the foe?"

Conan was on his feet now but still wary. He nodded. But the skeleton had already turned around.

"Ah. Eggs," he said. He strode toward the nearest nest. Actually he lurched for his first few steps, then walked, then strode out like a captain coming to inspect a regiment, or a banner-bearer leading a regiment on parade.

Other skeleton warriors, including the leader, turned to stare. Conan grinned and mouthed to the leader, "You wanted strong blood?"

As the newcomer approached the nest, a hatchling crawled out from under it. The skeleton looked at it, then picked it up by the tail and cracked its head against a wall. A moment later he was at the nest—and by now everyone who had not gone in pursuit of the other serpents was watching him, Conan among them.

The skeleton warrior picked up a wad of the nest material and looked at it. Then he stepped to the wall and raised his free arm. A moment later sparks flew, as he struck his arm against the wall.

The sparks burst in all directions, but enough of them fell on the wad of nest material to ignite it. Smoke rose first, then little flickers of flame.

Then the skeleton flung the wad in among the piled matter of the nest.

Even he seemed to recoil from the stench that arose as the nest took fire. Conan felt rather as if he had been flung headfirst into a midden pit long ripened under a hot sun. He still retreated at a walk, despite the fact that his nose and lungs were urging his feet to run.

Conan sought the open air near the cave's mouth, while the other skeletons joined in the work of burning the nests. The skeleton warriors ran about, striking sparks and hurling tinder. Black smoke poured up and out, reeking and fouler than Conan had words to describe. Amid the smoke red flames glimmered, and Conan heard them crackling.

He also heard, slowly at first and then coming in rapid succession, the pops and bangs of the serpents' eggs bursting amid the flames.

That sound brought the fleeing serpents back, attacking in a frenzy to save their eggs and their race from the flames. Conan had to plunge into the smoke to join the skeletons, though he could barely breathe.

In the end, his sword was not much needed. Against opponents who took no breath, the serpents were hopelessly burdened by the smoke. They could hardly breathe, they could see less well, they could hear or feel nothing whatever—and the skeletons had a merry slaughter.

When the last serpent was dead, the skeletons began joining Conan in the open air. Most of them had turned from grayish-white to sooty black, with occasional spots of charred ichor. Few of them still had their weapons, and some of them swayed on their feet in a way that told Conan even warriors of stone could reach the limit of endurance.

The Cimmerian leaned on his sword and looked outward into the Thanzas without truly seeing anything. He felt rather as he had in Vendhya, when he

and his friends had hunted down a man-eating tiger
that had devastated whole villages. They had finally
slain her by getting between her and her cubs and
taking her as she came to their rescue.

It was work that needed doing, or people would die.
It was work that demanded a warrior's skill and
courage. But it was not work that a warrior could look
back upon with pleasure or that he would care to boast
about over the wine in taverns at night.

None doubted any longer that the ichor of the serpents was "strong blood" enough for the skeletons'
needs. The problem was how to bring it to the still-
inanimate skeletons far below—or bring the skeletons
to the ichor—and to do one or the other before the
blood lost its strength.

Luck, which had so long eluded the warriors
charged with overthrowing the Death Lord of Thanza,
now turned their way. They found a crippled but living
snake, and almost at the same time, a nearly-vertical
shaft that plummeted deep into the mountain.

He shouted, echoes replied—and then so did one of
the skeleton warriors who had been left below, guarding their as yet inanimate comrades and procuring
more weapons. The shaft lay within a hundred paces
of the remaining skeletons.

Not that using this luck was entirely easy. It meant
making rope of the hide cut from the dead serpents,
and lowering the moribund one down the shaft. Twice
it stuck, but two of the skeleton warriors had prudently
climbed down after it and were able to pry it loose.

One of them fell during the descent, and once again
the dirge for a shattered comrade rose from the
skeleton warriors. The Cimmerian would have

silenced them had he known how, but an appeal to the leaders that hostile ears might be listening was in vain.

"It is a custom from the days when we were men," said one of them. Considering how long ago that must have been, Conan decided that the custom might be several thousand years old.

If anyone was going to argue the skeleton warriors out of their customs, it would have to be someone with a quicker tongue than his. He also had to admit that if the uproar of the battle and the smoke from the burning of the serpents' nest had not warned enemies, none were there to be warned.

Even while they sang the dirge, the skeleton warriors were hauling up the first of their comrades reanimated by the serpent's ichor. The newcomers seemed more befuddled than the earlier ones, being reanimated amid the slaughterhouse scenes of the serpents' nest. But the leaders told off one of the first party to advise and counsel each of the newcomers. They were soon snatching up weapons and doing what in living men Conan would have called an arms drill.

Sleeping a few thousand years clad only in your bones would, he supposed, render a warrior somewhat out of practice.

Around the time that the fifteenth reanimated warrior from below rose into daylight, Conan heard a sound in the distance. It reached his ears as a low-pitched humming, as if a swarm of enormous flies had passed overhead. The Cimmerian called the leaders' attention to it, but they merely posted extra sentries and continued retrieving their comrades.

By now there were too few inanimate skeletons below to require the help of all their animate comrades. Many of those whom Conan had first encountered began their climb. Some rode up the shaft on the ropes, others followed the path of Conan and the snake-killers.

The first of these had just reached daylight when the mountain quivered. It was not a violent movement, but for a moment the solid rock underfoot seemed to Conan to be as mobile as jelly.

At the same moment, the distant droning grew louder. Now the flies might have been swarming toward Conan. It nearly drowned out the next sound, which was the rumble and crash of falling rock, far away and far below.

Conan and his skeletal comrades looked in all directions, from the sky to down the tunnel shaft. The skeleton warriors in the tunnel hastened their pace, five of them dashing out almost in a single body.

Then a roar like a waterfall swept over them. The mountain no longer quivered; it seemed to be dancing. Loose rock cascaded everywhere, and dust poured out of the tunnel and up the shaft. Mingled with the ashes of the fire, it formed an opaque cloud through which the Cimmerian could scarcely see his hand at the end of his outstretched arm.

"Out!" he roared, and the leaders echoed him, in so far as anyone could make himself heard over the groaning of the mountain. The open slope might be shaking; it might be swept by rockfalls; it might harbor live serpents or other unknown perils. But it was safer than in the caves and tunnels or under overhanging cliffs, where rock might fall at any moment and crush flesh and stone alike.

Conan did not head the withdrawal. With the other leaders, he remained coughing until he thought his ribs would crack from the dust and ashes.

At last none of the other skeleton warriors seemed to be lagging behind. The three leaders turned—and as they did, the mountain heaved again, causing both shaft and tunnel to collapse with a roar that eclipsed everything before it. A blast of dust and heat that made Conan think of erupting volcanos filled the air.

He and the leaders dashed out on to the open mountainside—and saw their band standing about, all looking downward and some pointing, while others waved their arms frantically. One could not say that their skulls showed any emotion, but Conan had seen similar poses in men stricken with horror at some indescribable sight.

Conan pushed through the ranks of the skeleton warriors. Then his own mouth dropped open, and for a moment words failed him.

A vast hole yawned below where the mountaintop had been. In those moments of quivering and uproar, the entire top of the mountain had lifted from its base into the sky.

Already they were nearly clear of the hole. The flying mountaintop seemed to be drifting aimlessly as it rose higher each moment.

Conan wondered what would happen if it reached into the clouds. A man could climb so high on an earthbound mountain that he died of cold and an inability to breathe. How high could one rise on a flying mountain—one sent aloft by the Death Lord of Thanza?

That thought seemed to have occurred to the skeleton warriors too. They sang the dirge for their comrades now lost forever far below, but they also posted sentries and set themselves to sharpening their weapons. It was with horror that Conan watched a skeleton sharpening a short sword on his own thigh.

"We have enough," cried the leader who had been the first to rise from the serpents' ichor. "None to spare, but enough for the work at hand. You yourself are worth ten of us or twenty living warriors."

"You flatter me," Conan said, then realized that he had no names for the two leaders. He could barely tell them apart.

"Do you have lawful names?" he asked.

The leader below nodded. "I may be called Iom. He is—I think—Ruks. The gods allow us no other names."

Those were odd names, but then these folk might have worshipped odd gods. Conan was content.

"Iom, Ruks. When your—men—have their weapons ready, it is time for us to go hunt the Death Lord of Thanza in his lair. Unless you think some other power has sent this mountain kiting off like a piece of thistledown?"

Both Iom and Ruks shook their heads eloquently.

Sixteen

It had not been easy for the Death Lord of Thanza—who now thought of Baron Grolin as a man who had died to bring the Death Lord to life—to decide what to do next with his powers.

Once he made the decision, however, it was easy to wield the power to turn the thought into a reality.

He merely imagined rock splitting all around and all through the mountain, far enough down so that a large solid mass would rise into the sky. He also wished to divide the mountain high enough so that perhaps some of its unwanted visitors would not go with him.

He was not, after all, a trail guide giving rich city folk a safe view of the forest. *He* was the *Death Lord of Thanza*. He flew over forests, so that no one had a safe view of him; and what he wished, he asked for—his flying mountain would descend and crush the obdurate until wiser survivors yielded.

What should he ask for first? It was unimaginable that he should need to eat, drink, sleep, or perform other merely human actions. That also made it needless to ask for women.

Silver, gold, jewels? Toys, all of them.

The Death Lord allowed the mountain to rise slowly and drift on the wind while he pondered his needs. At last he decided that he most needed more living folk to give up their lives to increase the power of the Death Lord.

A few hundred would do, and of course they would require food, water, quarters, and discipline while waiting for death. He would demand the first two from the worms below, offer caves for the third, and see to it that the victims provided their own discipline. There were always folk who would play tyrant over their fellows, even in the most hopeless of situations, merely to gain the privilege of being the last to be destroyed.

Or they might gain the privilege of watching their fellows die exotic and horrible deaths. That too would be a simple matter to contrive. Perhaps that would give the Death Lord a hold over certain humans, so strong that they would raid the ground for their master's prey.

If he wanted several hundred people, however, the mountain would need to leave its native Thanzas. He trusted that his power would still work outside the range; if not it was hardly worth having.

Before Grolin died, he had held a map of this borderland region in his mind. His memories had gone to the Death Lord when Grolin ceased to be. They told the Death Lord that there was a town about a day's ride to the northwest, that held enough people to provide the first few hundred inhabitants after the inevitable death of the others in the destruction of the town.

The town would have to be destroyed, of course. No one would believe that the Death Lord really meant what he threatened, unless he used his power at least once.

He could, when appropriate, slay many more for his own pleasure, but this first destruction of a town was a matter of stern duty.

Lysinka, Klarnides, and their fighters had a much better view of the mountain's rise than had the Cimmerian. They saw the cracks girdle the mountain then turn into crevices that swallowed slabs of rock the size of small temples. Lysinka crammed her hand into her mouth to keep out the dust.

When she finally pulled her fingers out, she saw that she'd bitten her knuckles bloody. She flexed her wrists, drew her sword, and looked downhill.

The dust was still rising too thickly from the gaping cavity where the mountain had stood for her to see the place where she had left the wounded. She only hoped that they had been lying below the crack, so that they had not been ground to bits by falling rock or carried off on the moving stone. Since she herself and those around her were clinging to the shaking rock by their fingertips, the wounded fighters would surely lose their grip and fall to their doom.

Presently the shaking ended, and the dust blew away. But by now the mountain—mountaintop, as she now saw it—was moving away from its original resting place. She could no longer make out the spot where she had left the wounded clearly enough to tell whether or not they were safe.

One small blessing, though: the mountain was moving away from Lord Grolin's citadel, instead of returning to crush it. Fergis and those left behind would be safe—until the mountain finished whatever tasks its new master had in mind.

"It seems we are going for a ride with the Death Lord of Thanza," Klarnides said. He was sitting up, polishing his helmet with the sleeve of his tunic. Only the fact that his face was the color of chalk spoiled the impression of his complete self-control.

"Yes," Lysinka managed to say. "I agree. So the first thing to do is to find out if we have any fellow passengers and if they are friends or foes."

She found that she could not utter the name "Conan," any more than she could say "Death Lord."

"Then we go hunting the master of this mountain," she concluded.

"What if he is down below, sending this rock on its wild flight?" Klarnides asked.

Sometimes Klarnides's habit of expounding on the tactical possibilities annoyed her. There were times to parade new knowledge and times to keep to the point at hand. She said shortly: "Then we jump off and go hunting for him on the ground."

She felt like laughing at Klarnides's face, as he plainly wondered if she was jesting or not. It was the first time she had felt like laughing in a long while, so on impulse she bent over and kissed him. His face turned from white to red, and he seemed to have inhaled a cloud of dust. Then he too laughed.

Lysinka wondered if this was to be her last laugh in the world. If so, she could have had worse company for it. And now her thoughts flowed again, so that at least she would not die with anyone thinking her a witling or a coward.

"Up!" she shouted. "We still have a mountain to climb, even if we can't climb down again!"

Conan, Iom, and Ruks led some fifty skeleton warriors to the mountainside. Conan wanted to march straight to the top, but Ruks reminded him that they should search for friends and foes while the Death Lord was occupied with his magic.

"Unless all we were taught about him is false, this levitation of a mountain must be a burden for the Death Lord," the leader said. "We may not have another such chance, before he grows into his power like a root growing into a crack in the rock."

Conan could see that Iom and Ruks were hoping—in vain, he thought—to find more of their animated or at least intact comrades and give them the honor of joining in the final battle. It went against his notions of war to give a foe as powerful as the Death Lord one unnecessary heartbeat's worth of time, but Iom and Ruks clearly had made their decision.

Also, while they were searching for their comrades, Conan might be able to learn the fate of any of his followers who had come in search of him.

At least he could, if they had climbed high enough on the mountain before it rose to the sky.

After a while, commanding the flight of the mountain became such a simple task that the Death Lord grew bored. He glazed one wall of his chamber into a mirror and studied himself in it.

He appeared to be a larger and stronger version of Grolin, except that he was clad all in crimson—if he was clad at all. It was hard to tell whether the shimmering substance that covered him from crown to toe was clothing, armor, skin, or a shell like that of a lobster.

Only in two places did other hues intrude on the blazing crimson. In the center of his chest was a space that he could cover with his two hands, that pulsed a

virulent green. He knew without being told that there
the Soul of Thanza had taken its seat.

His eyes were also something other than crimson.
At times they glowed the same green as the Soul. At
other times they took on the hue of tarnished gold or
shone jet black flecked with silver.

The Death Lord wished the mirror out of existence.
He did not much care to look into his own eyes or at
what his chest now held.

Grolin, when a living man, had sought the Soul to
gain power that would be his alone. It displeased
the Death Lord to have to wonder if Grolin had died
in vain.

But the power was real. He toyed with it, making
the mountain rock gently, like a boat on a river. Then
he sent it out searching the mountainside for signs of
life. If there were persons riding the mountain through
the sky, they could scarcely harm him.

But their lives might feed and strengthen him while
the mountain journeyed toward the first town it would
destroy.

Lysinka did not cry out when she saw the armed,
walking skeletons emerge from behind a rocky out-
crop. Some of those behind her had less fortitude.

The skeleton warriors halted, formed a line with
their weapons at the ready, but made no hostile move.
One of their number turned and withdrew briskly.
Lysinka's gaze followed it until it was out of sight.

Meanwhile, her fighters had formed their own line,
with Klarnides on the other flank. She saw many pale
and sweating faces, suspected that hers was among
them, and knew that fear needed little encouragement
to rampage through her as well.

These had to be creatures of the Death Lord, sent to

scour the mountainside. Who else would send out as soldiers those from whom life had departed so long ago that nothing remained of them but bones?

Then the messenger returned, with two more skeletons and between the skeletons—

If Rasha had not held her upright, Lysinka might have fallen. As it was, she swayed, blinked, and only then allowed herself to believe that what she saw was reality.

Conan. Her comrade of bed and battle, Conan the Cimmerian. He stood between the two skeletons, staring at her as if contemplating a ghost. She saw that he seemed on easy terms with the two skeletons, as if they were three soldiers who had met the night before at a tavern and were now new friends back on duty.

"Crom!" the Cimmerian exclaimed and rushed forward to embrace her. His arms nearly lifted her off her feet, while she could have sworn that the fleshless faces were smiling.

Then he introduced the two skeletons with him as Iom and Ruks.

"They lead these warriors, who are sworn to the destruction of the Death Lord of Thanza. They can tell you more about what they and I have been doing. Then you can explain what brought you to the mountain, and we can all go hunting."

The Cimmerian looked around. "Oh, good day, Klarnides. How fare you?"

Lysinka wanted to giggle, but feared she could not stop. Klarnides was looking at Conan as if doubting his own eyes. At last he stepped forward and gripped the Cimmerian's forearm.

"No stone there, or even between my ears, as you once thought," Conan said, with a gusty laugh. "I'm as much flesh and blood as I ever was."

"If you've lived to meet us here, you're something more," the young captain said. "Will it suffice if I believe in you enough to follow you?"

"Fair enough," Conan replied. "Now, Iom and Ruks can tell their tale while we move. We've a bit of shelter yonder; a cave that didn't fall when the mountain rose. But we can't stay long. It looks to us as if the Death Lord's bound for somewhere and meaning no good when he reaches it."

Lysinka forced herself to look downhill. Beyond where the mountainside ended abruptly, she saw treetops—so far below that they looked like a green carpet. She shuddered at the thought of being so high in the air, sustained by nothing save evil magic.

Then she shuddered again at the thought of this mountain descending on some peaceful town and holding it for ransom by the threat of crushing it to rubble. She could no longer think of stepping out of the Death Lord's path and letting him do as he pleased if he did not harm her and her band.

Somehow she knew that she would not leave the mountain alive without destroying the Death Lord.

It made it still easier to know that Conan—yes, and those skeleton warriors—would be fighting beside her. They *might* even have some notion of how to fight a Death Lord.

The warrior Conan had introduced as Ruks stepped up to her and bowed with a good deal of scraping and grating. He must have been at least Conan's size in life, and retained a courtly grace even in his skeletal form.

"Lady Lysinka, comrade of our leader Conan, let us march while I tell you the tale of the Death Lords of Thanza."

* * *

Conan listened almost as intently as Lysinka when Ruks told his tale. He did his best to listen with more outward calm.

Truth to tell, he was hardly more pleased than Lysinka to be challenging such magic as the Death Lord could command. Nor was he overly hopeful that this would not be his last battle.

But no one else seemed able to fight it at all. Nor was it in Conan to leave folk like the Death Lord to wreak havoc with their magic. A man who did that was no warrior but instead the sort of murderous wastrel who butchered women and roasted babies on spits over the burning timbers of ruined villages. Conan had never been one of those who even cared to consort with such, and it would be a pleasure so to end the career of the Death Lord of Thanza.

The Death Lord's extended senses had encompassed the greater part of the mountainside before he realized that he was not alone in the sky.

Life was there, moving in a way that suggested a human presence. There was too much strength for it to be anything but the largest flock of birds, and he thought he sensed minds far beyond the level that birds possessed.

Not that human beings were worth so much more than birds when one looked at them from the position of a Death Lord. But they could give service that birds could not, and their life was stronger than that of birds and strengthened him more.

If they were on the mountain, it was likely that they had come with hostile intent. Therefore he had no reason to doubt that they would come within easy reach long before he needed to deal with the town.

Attacking him, they could be destroyed at close range, as he drew their lives into himself with little exertion.

He might even be able to fly past the town, panicking the people but not otherwise harming them. Could he fly on to a larger, richer source of lives? It was worth contemplating.

At the extreme limit of his senses, the Death Lord felt something else. It was movement but not living movement. It was also curiously familiar, and he spent a frustrated moment realizing that he ought to know what it was.

Perhaps he should ask the Soul of Thanza?

Yes. He had done that before, after it took its place in his chest. But it demanded all his strength to get its attention, and sometimes a long while passed before he gained an answer.

Best start now, he thought. The people outside could scarcely draw close enough to harm him in the time he would need to speak to the Soul.

The Death Lord closed his eyes, placed his hands over the place where the living human Grolin's heart had been, and formed in his mind the questions he needed to ask the Soul of Thanza.

Seventeen

Conan had felt what he now felt too many times for his peace of mind. It was the sense of marching about under the gaze of a foe who has the patience of a cat waiting for a mouse—and the same willingness to toy with its prey.

He had lost many comrades and more than a little of his own blood in such ambushes. His own blood was between him and the gods, if perchance they cared at all, and most comrades put themselves in harm's way of their own will. But one could still grow weary of burying them.

The Cimmerian also remembered the times that this feeling had led him astray. He had walked in silence, wishing he had eyes in the back of his head, for entire days—and in the end nothing happened.

He took little comfort from those memories, however. Magic could strike with less warning and far more swiftness than any natural foe. Something that Ruks had said led him to believe that some of the

skeleton warriors—the Slayers of Death, they now
called themselves—had the power to sense magic of
the kind used by the Death Lord.

Something else that Iom had said, moreover, made
it likely that the new Death Lord had new powers. The
senses of the Slayers might not warn against these.
Nor was it certain that all their senses had survived so
many inanimate years.

Indeed, there was no certainty but one: Conan,
Slayers, Lysinka, Klarnides, and everyone else abroad
on the mountain was staying there until they closed
with the Death Lord of Thanza and slew him or perished at his hands.

The Death Lord's quest for answers within the
memory of the Soul of Thanza was long, seemingly
measured in days. It was wearying, for his senses
recorded every moment of those days, however much
time actually passed in the outside world from which
he had fled to embrace the Soul.

He had ample resources within himself, let alone
the Soul, to contend with mere flesh-and-blood opponents. If he faced something unnatural or magical, he
at least wanted to put a name to it before it reached
close quarters.

He asked the Soul whether it could enhance his
senses so that he could actually *see*, as if he had been a
living man, what lay out there on the mountainside.

The answer came: it could, but it would weaken
him. He was already wielding great power, keeping
the mountain aloft. Did he wish to involve himself in
another potent spell?

The Death Lord pondered the question, and in due
time delivered his answer:

He did so wish. The spell might weaken his power

for defense. Being surprised would weaken it still more. He and the Soul both had to look to their own survival.

Therefore it should help him.

Lysinka was the first to actually see someone watching the climbers. She was looking toward the summit when she saw what seemed to be a single vast eye open, look briefly at her from under heavy lids, and then close again—but not as if in sleep.

The eye was green, slit-pupiled like a serpent's, and seemed to have silvery smoke curling out from one corner.

"What did you see?" Conan said. She thought he had read her mind or seen something himself; then she realized that she had clutched his arm hard enough for her nails to dent even his tough hide.

She described it. Conan and Klarnides listened intently. So did Iom and Ruks, in so far as she could judge anything about the Slayers' leaders.

Iom broke the silence that followed Lysinka's tale.

"The Death Lord may now know what he faces. But he has also used much strength in learning about us. So what Lady Lysinka has seen is both good and bad."

"Spare us riddles," Klarnides grumbled. "Do we run upward faster, creep downward on our bellies, or do something else entirely?"

Iom and Ruks would have glared had they been capable of facial expressions. That was plain to Lysinka.

Conan, on the other hand, laughed.

"Don't flaunt new knowledge in the face of men who were bones when your forefathers were yet unconceived," Conan said. "But Captain Klarnides has the right of it. What do you suggest, my friends?"

"Haste," Iom and Ruks said together. "Also, that we

the Slayers of Death surround you fighters of flesh and blood. Each will need the other before this day is over, but for the moment you need our protection."

The only "fighter of flesh and blood" who looked content with this arrangement was Conan. But his opinion carried weight with Lysinka. He knew the Slayers. She and Klarnides did not.

"As you wish," she said. The Slayers clashed their weapons together or banged them on their ribs. The wind of the mountain's passage through the sky blew away any echoes. Then they ran to form a circle around the human fighters.

One Slayer lost his footing from moving a little too swiftly. He went down, began to roll, and could not stop himself. He kept on rolling, leaving a trail of dust that blew away in the wind, until he was no longer there.

For the first time, Lysinka heard the Slayers' dirge for one of their own slain. It was the most fearsome sound she had ever heard—even the death cries of one of her fellow concubines had not been so terrible.

Yet oddly, it made her feel more at peace with the Slayers and safer in their company. They too felt enough comradeship to mourn their dead. None who did that could be so far beyond human ken that she needed to fear them.

This time her grip on Conan's arm was almost a caress.

"We will sing for their dead when we come down, will we not?" she asked.

The Cimmerian grinned. It was a more wolfish grin than usual, and his teeth blazed white in a face as dark as a Stygian's with soot and dust.

"We shall. But we will also make the Death Lord do a trifle of singing before that!"

* * *

The Death Lord's study of his enemies had told him who they were—or rather, allowed the Soul of Thanza to tell him. The humans were food, no more and no less—if he could feed upon their lives. But the others were the Slayers of Death, sent into the world by who could tell what cunning trick. At least that was what his eyes and Grolin's memories told him, and he preferred not to doubt either.

The Slayers of Death being on his trail again was not welcome news. Nor was it welcome that he had depleted much of his strength. Keeping the mountain aloft was becoming a burden. Add fighting the Slayers and their allies to that, and his strength might fail.

It was time to devour more lives, the nearest first. Once he had strengthened himself, he should be equal to the task of fending off the Slayers until he had crushed the town and fed on its lives.

If necessary, he could keep the mountain on the ground until he dealt with the Slayers. With renewed strength and no remaining enemies, he could then resume his journey, knowing himself invincible.

To the north, Conan saw a broad lake with marshy borders. If the mountain landed there, his people would have a wet journey wading ashore, but they would be more likely to survive the landing.

To the west he saw a fair-sized town, with roads gleaming yellow-white amidst the green fields and the villages surrounding it. He even thought he could see people scurrying about in the streets and on the roads. Doubtless they had seen the flying mountain by now. Equally likely, they were half-mad with fear.

No help to be had from those poor wretches, even if the mountain by chance landed close to the town without crushing untold numbers of innocents under its mass. The Slayers and their companions on the mountain would have to do the work themselves—and quickly.

It was then that the Death Lord of Thanza struck hard for the first time. Crimson and emerald bolts of raw magical power poured down from the summit, curved around the marching fighters, and formed a whirlwind of colors that completely engulfed them.

Or rather, it would have, except for the circle of Slayers around the humans. The Slayers seemed to repel the whirlwind as two lodestones repel each other. They neither chanted, cried out, danced, nor made any other gestures that he thought of in connection with working magic.

They merely stood, and the crimson and emerald tide roared in frustration, dancing more wildly and churning up the air until the humans felt as if they were in the middle of a whirlwind. Gravel, dust, and dead grass flew, stung and scoured faces, and forced most to close their eyes.

Through eyes closed to slits, Conan saw one of the Thanza Rangers knocked off his feet. He rolled downhill, through a gap in the Slayers' circle, and out into the wind.

He had just regained his feet when his eyes bulged out and his mouth opened in a soundless scream. At the same time, two of the Slayers reached into a mass of crimson light that seemed almost liquid incandescence, and pulled on the man's arms.

His eyes were open and staring but without sight when they pulled him back. He was bleeding from the nose and mouth—and Conan saw the two Slayers each dip a finger of their free hands into the man's blood.

A howl of outrage rose from the Rangers, joined by

the bandits, the two together almost outshouting the whirlwind of light. Weapons flew free, and one man had a spear ready to cast at Ruks when Klarnides gripped the spear and thrust the point of his sword almost into the man's stomach.

"Stop it, you fool!" he roared, shouting down both the whirlwind and the angry fighters. "Tolos is dead. But his life can go to strengthen the Death Lord or to feed our friends the Slayers. Which do you want?"

"Vampires are no friends of mine!" someone shouted. Conan heard a ragged chorus of assent and took a deep breath when he heard Klarnides speak.

"Iom! Ruks! Can we give rites to the man whose blood you took?"

"Of course!" Ruks shouted. "Do you think we Slayers are barbarians? Look at Conan. He gave us blood and stands here hale and strong."

Conan drew his sword and added, "I'm also ready to kill the next fool! Do you think the Death Lord will allow rites for Tolos or anyone else, if he captures them? Gods above, don't make your comrades die without rites or purpose to strengthen our enemies!"

That seemed to renew the men's courage or at least to reduce them to silence as the whirlwind continued. Under cover of its whine and roar, Conan put his mouth close to Ruks's earhole and muttered:

"What we've said had better prove true, or you'll be fighting the Death Lord by yourselves. I thought that once you folk were animate again, you had no more need for strong blood."

"We do not need it," Ruks replied. "Indeed, more than a little of it will kill us. But even as it begins to kill, it also makes us stronger for a brief while."

Conan studied the eyeless, fleshless face, that seemed the face of death itself yet was prepared to fight off something worse. "Then I suppose you want the blood of our dead?"

"If we are to win, that may be needed."

"I fear you will have to fight enemies on both sides," Conan said. "But you may have my blood if I fall."

"If I could still pray, I would pray that would not be needed," Ruks said. He looked outward, and Conan saw that the colors of the whirlwind had faded to pink and a pale green like sun-bleached seaweed. Also, the debris cast into the air by the wind was pattering down again.

One attack was foiled. How many more?

Conan looked up at the summit. It showed no sign of the powers just unleashed, but he had not expected much. The answer to his question, however, surely lay up there.

"Up!" he shouted. The men must be bone weary of that command by now, the Cimmerian thought, but they would cease to hear it only when they or the Death Lord were gone.

The Soul of Thanza beat within the Death Lord's chest like a heart gone mad. Both the beat and the madness flowed from it to every part of the Death Lord's body.

He had the fearful sense that though he might be invulnerable from without, he might perish through the work of his own long-sought ally.

Had the Soul grown stronger or he become weaker through the battle just ended? Perhaps both. Certainly he had needed all his power to batter desperately at the Slayers—desperately and ultimately without purpose. He had regained much of it, but not all.

When death struck at the living, it took lives into

itself. When death struck at the dead, it was *they* who took it into themselves. Took it in—and did not give it back.

The Death Lord would have cried out in rage had he not known that the Soul would use the strength he spent in that cry. He willed the mountain to fly faster toward the town. Perhaps if he was above the town and could threaten to crush it if the Slayers came at him, their human companions would oppose them.

Then Slayers and humans would be at odds. Without the protection of the Slayers, the humans would die. Their deaths would add to his strength, so that he could fend off his enemies until all the lives in the town were his.

He could still become invincible.

He willed the mountain to increase its speed toward the town. The Soul of Thanza hammered within him; for a moment long enough to give him hope, it seemed to be yielding to his will.

Then the Death Lord felt the mountain lurch and change course. He risked a glance at the outer world and wanted to cry out even more loudly than before.

A wind from the southwest was blowing upon the mountain. It was stronger than he could fight, and now the mountain was wandering in an immense curve *away* from the town.

Away from the lives that he could feed on. The Death Lord struggled to keep the mountain in the air as he sought lives on the ground below.

Even a flock of sheep or the shepherd would be better than nothing!

No more attacks came as the Slayers and humans breasted the slope. Even the skeleton warriors seemed to be moving more slowly, except for the one who had taken Tolos's blood. He was well out in front, almost dancing over the rocks.

Conan knew that baleful looks were aimed at the Slayer. But the worst he heard was, "I hope the stone-head can do more than dance from Tolos's blood when it comes to the fight."

Conan felt likewise.

The cave that Iom said was the seat of the Death Lord was just below the summit. It seemed to have three or four entrances. Conan considered dividing his force to launch the attack at the Death Lord from various directions.

Ruks shook his head. "We must all stay together to protect one another. The wisdom of war against men is not the wisdom of war against the Death Lord."

"I am grateful for that knowledge," Klarnides said. "But I pray that I will have only this one opportunity to use it."

"Who knows?" Iom said. "Perhaps Aquilonia—the new name of this land, I am told—perhaps it will face a Death Lord once every ten years for the rest of your life. Consider, Klarnides, how far advanced you are in learning, now ready to become leader of the new Slayers of Death."

Klarnides turned from pale to red before he realized that a living skeleton was making a joke at his expense. Then he laughed.

"I would rather celebrate the life of Slayers at a grand party," he said. "My father's cellars are famous."

"No doubt, among those who can drink potions other than blood," Ruks said. "We, on the other hand——"

"—have serious business on *all* our hands, be they ever so many," Lysinka put in, with mock severity. Both Iom and Ruks slapped her on the shoulder—

checking their blows, Conan noticed, so that they neither bruised her nor disturbed her balance.

She gripped their hands, and looked almost ready to kiss the fleshless skulls where their cheeks had been.

Then the mountain shook again, a man went down, and a Slayer snatched him to his feet.

"Run!" the leaders shouted in chorus and began the trek themselves. Weary as they were, fighters in both flesh and stone followed.

The shaking returned, and this time it did not cease. As Conan tried to keep his balance at a dead run uphill over ground that would not remain still, he saw the town off to his left. The mountain had changed its course. Now it seemed bound for the lake.

That might save the town, but it gave no help to those on the mountain.

Conan continued to run, and now even his breath came rasping and hot within his massive chest.

The Death Lord knew that the last battle was close at hand, for his sense revealed that the enemy was closing in around his cave. Soon they would try to enter.

Then he must fight and win. It would be the last battle whether he won or not, but he *would* surely win.

Then, with the Slayers slain, nothing less than a god could oppose him.

He pressed both hands against the Soul of Thanza—lightly, almost caressingly, as if he were reassuring a nervous puppy on its first night in a new home. He thought he felt warmth radiating from the Soul.

At least they would not go into the battle at odds with each other. Death Lords and whatever kind of being the Soul of Thanza might be lacked friends, but they need not fight alone.

Then the Death Lord knew his enemies were entering the cave. By a single entrance, which was both good and bad—but he would have to fight them however and wherever they came.

The body took a deep breath. The Death Lord cleared his mind of doubt and fear, leaving only battle skill and rage.

The Soul of Thanza glowed more brightly.

It was the glow that Lysinka saw first, as she stormed into the cave at the head of her fighters. She saw just behind Conan and just ahead of Klarnides. They would have gone in abreast had the cave mouth been wider.

Iom, Ruks, and the blood-strengthened Slayer entered ahead of Conan. They met the first blast of the Death Lord's magical energy, which sent light and heat pouring out of the cave until Lysinka felt as if she had been dipped in boiling water. She closed her eyes.

When she opened them again, she found that her feet had carried her into the cave. The blood-strengthened Slayer flung himself at a glowing crimson figure with the most appalling eyes Lysinka had ever seen. The eyes were jet black with silver tints swirling in them—and now the silver orbs formed long glowing threads and streamed out to surround the Slayer.

They did not grip tightly but neither did they recoil as the whirlwind had done. They enveloped the Slayer without slowing his rush toward the Death Lord.

The Slayer came within a mace-length of his enemy and swung. The mace melted as it struck, and Lysinka heard screams as molten metal tore into living flesh. It also fell on animate bone, and she saw one Slayer collapse with his leg completely incinerated.

She turned her eyes away as he crumbled into dust. She led her people forward.

Death met death in a rock-walled chamber not much larger than the common room of the Golden Lion in Shamar. That gave the attackers an advantage, for the Death Lord could not strike at vulnerable humans without his powers meeting at least one Slayer.

Each time those powers met a Slayer, they returned to the Death Lord somewhat diminished. The Slayer was hardly touched at all.

Still, the sheer physical impact of the Death Lord's power would hurl a Slayer against the wall hard enough to shatter bones. Thus, it was not long before dust deep enough to show footprints lay on the floor of the cave.

That same dust soon mingled with blood. Five humans were down and more were out of the fight. But the Slayers found no one opposing their taking blood now. They took so much that indeed one Slayer with a broken arm healed himself and returned to the fight.

Iom had long since gained blood-strength. Now Ruks was pushed back until he was face-to-face with Rasha at the moment when another pulse of raw magical energy streamed from the Death Lord.

It took Rasha with all its force, tearing her apart from throat to belly so savagely that she had no time to feel pain, or even to scream. Ruks not merely took her blood, he was almost bathed in it.

Lysinka screamed one curse at Rasha's death, then another at Ruks. She screamed a third time as Ruks seemed to grow still more. She could have sworn that he was *glowing*.

He rushed forward with unstoppable fury. The magic of the Death Lord threw him to one side, hard enough to have shattered him moments before. But now he merely bounced off the wall, flung himself on the Death Lord from behind, and gripped the magic-wielder in bonds that seemed forged from the mountain itself.

"Strike!" Lysinka thought she heard Ruks cry.

She saw Iom stagger and realized that he was standing on one leg, the other shattered beyond even the power of blood-strength to repair. She saw him grip his right arm with his left, and pull it out of its socket.

The arm fell apart as it came free, but Conan snatched up both the upper and lower bones. He dropped his sword, swung the upper arm bone at the Soul of Thanza, and stabbed with one of the lower bones straight at those silver-shot jet eyes.

The Death Lord of Thanza spasmed. The Soul of Thanza shattered like a glass goblet flung down upon a stone floor. Smoke poured from the eye socket that Conan had emptied. Lysinka gagged at the smell.

Then the Death Lord spasmed again. He flung himself backward against the wall of the cave, catching Ruks between his body and the stone. Ruks disintegrated into bone fragments and dust—but the dust rose to the roof of the cave as the Death Lord fell.

The dust floated down on the Death Lord's body as it continued to spasm—and burst into flame as it touched the Death Lord's wounds. No smoke arose with the flames, but another gagging stench filled the air as it burned into the Death Lord's body.

At last the Death Lord stopped moving—and with him, his magic died, and the mountain fell out of the sky.

Had the mountain fallen elsewhere than in the lake, it would surely have shattered, crushing everyone under falling rock. But the lake bottom was composed of ooze that sank as far below the surface as the mountain's tip rose above it. That was enough to cushion the fall of even such cosmic masses as the Death Lord's flying mountain.

The waves stirred up by the mountain's fall scoured the lake shores clean of life. But those within the cave of the mountain's late master, the Death Lord of Thanza, survived. A few lay senseless. All were battered and bruised; but most were fit and well.

Lysinka struck her head and was one of the senseless for a while. When she awoke to find Conan bending over her, her eyes stung. Not only from the stench and the dust but from knowing that even if she had survived, anyone outside the mountain must be gone. Even if her wounded followers had survived thus far . . .

"Come on, Lysinka," Conan said, lifting her to her feet. "You can nurse your headache once we're safely hidden in the forest."

"Safe?" To Lysinka, it was a word without meaning, or at least past belief.

"The Death Lord's gone to meet his namesake," Conan said. "And when the mountain came down, it made a thorough mess of the lakeshore. I doubt the kin of those who have drowned will come bearing garlands."

Lysinka pressed her face into his shoulder a moment then jerked it back at the smell of the soot and filth that covered him.

"We all need baths, Lysinka. You'd clear a whole market square if you stripped down now. And the lake's not going to help much, with all the mud we've stirred up.

"But Klarnides is out there, and he's got men at

work pulling in floating logs and overturned boats. We'll be off before anyone comes to trouble us, if you don't dawdle."

Lysinka looked about the cave. She saw more bodies than she could count, including Rasha's. But the dead were all human, none of them Slayers.

"Our comrades started crumbling to dust the moment the mountain struck," Conan said quietly. "They were all gone before you regained your senses. I've never fought beside better comrades, and I wouldn't have had it end that way." He paused then added "But their work was done. The magic that bound them let them go."

Lysinka looked up at the Cimmerian, whose ice-blue eyes still blazed in the darkened face.

"Will you bind me, Conan, and not let me go?"

"That's the sort of thing that ought to be done in private, you perverse wench! But if you wish, I'll buy only the best Khitan silk for the cords, and bind you as you've never been bound before!

"Now you'd better ready yourself to walk, because I doubt I can carry you without cracking your head against the cave roof, and small gratitude that would show!"

Lysinka turned and leaned against the wall, gazing at the open air and the sunshine, neither of which she had expected to see again. Only after she dried her tears did she have the strength to walk into the sunshine ahead of Conan.

Eighteen

It took enough time to strain tempers before it was known who lived and who had died.

Fortunately, most of the surprises were pleasant ones.

Tharmis Rog and the rest of his people saw smoke in the sky, felt earth tremors, and observed what they later learned was the flying mountain. This they learned from panic-driven fugitives who poured past the camp, mostly bandits and hunters. A few of the hunters offered to remain with the camp and provide it with food, and without their aid the wounded might have been in dire straits.

Meanwhile, Fergis and the garrison of the late Lord Grolin's citadel had a fine view of the mountain's departure. As soon as he felt it was safe, Fergis sent scouts to the mountainside. They found the survivors of Lysinka's wounded and summoned help.

Before Conan and Lysinka waded ashore, her wounded men were safely in the citadel. As soon as these could travel, Fergis set out for Tharmis Rog's camp.

Meanwhile, Conan, Lysinka, and Klarnides were leading their fighters home. They had farther to travel even though they were less burdened by wounded, so arrived only hours before Fergis did.

They had been delayed by the need to move mostly at night. The countryside farther west was swarming with people, both soldiers and the curious, who wished to learn why mountains had suddenly gone wandering across the sky instead of remaining on the ground where the gods had placed them.

After the first celebration, the leaders realized that this was indeed a question for which people would be seeking answers for some time.

Klarnides offered what seemed to be the best solution.

"The governor of the province is an old friend of my mother's," he said. The look on his face dared anyone to ask for details, so he continued in silence.

"I can gain his ear and, I trust, keep the Rangers in force without questions being asked. I will appeal to him for a pardon for anyone who needs it and wishes to take it. Anyone else, I advise to lie low, preferably on the Nemedian side of the Thanzas. Ophir seems a trifle chancy right now."

Conan confirmed that last remark, then added, "And what if you fail?"

Klarnides shrugged. "Let us set a meeting place, to which I can come with the message. If I come lightly accoutered, all will be well. If I come with my baggage packed for flight, march for the border, and be assured that I will be with you."

He smiled, a man's smile rather than a boy's. "If I am to spend my life in exile, I am fortunate. I have already met men and women with whom I could spend that life."

"Three cheers for Captain Klarnides!" Rog shouted.

The cheers lasted much longer than that, and if anyone had been looking for the camp, their search would have been at an end.

Conan and Lysinka saw off those who were border-bound, then retired to an inn in a small town not far from the intended meeting place.

Lysinka received her Khitan silk—in the form of a bedrobe so thin it hardly seemed worth putting on at all. But she loved the feel of it on her healing skin, only a trifle less than she loved the feel of Conan's hands removing it at night.

She wondered where he had acquired it, having always doubted his tales about being so bumbling a thief that he had given up the trade. But then, if she did not ask about where he won the silk, she would not have to tell him where she found the silver flask of scented oil.

Conan refused the oil but made no objection to rubbing it into her skin. That became a bedtime ritual for three nights in a row.

Early on the morning of the fourth day, with dawn not yet warming the sky, Lysinka awoke to find Conan's side of the bed empty and already cold. Instead of the Cimmerian, a fur robe lay, with a scrap of parchment pinned to it with one of Lysinka's needles.

The writing was Conan's, the strong, rough script of a plain man who had come to reading and writing only when grown but had applied his keen wits to the job as to everything else. She was grateful that she did not have to puzzle out the words.

Lysinka,

I am going to Turan. I still owe King Yezdigerd more than I have paid him. I will ride with
the *kozaki,* who remember me well. With them, I
can finish paying the Turanians.

It would be good if I could stay. I cannot. You
are too like Bêlit, and I would want to make
you more like her. You might even want to
do this.

Then you would not be you any more. You
would know it in time and come to hate me.

Also, two thieves under one roof is bad luck.

I bought the silk bedrobe but not the fur.

Klarnides says all goes well. This means you
can have a pardon if you want it. I hope that you
can find a place to live and a good man to live
with in it.

Conan, always a friend

Lysinka wished she could say that she was surprised, but whatever she had wanted from Conan, she
had not truly expected much more than she did.

So she did not weep, or throw the fur on the floor.
The hour being what it was, she prudently went back
to sleep, after hiding the letter under her pillow along-
side her dagger.

But when she slept again, strange dreams came. . . .

A boy toddled down a dusty garden path, a boy with
her dark hair but much of Fergis in his face.

The boy grown into a young man and practicing his
archery.

A battlefield, well to the north. An older Conan and
an older Klarnides, leading Aquilonian soldiers against

short dark men—Picts, she judged. Some of the soldiers wore the badge of the Thanza Rangers, although she recognized no faces under the crested leather helmets or wielding bows and short swords.

Conan and Klarnides, still older. Conan stood with a tall, dark-haired woman, of surpassing beauty and far younger than he. They gazed fondly at a boy, playing on a tile floor. Squatting beside the boy was the young man who had once toddled down the garden path, now with a bushy mustache and scars on face and arm.

Will this come true? Lysinka's thoughts asked.

The answer came, in Conan's voice:

Do you want it handed to you on a platter? That's not the Lysinka I know!

It seemed rather strange for the gods to speak with Conan's voice, but hearing him one last time eased Lysinka back into a dreamless slumber.

The End